DRAG QUEEN
IN THE
COURT OF DEATH

MLR PRESS AUTHORS

Featuring a roll call of some of the best writers of gay erotica and mysteries today!

Maura Anderson
Victor J. Banis
Jeanne Barrack
Laura Baumbach
Alex Beecroft
Sarah Black
Ally Blue
J.P. Bowie
P.A. Brown
James Buchanan
Jordan Castillo Price
Kirby Crow
Dick D.
Jason Edding
Angela Fiddler
Dakota Flint
Kimberly Gardner
Storm Grant
Amber Green
LB Gregg
Drewey Wayne Gunn

Samantha Kane
Kiernan Kelly
JL Langley
Josh Lanyon
Clare London
William Maltese
Gary Martine
ZA Maxfield
Jet Mykles
L. Picaro
Neil Plakcy
Luisa Prieto
Rick R. Reed
AM Riley
George Seaton
Jardonn Smith
Caro Soles
Richard Stevenson
Claire Thompson
Kit Zheng

Check out titles, both available and forthcoming, at
www.mlrpress.com

DRAG QUEEN
IN THE
COURT OF DEATH

CARO SOLES

mlrpress

Copyright 2009 by Caro Soles

All rights reserved, including the right of reproduction in whole or in part in any form.

Published by
MLR Press, LLC
3052 Gaines Waterport Rd.
Albion, NY 14411

Visit ManLoveRomance Press, LLC on the Internet:
www.mlrpress.com

Cover Art by Deana C. Jamroz
Editing by Judith David
Printed in the United States of America.

ISBN# 978-1-60820-011-5

Re-issued 2009

ACKNOWLEDGEMENTS

Where would we be without our early readers? In the first edition of this book, this list of thank-yous was lost somewhere in cyberspace. I'm taking this opportunity to reinstate that page.

A big thank-you to my first readers, who pointed out all the little inconsistencies of earlier drafts.

And to Nancy Kilpatrick, Helen Lightbown, and Pam Watts, whose combined eagle eyes saved me from a red face many times over even after I thought I was home free. And to Jan Archibald, who hears about every character and every twist of plot, sometimes long before they reach the page, and whose interest helps me go on.

CHAPTER ONE

The last time I climbed up these stairs was exactly three weeks ago. I would have stayed away longer, but Ellis was insistent, pining over all those gorgeous gowns and shoes and wigs; imagining great bolts of flashing silks and glittering lengths of magical cloth that ran through your hands like a sigh.

"And the makeup," Ellis said, behind me on the stairs. "There's probably mountains of the stuff."

"No doubt," I said. "Remember, he left most of it to Wilde Nights."

"Well, I'm in Wilde Nights," Ellis said.

"So am I." That was his friend. Some young thing named Jaym or Jayce. A non-name. An effort at re-creation that I might have appreciated in my younger days. Now it just annoyed me.

I paused at the landing, the key warm and moist in my hand. The air danced with dust and heat. I didn't understand why Ronnie had stayed so long in this place, the top-floor apartment of an old converted rooming house in a part of the city that was finally becoming fashionable again. When he had moved in, he was just a student. In my homeroom. It was the '60s, and we thought anything might happen. Anything might become something else entirely. Something wonderful and engaging and strange. Like Ronnie himself. At least, to me.

"Come on, Michael." Behind me, the heat from Ellis's tight body radiated close to my back. "I'm dying here."

Immediately he caught his breath and I felt the air go still. Dying. But it was Ronnie who was dead.

For a moment I rested my hand flat against the painted door. The deep purple surface was warm. I put the key in the locks, all three of them, and stepped back. The door opened outward, making it awkward for a moment, balanced on the steps. Behind me, the other two muttered and shifted to make room as the plum door swung to the left and I walked into Ronnie Lipinsky's apartment.

Hot, dust-filled air hit me in the face. It was like pushing into a wall of solid heat.

Ellis coughed. "Hell on wheels! Air! Air!" He rushed towards the full-length window, which opened onto the fire escape. We used to sit out there on hot nights, Ronnie and I, wrapped safe in the darkness and liquid emotion, talking the night away. Ellis struggled with the old, much-painted wooden sash and finally forced it open. He stood for a moment, panting in the heat, the sunlight dancing on the frosted tips of his short hair.

Beside me, Jaym was looking around at the eccentric decor, his dark eyes taking in every detail. "Cool."

Some time ago, Ronnie had remodeled the top floor, which was originally three separate rooms, into a small apartment. I didn't understand why he'd bothered, but he loved the place. It had memories, he said. Associations. It gave him back the roots he had voluntarily broken when he left the US and came here twenty-five years ago at the age of seventeen. Technically, he was not a draft dodger, since he hadn't been called up yet. But he would have been. Here, in this eccentric top floor of an old house in Toronto, he re-created himself over the years, till at last, when I met him again, he was a different person.

The sloping walls were a deep midnight blue, the ceiling silver. The furniture was all upholstered in white, with painted cushions on the sofa and piled on the window seat. Near the dormer window hung five or six mobiles Ronnie had made from bits of colored glass and crystals and sparkling ornaments. They moved gently, emitting a soft tinkling sound that set my teeth on edge.

"What's that about?" Jaym asked, pointing at one wall. It was covered with pictures of angels and saints, Madonnas and plaster cherubs and dried flowers with dusty ribbons hanging from their stems. There were pictures of men, some formal, some snapshots. Some were very old. There were also antique in memoriam cards bordered in thick black, with people's names in spiked Gothic script. On the floor stood two large painted wooden candlesticks, holding squat beeswax candles.

"It's a memorial to friends who have died of AIDS," I said.

"It's creepy," said Ellis, with a mock shiver.

I shrugged. It was just another theatrical touch in a room filled with dramatic flair. "The gowns are through here," I said, opening the door to the room at the back of the house.

This one was painted white, with a wall of mirrors along one side. The lighting was bright but muted, so that the effect in the mirrors was flattering. Rows of clothes hung in plastic bags along both sides of the room.

Ellis descended on the gold mine with cries of delight. Jaym merely stared as the light bounced off the sequins and satins, the bugle beads and seed pearls. It was as if the room winked at us.

I left them to it and went into the bedroom across the hall. Here the walls were sky blue. Someone had painted clouds on the ceiling. A mobile of stars hung in the window. This closet, I knew, was filled with sober, expensive suits, which Ronnie wore to work at the accounting firm of Shaw and McGinnis. It was not one of these suits he had chosen to be buried in, but a gown of old rose with beadwork on the bodice and a high, almost Victorian neckline. I knew because I had taken it to the funeral home, per his request.

Across the hall I could hear Ellis's laughter, his delighted exclamations, the *ohhhs* of appreciation. Jaym's low voice answered him, and occasionally he would laugh too. I pulled myself together and collected the mail from the box downstairs, took it back to the living room to sort. There was the usual junk, some bills that needed attention, a few letters and notes I put aside to answer later.

My concentration kept wandering, and I soon gave in. I wasn't ready for business. I took a box of photos from the top of the desk and sank into the couch to look through them. Some of the pictures I recognized, but they were mostly of people I didn't know, taken in bars and during drag shows, at parties where Ronnie smiled and talked with wide-shouldered transvestites and men holding wine glasses or cans of beer.

Ellis and Jaym were piling selected gowns on the brightly painted chest in one corner of the living room. I vaguely remembered the chest, a trunk, really. In the old days, it had stood in the middle of the room, used as a coffee table. Seeing it now brought back unpleasant memories of our breakup, an abrupt and painful wrenching apart of something I had assumed solid. I was a fool, but I had never really been in love before, and Ronnie's sudden, erratic behavior was incomprehensible to me.

The laughter and screams of delight from the other room had faded now as the two became serious in their winnowing of the treasures that crammed the racks. I raised my head to watch, catching alluring glimpses of Ellis posturing and pouting in one gown after another, his short, spiky blond hair almost glittering in the bright light. Occasionally Jaym would try something on, but mostly he seemed to see his role as valet, the one who puts everything away, smoothing out wrinkles and zipping up the garment bags. I was glad he had come along.

"What a bitchin' collection," Ellis said, arms akimbo as he looked at the gowns he had piled on top of the old trunk. "How the hell can I choose just three?"

"Find a way," I said. Three had been an arbitrary number, but having chosen it, I felt bound by my own careless words, something that often happened to me.

"Shit," said Ellis. He passed several of the gowns to Jaym, who obediently hung them up. I was sure in the exact same place they had come from. "I'll have to shorten them," Ellis went on, "but other than that they fit great. What's in the trunk?"

I shrugged. "How would I know?" I glanced pointedly at my watch.

"Okay, okay. Just let me take a look in case he was keeping some gems hidden, for some reason. Jaym, give me a hand here. It seems to be stuck or something."

I watched the two of them struggle with the trunk for a while. Irritated that it was taking so long, I got up and went over to help. The lock had sprung open, but the top refused to budge.

"What the hell has he got in here?" Jaym asked. "His tiara collection?"

"Hold on." I went into the tiny, immaculate kitchen and came back with a screwdriver and a hammer. I resented that trunk. It had always been there, changing slowly as Ronnie changed, painted, repainted, covered with pictures or draped with shawls, while I had been banished, my life broken apart.

As I tried to force the screwdriver under the lip of the top of the trunk, I realized Ronnie had sealed it with something.

"Weirdness," murmured Ellis.

Jaym had discovered the end of a tape and slowly and carefully removed it. Underneath was another kind of sealant, but with three of us working on it, we chipped and peeled it off too. By now, we were all determined to discover the treasures within. I felt the faint beat of an excitement I hadn't experienced for many years. Anticipation. Adventure. I smiled at Jaym as he handed me the hammer. It was warm from his touch.

"One more whack should do it," he said. "Go for it."

I did. The top swung open with a creak. They cheered. Paint chips from the hinges flaked onto the deep blue rug. A heavy smell of dust and mold rose from inside.

Ellis pulled back, coughing. "I don't think I want anything that's been in here," he said.

"Don't be too hasty," I said, pulling out the heavy green tapestry material that lay on top. It was just material, nothing else. Underneath was something that looked like old leather, cracked and brown, discolored with neglect. I tried to pull this out too, but it wouldn't move. Jaym reached in to help, and we both pulled at the thing, finally getting it half out. It appeared to be sewn together, so that the entire bundle filled the large trunk in a mass of stiff, dusty leather.

Ellis coughed again. "What it this? Bondage gear?"

"You wish," said Jaym, his dark eyes dancing. He flashed a sudden grin. "Let's heave it out on the floor."

It wasn't that heavy, no more than you would expect from a package of leather, but I was beginning to sweat. Something wasn't right about this. I had never heard of Ronnie being into anything leather before. The thought that there was a lot about Ronnie I might not know was surprisingly painful.

We crouched on the floor, looking at the awkward package. Whatever it was, it had been in there a long time.

"Turn it over," Ellis said.

When we did, he pointed to a row of heavy stitches. "So where are the scissors?"

I shrugged.

Jaym got up and went into the room where all the gowns hung. There was a sewing machine in there. He had remarked on it earlier. Now he went unerringly to the box where the scissors and such things were, and came back triumphant.

"Piece of cake," he said, and began to snip away. When the scissors proved too slow, he picked out a utility blade and sawed through the thick stitches.

The heavy leather peeled away from the package slowly, almost reluctantly. It took a while, turning the bulky package around, moving it farther into the room to give us more space. The dust was heavy, smelling strongly of mothballs now. I turned away to sneeze.

Ellis screamed.

Jaym dropped his side of the bundle and jumped backward, knocking over the telephone table.

I swung around and stared. The air rushed out of me, as if someone had hit me hard in the stomach. Staring up from the leather cocoon was a mummified face, the skin shriveled and brown, pulled back over yellowed teeth.

"Christ!"

Jaym rushed to the window and opened it. I thought for a moment he might crawl through to the wide ledge outside, but he didn't. Ellis had scooted back till he was against the farthest wall. He held both hands over his mouth, still staring at the corpse.

"Holy Christ," I said, my mind whirling in confusion.

A body. A mummified corpse forced into the confines of Ronnie's trunk. A full-grown man crammed into a space that would barely fit a child. Or so it appeared.

There was no rational explanation for this atrocity. All I could think of was seeing this trunk all those times over the years when I had visited Ronnie. Was this monstrosity inside while we made love on the floor beside it years ago? I felt my insides well up, and rushed to the bathroom. Nothing came up.

I threw cold water on my face, went back into the living room, and dialed 911.

CHAPTER TWO

Ellis uncoiled himself from the floor as if released by a spring and whirled into mindless action. All the time he moved he was talking endlessly, words meant to center himself, organize his suddenly chaotic world: "All right, all right. We'll just get these things cleared up. Just keep busy till they get here. Nothing to do with us, really. Like, nothing. Just get these things put away. Come on, Jaym. We'll just get these things in the car."

He was scooping the gowns up in his arms, rolling them up and under, any old way. The turquoise and silver and deep red silks and satins slithered out of his grasp as if they were alive. Sequins and beads winked and sparkled in the sunlight.

Jaym turned from the window. His face was drained of color, his dark eyes glazed with shock.

"We have to wait for the police," I said.

"I know!" snapped Ellis. "I just want to put these in the car, okay? Shit, I need a cigarette." I handed the car keys to Jaym without another word. I felt stiff, even the muscles of my face clenched and slow to react.

Together, Ellis and Jaym swept up the gowns from the coffee table where they had been flung in our rush to get the trunk open, and almost tumbled out the door and down the stairs, leaving me alone.

The heat and dust and sudden silence closed around me like a liquid wall. I felt trapped, buried alive. I realized that, except to stand up, I hadn't moved since we found our grisly discovery. The mummified corpse still leered at my feet. My heart tightened in my chest. I couldn't breathe. A sob strangled in my throat as I finally wrenched myself away, almost running across the hall toward the bedroom. At the last moment, I veered away and ducked out the window to stand on the fire escape. I concentrated on nothing but breathing…in and out…in and out…

Below through the branches of the maple tree, I could see Jaym leaning against the trunk of the car, swinging my keys nervously in one hand. Ellis was pacing back and forth, smoking and talking, gesturing with his cigarette. For the first time in many years, I felt the urge to smoke. A useful vice, I thought, like drinking too much. Oblivion. That's what I craved right now.

I didn't want to think of what was in the other room. What had obviously been there for a very long time. The feeling that overwhelmed me, however, was not revulsion but a shattering sense of betrayal. I blinked in the dappled sunlight, and for a moment I saw two of Jaym. Two of Ellis. I blinked again.

Minutes crawled on. By the time the police arrived, my bones seemed locked in place from hours of standing on the fire escape, although I knew it had been less than fifteen minutes. I listened to the tramp of their feet on the narrow stairs and opened the door slowly, so as not to knock into them.

"It's in here," I said, leading the way into Ronnie's living room.

The first cop was large and pink, his partner, a woman, tanned and fit, her uniform crisp even in the wilting heat. They both moved with a solid tread, weighted down with the equipment attached to their belts. They kept me standing in the hall while they checked out the corpse, then the male officer politely asked if he could use the phone.

The woman, Officer Dio, came out into the hall with me and began asking questions in an irritatingly calm voice, as if there was nothing out of the ordinary about having a mummified corpse in your living room.

"My name's Michael Dunn-Barton," I said, spelling the last name. I gave her my address. My phone number. "This place belonged to Ronnie Lipinsky, who died three weeks ago. I'm his executor. We came to pick up some clothing he had left to Ellis, the young man downstairs." I saw another police car arrive, along with an ambulance and a fire truck. There were more heavy treads on the stairs. "There's really no need for all this commotion," I said.

Officer Dio went to the door and talked to the others in a low voice. I wished I was downstairs with Ellis and Jaym.

"Step in here for a moment and give them room to work," Officer Dio said, herding me into the bedroom with the expertness of a border collie. The small room with its intimate associations made me even more uncomfortable. The trunk used to be in here, covered with an old Spanish shawl Ronnie had picked up at the Sally Ann store for fifty cents.

"I don't know a thing about this," I said, with a quick gesture to the living room. I was annoyed with myself for feeling any sense I possessed slipping away in the cloud-painted room where I had first gotten to know Ronnie — or thought I had.

Officer Dio flipped open her notebook again. "How long have you known the deceased?"

"Know him? I don't know him!"

"I meant the man who lived in this apartment."

I took a careful breath. "We were good friends about twenty-five years ago," I said. "Then I moved away from Toronto, and after that, I only saw Ronnie occasionally."

"But you're his executor," she said, pencil poised, the unstated question hanging in the air.

"I moved back to Toronto in the fall."

"The fall of 1989?"

"Yes, last year. I'm a history professor at the University of Toronto." She seemed unimpressed. She had stopped writing, waiting for me to get to the implied question. I shifted uncomfortably, feeling trapped, guilty of some unspecified crime.

"When I met Ronnie again, he was quite sick. I joined his circle of friends to help out. I had no idea he had named me as his executor until I was contacted by his lawyer." I heard the anger in my voice. I was sure she heard it too.

"Have you any idea of the identity of the body?"

"None whatsoever." I glanced out the window and saw a crowd gathering, gawking at the police cars, the ambulance, the fire truck. Another cop was talking to Ellis and Jaym.

Officer Dio kept me a few minutes longer, asked a few more questions. I gave her a set of keys to the apartment.

"I guess I shouldn't leave town," I said.

Her reply wiped the smile off my face. "That's right, sir. The detectives handling the case will want to talk to you."

"But this is absurd," I sputtered. "I don't know a thing about…about…"

"I'm sure you don't, sir. It's just routine."

Routine? What was routine about this? I watched the ambulance crew maneuver their gurney through the hall and out the door to the stairs, the obscene bundle stuffed into a body bag and strapped in, as if it were some unpredictable alien life form that might attack at any moment. I felt hysteria rising as they said their solemn good-byes and locked up the apartment, sealing the door with police tape. It was all I could do to keep the mad laughter at bay.

Outside, the crowd was growing. Who were these people? What did they expect was going to happen? For a moment, I felt disoriented as we emerged into the bright sunlight. Everyone was looking at me as if I was the new Ted Bundy. I saw a City TV news truck slewed across the neighbor's driveway. How did they know? What did they want? A young woman in a tight black skirt was hurrying toward me with a microphone. I bolted to my car, flung open the door, and took off, narrowly missing a fire hydrant. Only when I was a few streets away did I realize Ellis and Jaym were in the backseat.

They seemed to have regained their youthful exuberance and were both full of talk, a chatter that jangled my nerves even more.

"Was that weird or what?" Ellis said. "Did you have any clue?"

"Unbelievable," Jaym murmured, over and over. Finally he leaned forward from the back seat. "How well did you know this Lipinsky guy?"

"Not well enough, it seems."

"I thought I knew him too," Ellis said.

"I only met him a few times, myself," Jaym went on. "Just around, you know. I saw a few of his shows, last year while he was still performing. I was never invited to the really intense parties."

"Neither was I," I said, trying to imagine what Ronnie's "intense" parties might be like. "I'm sorry to disappoint you, but I didn't know him well at all."

"But you're managing his affairs. You must have —" Jaym's dark eyes met mine in the rear view mirror. "That's none of my business," he said quickly.

"Damn right it isn't."

He drew back, slumping into his seat in silence.

"A different sorta skeleton to have in your closet, right?" Ellis prattled on. "Trust Ronnie! So, you never saw that trunk before, Michael? Where do you suppose it came from? Who would do that?"

"Enough," I said. "I don't know a damn thing about the fucking mummy. No idea who it could be, where it came from, or who put it there."

"Okay, okay." Ellis looked at me, startled. "I was just wondering how long it'd been there."

So was I. Anger rushed in as my shock abated. I could feel the heat of it and the energy, coursing through me, heightening my color, making my hands almost shake on the wheel.

Luckily it was a short ride to Ellis's. The last I saw of them both, they were struggling through the front doors of the apartment building, holding the gowns between them, talking animatedly. I wondered briefly if they had made off with more than the allotted three.

I drove away quickly, breathing fast. I hung a left across traffic, narrowly missing a cyclist. "Damn Ronnie," I muttered, my jaw tense. If only our paths had never crossed again!

I glanced at my watch. It was four sixteen. I had planned to visit Logan this afternoon. An image of his ravaged skeletal face flashed into my mind. The wheel jerked under my shaking hands as the mummy's grinning skull superimposed itself on top of Logan's face. Shit! I swerved onto a side street and glided to a stop. I felt the adrenaline seeping away, leaving me cold and shaking. I needed a drink.

On autopilot, I made my way to the Mason's Arms, a nearby pub that was usually crammed with students. In late June I felt I would be safe. I ordered a Heineken, then changed it to a scotch on the rocks.

It was Logan's fault Ronnie had entered my life again. It was all because of him and his accident.

I met Logan the first month I moved back to Toronto. He and two other men were trying to move a full-size grand piano into his apartment above a store on the corner down the block from me. I stopped to admire it and offer my help. They ended up using a crane to swing the thing into the upstairs window, and afterwards, Logan invited us all up for beer and pizza. The movers soon left but I stayed, drawn by his warmth and interesting conversation. I envied him his piano and his skill in playing it. I envied him the path he had taken to a career in music, whereas it had been denied to me. Music was a frivolity in the Dunn-Barton home.

Logan had quite a collection of musical instruments, but he made his living playing clarinet and flute as a studio musician, and in the pit of musical theaters. After that we would meet occasionally. I invited him in to check out my spinet harpsichord, and we played a few impromptu duets, with him on recorder. It was during one of these evenings he told me about his young brother who had died of AIDS two years ago. Then he told me about doing the music for Wilde Nights, the drag show AIDS fund-raiser, playing the piano during rehearsal as well as working on the orchestrations and getting the musicians to work for free. And then some after-hours place he was playing in was torched, and he was caught in the fire. That night, he had invited me to drop in and hear some visiting musician who was playing with the group. Instead, I had fallen asleep at home, watching the news at eleven.

Logan had been in the burn unit at the Toronto Hospital for months. At first he wasn't allowed visitors. Then, one at a time, we could go in, fully gowned and masked. By now there were few who still went to spend time with him. I used to go almost every evening, taking papers to correct or notes for my book to write up on my laptop, anything to keep me busy but still there. I played music on CDs I brought with me, all kinds, some I bought just for the purpose. I had this insane sense of guilt, as if my being at the club would have made a difference. Of course it made no sense, and I never mentioned it to anyone. Not even to his sister, who was his one faithful visitor. His girlfriend had drifted away weeks ago. So much for love.

The scotch warmed me. I felt my body relax into the fake leather armchair. I could weather this. I could deal with Logan this evening, keep as much to my routine as possible. I wouldn't let Ronnie's nasty trick disrupt my life. Everything would blow over quickly. In a city this size, there was always something bizarre happening to catch the headlines. I drained my glass. As I raised my head, looking around for someone to give me a refill, I noticed the TV over the bar. The sound was turned down, but I recognized Ronnie's house. The police cars. The gurney and its awkward alien burden. And me, my face a mask of shock and anger. I paid my bill and left.

CHAPTER THREE

As I walked in the front door, the phone was ringing. I rushed across the hall to answer it, slipped on a scatter rug, and skidded to a jarring stop. What if this was the police? But the voice I heard when the answering machine picked up was that of Julie Kates, telling me she knew I was here, had just seen me come home, and if I didn't answer the effing phone she would come downstairs and lie across the front door, howling at the moon.

I picked up the phone. "It's too early to howl at the moon," I said. "It's still light outside."

"Bullshit. Never too early. Okay, Michael, what's the poop? Since when do you run around discovering dead bodies?"

I felt the jolt go through me. "I forgot you were a reporter," I said. I looked at the flashing light of the answering machine. Eighteen messages. Of course. The fourth estate.

"Michael?" The voice sounded very close. I turned around. She was standing in the hall, her new cordless phone in one hand. "You left the door open," she said.

I dropped the receiver back on the cradle.

"I'm a pushy broad." She grinned and shoved back her mane of untidy red hair. "But we're friends, right?"

I looked at her. She had the grace to look sheepish.

"I'm curious," she said. "Shoot me."

"Not till you pay the rent," I said. "It was due last Wednesday."

"Shit. I forgot." She dropped into a chair and stretched out her long legs, resting her Doc Martens on my footstool. "So what's the story?" she said, cracking open a package of Chicklets.

"There is no story."

"Oh come off it. I saw you on TV."

"Fifteen seconds of fame I could have done without."

"I guess. Bummer for you, but still a great story." Her eyes gleamed. "So who was Lipinsky to you? Friend? Partner? Lover?"

Good question, I thought. But not one I was about to discuss with Julie. "Not now," I said. Maybe not ever.

"Ah, come on."

I shook my head.

"Hey, this is the topic du jour, Michael, and you're the only one with the answers."

"But I don't have any answers," I said. "Let's talk about something else."

"Okay. I want to know about the trunk. Did the cops take it? What else was in it? Will they look for fingerprints? What?"

"This is your idea of changing the subject?"

She shrugged. Her eyes strayed to the big cardboard box I had lugged over from Ronnie's place just before he died. Had I unconsciously glanced at it, tipping off her well-honed instincts? I don't know why Ronnie was so insistent about me bringing it home then. I kept telling myself I would look inside soon, but something kept pushing me away, not wanting to open old wounds, painful memories. It stood where I had left it, pushed almost behind the chair Julie slouched in. Ronnie's name and mine were on the side in thick neon pink. Underneath, in ornate printing, *Oh best beloved...* After all these years, he still remembered how I used to read him the *Just So Stories*.

She turned back to me. "So, more than a friend," she said with a smile.

"Look, I've had a rough day. What I want now is to forget about this nightmare."

"Oh come on. Talk about it. Let it all out. You'll feel better."

I stood up. "Julie, I'm going out tonight," I said abruptly. "I have to shower and change."

"Hell, it's only five thirty, far too early for the fashionable set you hang out with." One hand ran over the peeling glitter stickers and rainbow ribbons decorating Ronnie's box. "So what's up with this?" Her fingers slid under the flap of the box and flipped it up and down, playfully.

I stiffened. "It's none of your business."

She grinned at me mischievously. "Oooo, no more Mr. Nice Guy, eh?" She pushed back the flap and pulled out some photos. "Look, pics."

"Put those back at once. Then leave."

Her playful air dropped away suddenly. "Okay, okay. But can I talk to you later? Before you talk to anyone else?"

"I'm not talking to anyone. Period." I walked over to the door and opened it. "Out. Now."

She got up and walked towards me, eyeing me closely, as if trying to read my thoughts. Then she shrugged. "I'll drop the check off tonight," she said and slipped past me.

I slammed the door after her and walked back to the box, the anger hard inside. I laid my hand on the cardboard surface, as if this contact would erase Julie's invasive touch. After a moment, I pushed the thing completely behind the chair. I poured a Cinzano and vodka and listened to the messages. Sure enough, word had spread. The fourth estate was out for blood. So was my sister, Trish, but that was not unusual. This just gave her more ammunition. I erased the messages and took a shower, trying to wash away the sour taste of the day. I needed to clear my mind for visiting Logan tonight.

I hated hospitals. Ever since my mother's long, lingering death when I was fourteen, I have avoided them as much as possible. Friends knew not to expect me to visit should they be unfortunate enough to land up there for a time. Members of my family wouldn't want to see me anyway, so that was a useful excuse when my sister had complications with her pregnancy. But with Logan, my strange sense of responsibility pushed past all these long-ago barriers. Once my university classes were over, I went to see him on Mondays, Wednesdays, and Saturdays. Gradually he had pulled me into his world, dictating letters to the insurance company he was suing for more compensation, asking me to pick up envelopes to stuff for the fund-raising mailing for the hospice where his brother died; suggesting that while I was there, I could bring along the labels and put them on too. And would it be too much to write up an ad for auditions for Wilde Nights in XTRA? When he explained about the musical drag extravaganza, I agreed to fill in for him, playing the piano for rehearsals. And that's when I met Ronnie "Luna La Dame" Lipinsky again. On stage. In full drag. Showing the girls how to be a star.

By the time I found a parking space and walked all the way to the hospital, it was almost eight o'clock. At least I was reasonably sure he wouldn't know about Ronnie's little surprise. He rarely watched TV.

Over the months, Logan had lost weight. He lay with his gaunt face turned towards the window, and from this angle, I couldn't see the scars and tight, angry red skin that spread across one cheek and down to his chest and arms. Luckily his hands had been spared, and he continually worked with a rubber ball to keep his fingers supple. He was doing it now with his left hand.

"How's the world treating you?" he asked, turning towards me. "Not good, by the looks of you."

I shrugged. "I've had better days." I sat down on the orange armchair and handed him the bag of fruit I'd brought. "Picked fresh from the crates outside your apartment," I said.

He smiled, an odd effect, since the skin on the right side of his face twisted that side of his mouth down slightly, giving him a cynical air. "Thanks. Tell me how the book is progressing."

"Well, it's slowing down a bit now. I'm writing the part about Greek hoplite shields and how the shape tells us what kind of weapons they were going up against in battle and that brought me up against the theory of artistic license. A lot of what we know about the period comes from a study of Greek vases, and I wonder how much of that is meant to be accurate. It was decoration, after all."

"Not a Kodak moment?"

"Exactly. Like Kane and the Indians."

"The painter?"

"Right. The Canadian icon. We use his paintings to illustrate history books, or we used to anyway, but how accurate are they? Not very. If you look at his sketches and compare them to the paintings, you can see the artistic license at work. In one painting he even has the Indians paddling the canoe backwards, but it makes a great painting. That's all he cared about, and his contemporaries appreciated them that way. Why not the Greeks?"

"Very persuasive. Are you allowed to range far and wide like that?"

"I can do whatever I want. It's my book. Of course they might not publish it, but that's not what this is about."

"Ah. Lofty sentiments. Scholar as artiste. Screw commerce."

I opened my mouth to protest and stopped myself. He was always doing this, his low, hoarse voice leading me on with interested questions, then throwing something back in my face that struck him as pompous or false. His moods changed suddenly too, probably as the pain washed over him or the drugs he was taking tugged him this way and that.

"We found a mummified corpse in Ronnie's trunk today," I said abruptly.

Slowly, he shifted himself around so that he was facing me. "Run that by me again."

I did, filling in what few details I knew as I went along. His hand had stopped its constant squeezing of the ball and his tired eyes never left my face.

"Well, I'll be damned," he said when I had finished.

"Looks more like Ronnie who'll be damned," I said.

"So that's why you look like shit." Logan closed his eyes for a moment. "Imagine sleeping at night, knowing that's in the next room," he murmured. "If he knew."

"Un-huh. Someone walks in with a body one day when Ronnie's out and stuffs it in his trunk. That makes sense."

"Good point. Unless he brought it with him from his hometown. Where was he from anyway?"

"Albany."

"Guess it would be hard to get something like that across the border."

"So that theory makes even less sense."

"I doubt we'll get very far in this by trying to find much sense in it," he said quietly.

"I don't want to get anywhere with it, Logan. I just want to forget it."

"Ronnie doesn't seem like an easy person to forget."

"And he's made damn sure of that, hasn't he?" I said bitterly. I was still angry, as if Ronnie had dragged me into this on purpose to give me a hard time. "I don't want anything to do with this," I went on. "I'm calling his lawyers on Monday and resigning as executor."

"Is it that easy? And what about the money?"

"I had no idea he had so much money, and I sure as hell don't want any of it now! I've had enough of this fighting over estates with my own family. Fuck it."

"That's not what you said when you found out about it," Logan murmured.

"Well, that's when I thought it was a small amount of money with no complications."

"Anyway, by Monday it'll be too late to extricate yourself. The papers will see to that."

"No shit. It's a circus already!"

"More like *danse macabre*, I should think," he said, settling back against the pillows. "What a wonderful puzzle he left behind," he said. "A wonderful puzzle…" His eyes closed and I felt him drifting away. His breathing rasped in his throat.

Indeed. A puzzle I wanted nothing to do with. A puzzle that reached deep inside and pulled at long-dead feelings and confusion. It was all very well for Logan to look at the problem, all Spock-like and removed. He wasn't there. He hadn't been there in 1965 either.

I took my chapter eight draft out of my briefcase and started to proof-read it. After a few minutes, I gave up. I shivered in the warm room as my nose was suddenly filled with the dusty must of Ronnie's old trunk as we forced back the cover.

"Pandora's box," I murmured, shaking my head. "We've opened Pandora's bloody box."

CHAPTER FOUR

Detective Chan from the homicide squad of 52 Division called the next day. I was at home, working my way down the list of chores I had prepared before the Gay Mummy Case, as the papers were calling it, had blown up in my face yesterday. Soldier on, my father used to say, though I admit to being glad he was no longer around to say anything about this latest fiasco in my life. The detective was taciturn in the extreme, merely asking me to drop in to the police station tomorrow sometime and dictate a statement for their records. He apologized for calling on Sunday, then hung up abruptly. I went back to waxing the floors, wondering if he had called *because* it was Sunday, if he had wanted to intrude.

After lunch I went down to the basement and did some work on the current wine-making project, clarifying the Burgundy for the second time. It should be a full, rich flavor by the new year. It was soothing doing all these physical tasks, demanding enough to keep my mind from wandering, but not taxing. In this way, I managed to keep the world at bay for the whole day. Naturally I ignored the phone and paid no attention to the doorbell.

I had half expected a call from Laura, canceling our dinner for tonight, but she didn't call. Surprisingly, I was looking forward to our visit now, to being enveloped by the atmosphere of peace and stability that she always provided. There would be no embarrassing questions, no thoughtless probings into my tenuous stability. Perhaps that was what had really drawn me to her so strongly all those years ago, what I had naively believed to be love, the basis of a marriage.

Technically, Laura was still my wife, although we had had little contact for many years. Now that I was back, we met from time to time at parties, once or twice at the yacht club, where I now felt like an outsider. We talked of getting together, but I left it up to her and then when she did arrange something, I had to cancel. Tonight was long owing, as was the more formal dinner party she had set up for next Sunday. I was leery of the past. Although I had returned to my hometown, I told myself I was doing so on my own terms. But I had left almost a pariah; my wife in despair, my family not speaking to me, old friends avoiding me in the street. I was still not sure how much of the 'old' life I could handle.

Laura was firmly entrenched in that 'old' life. She lived in the house where she had grown up, where I had courted her in the formalized rituals of our youth. It was a large, generously proportioned home overlooking the Rosedale Ravine. It felt odd driving up that familiar road. Years dropped away as I passed the ancient tree in the middle of their lawn and pulled sharply to the right, directly into her circular driveway. As I got out of the car, I glanced around, looking for signs of the passage of time. Everything looked exactly the same; the roses between the tall front windows, the geraniums spilling out of the white urns on either side of the front door, the carefully tended grass. The house gleamed with new paint, but the color, even the trim around the windows, was the same. I hadn't been here for twenty-five years, and it might have been twenty-five minutes, except for the size of the Austrian pine that had been planted the year Laura was born. It now towered over the far corner of the front lawn.

I had barely touched the bell when the door opened and Laura stood there, trim, smiling, impeccably dressed in a simple white linen dress and gold jewelry. She held out both hands to draw me in.

"Michael," she said. "You poor dear. I can see what a shock you've had."

"It was…unexpected," I said, "and I'd rather not talk about it."

"Of course. How gauche of me."

Her skin felt cool and remote as I kissed her tanned cheek. She still wore Fleurs de Rocaille, and as the scent enveloped me, I felt a dizzying sensation of sliding back to a time when everything was bright and sure, and we had rules to guide our lives and keep us safe. I would stand in the hall watching her sweep down the stairs in one of her many long dresses, all with demure scoop necklines, watch her smile as she slid the short fur cape around her shoulder and come toward me, pulling on her elbow-length white gloves. But I had broken the rules, and that moment was long gone.

"Do you still like Saint Raphael Blonde?" I asked, handing her the bottle I had tied with a gold ribbon.

"Your memory is wonderful." She smiled. "But nowadays I add soda water. Let's sit on the terrace. Lupe made some sangria before she went to take her nap."

"God, she must be in her nineties by now," I exclaimed without thinking.

"She wasn't that old back then. We just thought she was, because she had so much more sense than we did. I think she's about twelve years older than I am, but she's not sure of her birthday, or so she says. We made one up when we went through all that trouble with immigration a while back."

"What was that all about? Didn't your father go though all that years ago? I seem to remember something."

"Well, that's what I thought. Apparently there are still miles of red tape left to wade through. Sangria?"

"Super." I winced, hearing myself slip back into the vocabulary of another life. I sank back into the chintz-cushioned armchair and took the ice-cold glass she offered. I sipped as she chatted on about people I used to know and had thought I cared about. It was all vaguely interesting, like hearing about someone's travels to a place you have never even thought of visiting. It felt quite detached from me, my life.

"I haven't seen Ed Summers since university," I said, trying to picture the man behind the name. I had a fleeting memory of glasses and carefully combed hair, of bad skin and well-cut clothes. "So he finally got married. Did you go to the wedding?"

Laura nodded. "It was nice to see some of the old crowd," she said.

"I thought you saw 'the old crowd' all the time."

"Not all of them. Goodness, some of these people I haven't seen since school." She sounded a little defensive.

"Ancient history." I laughed. "Not a place I want to live anymore."

"No one's suggesting you live there, Michael, but a visit now and then can be very pleasant."

Pleasant. Life was always pleasant for Laura, or seemed so. I know she worked hard to give this appearance of effortlessness, but I never understood why.

Laura set down her glass and leaned forward slightly, her back, as always, perfectly straight. "That was tactless of me," she said, her voice dropping.

I looked at her, into her eyes, clear gray with very dark pupils. I didn't say anything, but I was not relaxed anymore.

"I'm not a total boor," she went on, her voice speeding up slightly, as if she wanted to get this out of the way. "I've canceled the dinner party next Sunday. It's the least I can do to spare you."

"Spare me? What are you talking about? I didn't say I wanted out of the dinner party." I had been trying to think how to broach the subject and do exactly that, but now that she had sprung this on me, I rebelled.

"Dear heart, it's all over the news about…what you've been through recently."

"You mean Ronnie's grim little secret? What's that got to do with me?"

"It's your name that's linked to the whole gruesome thing. I thought it best to cancel, under the circumstances."

"I won't come, if it will embarrass you. Have your party. There's no need to cancel."

"Have you forgotten it was that…person who broke up our marriage?"

"But Laura —"

"I can assure you that no one else has forgotten. And if by some miracle they had, it'll all come back to them now!" Her voice, even her face, seemed to have sharpened. She looked older. Maybe it was that the sun had moved enough to fall slantwise onto her face, showing the fine lines around her lovely eyes, the occasional glint of silver in her carefully bobbed hair. It hadn't occurred to me how this whole thing might impact on her peaceful existence, how it might once again tear at her inside, as it had before, with such force that it had almost ruined her life. She had never really moved on.

"Laura, you don't have to worry about this. I'm getting out of it as soon as I can. I don't have to be executor for anyone, and I'm resigning the instant the office opens on Monday."

"The connection has already been made," she said quietly. "If anyone cares to dig at all, they'll find a much closer connection than that of executor."

"Oh for God's sake! The tabloids, maybe. Come on, Laura, it's 1990! Besides, in a day or two some other horrifying or scandalous thing will happen down at City Hall or somewhere to knock poor old Ronnie off the front page for good."

"One can but hope." Laura got up and took the empty cut glass pitcher in both hands. I stood up too and reached for it. "Let me take that for you," I said, my hands closing around the cool, damp crystal.

"No need, Michael, I can carry it. I've been carrying it for years."

"Point taken." My hands fell to my sides.

"Really? Do you really understand?"

We stared at each other, and I saw her hands tighten around the pitcher. Two spots of color burned red on her cheeks.

"Laura —"

"Shall we eat out here? There's a slight breeze, but it's still quite warm."

"Here would be fine." I moved over to the glass-topped table, set with hand-loomed mats I recognized as made by her sister. From this vantage point, I could see the small swimming pool that had seemed such a marvel when we first met. No one else I knew then had a pool. The turquoise water dimpled in the breeze. I turned, thinking I'd go in to help Laura carry out whatever was needed, but then thought better of it. She wouldn't want me there. I could see that this was a bit of an ordeal for her, entertaining me while headlines about my murderous old lover sizzled across the papers and TV screens all over town. Why it hadn't occurred to me earlier was one more instance of how out of touch we were.

The rest of the evening ran like a drawing room comedy of manners, without the comedy. We talked about theater and music, the plans for the new opera house, the guest prima ballerina dancing with the National Ballet. We discussed how her old family friend Rolly Paterson had had to sell his boat to pay his yacht club fees. Even Laura thought this was amusing, though she admitted she felt a little guilty about her laughter. But no matter what we talked about, there was Ronnie, looming over us like a bad-mannered ghost. Not content with tearing Laura's life apart once, he was obviously determined to do it again.

As I left that evening, I wondered suddenly if Ronnie had done this for a reason. Had he named me executor for the sole purpose of throwing my life into turmoil once again? Was it like him to harbor a grudge for years? This man — so apparently careless and free, living only in the moment -- was a successful accountant, shrewd enough to be a silent partner in the firm he had joined many years ago. I was only now finding out about this other life, this secret respectability that lay concealed underneath the laughing extravagant gestures of the drag queen. He was quite capable of planning this as an embarrassment to me and Laura.

"Not this time, buddy!" I muttered through clenched teeth as I drove down the steep hill from Laura's house. "You're not going to have the last laugh!"

After all this time, our last days together were muddled in my mind. But I was clear about one thing — *he* had left *me*! And that still rankled.

It was just after ten thirty as I drove into the gay ghetto. I felt the urge to immerse myself in the here and now, to wash away the clinging cobwebs of my past, to feel alive. The street jostled with men in short shorts and bright tank tops, walking in pairs, talking in groups, stopping to greet friends as the crowd flowed around them. I swung into a sudden U-turn and parked illegally close to the corner of Alexander. There were a few motorcycles outside the Black Eagle. Two men in leather lounged near the front door, silent, watching. I recognized one as the dentist I had been to a few times for that troublesome root canal. I nodded and passed on.

There were balloons tied to the brass railing outside Woody's. Three drag queens swept up the steps in front of me in impossible heels, calf muscles bulging. The place was huge, but the exposed brick of the walls, the polished brass and division of space into rooms, gave the place an air of welcoming coziness. So did the hum of masculine voices, the laughter and cheerful music. I knew there were many who hugged the walls, watching, appraising, longing for contact. Older men like myself often feel out of place in a society that idolizes youth.

I elbowed my way to the bar and ordered a Rickers Red. The bartender looked vaguely familiar, but he was more likely just a type I had seen hundreds of times before in places like this. I took my beer through to the back and watched a game of pool, this ritualized sex dance that lately made me feel rather like an old *roué*. Nevertheless, the bend and stretch of denim against a tight ass was aesthetically pleasing.

There were three of them around the pool table, one in his early thirties, one older, the third, a young-looking twenty something. The boy was lithe and sinuous, his hair the color of streaked sunlight. He looked good and he knew it, smiling up at me from time to time in a quick, sideways look. The older man was big, with a great chest and biceps that stretched his T-shirt sleeves. He reminded me of someone. A definite someone, not just a type. I let the half-remembered resemblance tickle in my mind as I watched the boy bend and stretch, sight down the cue, shift his weight.

When they invited me into the game, I was surprised. A flush of pleasure was, I hoped, not noticeable in all the heat and ruddiness of drink. We exchanged first names as we chalked our cues. The youngest, Ryan, flirted shamelessly with me all evening, sliding hot glances my way from under those thick eyelashes and standing very close as we watched the others play. I even gave him my card, during one of those lulls when someone was getting us drinks from the bar — drinks that I paid for. It was a good thing I didn't do this sort of thing often.

An hour or so later, eighty dollars poorer and pleasantly buzzed, I went out into the street and yanked the inevitable parking ticket off my windshield. As I drove home, I thought of Laura, in that big house with an aging servant, and a sudden rush of sadness flowed over me. In a way, I admired her, but I didn't want to be with her or share her life.

I was almost home when it hit me, and I finally remembered who the big man at Woody's reminded me of — Al Delvecchio. Al was Ronnie's new boyfriend for a brief time back in 1965, and the reason he had left me. They used to fight viciously, fiercely, going at it at full throttle. I was called by the neighbors once. The cops were called twice. With all that practice, Ronnie must have learned a few street moves from Al. One fight too many, perhaps? One final unlucky punch or shove that left Al dead on Ronnie's floor? And whom could he turn to? By that time I was desperately trying to lose myself in grad school, spending days buried in the dim netherworld of the stacks in the library, trying to forget all about the boy who had rammed into my life so spectacularly. But I couldn't forget that I was the one who had brought him out. And I was the one who had introduced him to Al Delvecchio. Was Al the shriveled, mummified corpse who had leered up at us so recently from Ronnie's trunk?

Chapter Five

"Well, you old devil," Lew's voice boomed over the phone, instantly recognizable even though I hadn't heard from him in months. "I see you and Ronnie are back together again. On the front page, at least."

"Lew, I know you think this is terribly amusing, but it's hardly in the best of taste. Please. It's too early in the morning. I don't want to think about it."

"Well, dear, everyone else is having a whale of time with it." He chuckled evilly, a sound that brought back some not unpleasant images from the past. It seemed I was doomed to walk down memory lane a lot lately, whether I liked it or not.

Lew and I had been an "item" in Montreal, years ago. I had found him attractive when I was with Ronnie, but at that point, I was into monogamy. Being with Ronnie was earth-shattering enough without piling an affair on top of that. Years later, when we met again in Montreal, where I was taking some courses, drowning myself in Greek and Roman history, with an occasional foray into the Middle Ages, we flung ourselves into it, hot and heavy. Lew claimed to be studying French, but he spent very little time in the pursuit of knowledge. His friends called him Loosey Goosey Gander behind his back, but his real name was Llewellyn ab Hugh. When I got the offer of a job in a small-town university, Lew remembered he had a law degree and came back to Toronto to become rich and famous as a criminal lawyer. I sometimes wondered if he might like to revive more than old memories.

"So who's the guy in the trunk?" he asked now, and I could almost hear him smacking his lips in anticipation of my reply.

"My guess is Al Delvecchio."

"Do tell. The one with the penchant for black silk shirts and skinny white ties?"

"And two-tone loafers. That's the one."

"Are you going to the police with this gem of deduction?"

"They don't need me to help do their work."

"Maybe you won't need to. I see by the paper this morning they plan to rehydrate the mummy-guy's hands and take his fingerprints. Isn't that delicious?"

I shivered at the thought. "Can they do that?"

"Apparently. It'll take a while, though. By the way, did you know Ronnie had a gun?"

"He didn't."

"Well, dear, he was an American. And he must have had one, because the mummy-guy was shot. Gotta run. Bye-o."

"What?"

But Lew had hung up.

I went to the porch and dug out the paper I had flung there that morning, refusing to read the front-page story. Now I did, and sure enough, they were going to juice up the corpse and take fingerprints. There wasn't much detail, but they did say there was what seemed to be a bullet hole in the skull.

I sank back into the creaking comfort of the old wicker chair, grudgingly donated by my sister from our family cottage. Who was Ronnie Lipinsky? I wondered. Had I ever known him at all? I threw the paper down on the floor and forced myself back into proofreading. At least all the violence I wrote about was centuries old.

Later that day, there was a knock at the door. I had been ignoring the phone and the door bell for a while, aware of the paparazzi hovering around my front lawn, but it was only Julie, holding a bag of bagels from the Harbord Bakery, a nervous grin and her rent check. Her kinky red hair stood out from her head like a messy halo. She always wore long, full, filmy skirts and Doc Martens. This time she topped off the ensemble with a tasteful, shiny black spaghetti-strapped item that I would imagine more at home in a Frederick's of Hollywood catalogue.

"Hey, hey, I brought the rent," she said, poking it at me with little stabbing gestures. "And some bagels, in case you're not busy and we can have coffee or something." She trailed off lamely. "And I promise I won't talk about the skeleton if you don't want," she added in a rush, "even though you're getting quite a fan club gathering out front."

I had to laugh, she was so anxious. I'd never seen her like this before. She always appeared quite self-possessed in a way I envied in someone of her age. Now her youth was showing and it was almost reassuring.

"I'm about ready for a break," I said magnanimously. "Come on through to the sun porch. There's coffee just ready in the kitchen and cream cheese and some apple jelly from Mrs. Whats'ername next door."

"Mrs. Goldstein? She been cooking again?"

"Bless her. I love it when she cooks. I'm taking a small jar for Logan, in case he feels the urge for something sweet."

"How's he doing?" she asked, holding the tray while I piled on the mugs and sliced bagels, cream cheese, plates, jelly.

I shrugged. "Up and down. But there *is* progress. The latest graft seems to be taking and he has whole stretches of time now when he's alert and interested in things."

I led the way back to the porch and cleared off the round table, piling the manuscript papers back into my briefcase. I was glad she had come with her peace offering. I tended to let things like this go myself, and slight rifts could widen imperceptibly until a great gulf yawned that I felt powerless to do anything about.

I talked about Logan some more as we both sank down into the wicker chairs and sipped our coffee, nibbled at the bagels.

"Scrumptious," I said, waving a piece at her.

She grinned. "Yeah. I love 'em fresh like this."

Finally I took pity on her. "Okay, I have a news flash," I said.

She leaned forward eagerly, her long hair spilling over one shoulder.

"But this is off the record. Agreed? Everything we talk about is off the record."

"Agreed." She nodded, sending her hair bouncing. "Anyway, I'm freelance, remember. The only piece I could sell on it would be maybe an interview of memories or something. You know, one of those 'He was such a sweet guy. Who'da thunk it?' kind of things, and I can't see you giving me one of those."

"Damned straight!" We both laughed.

I told about her about my Al Delvecchio theory as she nodded, one Doc Martened foot bobbing up and down. I tried not to look at it. "I met Al in the beer store one day, and he helped me carry a few cases I'd bought for a party Ronnie was having. I invited Al along, and he fell for Ronnie hard. Though I didn't realize it at the time, I guess it was mutual. About a month later, Ronnie told me to get lost. He said Al was more fun and more freethinking than me, which meant he was into drugs. They used to fight viciously. Once Ronnie got hurt so badly I had to take him to the hospital, but he still wanted Al. I left the city in the midst of their riotous relationship, rushing off to England to bury myself in atmosphere, study and close observation of British males."

"Bet that was boring."

"Shows what you know." I laughed, because it was expected.

"So you think they got into a fight and Ronnie killed him?"

"It's a theory. I was completely out of touch with Ronnie by the fall of 1965. That was the point after all."

"But are you sure this Al character is actually dead?"

That stopped me cold. I had become so attached to my theory that I hadn't questioned this basic precept. "Well, if he isn't that certainly blows my theory all to hell."

"Yeah. I'd say so. How about if I do some research to find out? I know how to do all that stuff, you know. I'm paid to do research, remember? And what I don't know I can find out about. I know this PI in Florida —"

"Different laws, Julie."

"Pretty much the same methods, though. Same databases. Everyone needs a death certificate, right? How do you spell that name again?"

She had pulled out a notebook from a suspiciously handy pocket and was looking at me expectantly.

"If no one knows he's dead, there'd hardly be a death certificate," I pointed out.

"After seven years someone may have wanted him declared dead, right? A wife or something? Maybe she wants to get on with her life, so she can marry someone else."

"Sounds pretty thin to me." I shrugged. "Why not? But this is off the record, remember?"

"Yeah, yeah! I said that already. I swear!"

"Okay. Al was Alonzo. That much I'm sure of. But the last name…. Now that I think about it more carefully, I'm not sure it's Delvecchio. It's more a sounds-like sort of thing."

"Michael!"

"I can find out, but it will take a while. I'll let you know, okay?"

"Like, soon, eh? I really want to find out before the police. Just for my own satisfaction," she added hastily.

I had to admit that I was intrigued myself. When she had gone, I thought about Al some more. I knew there would be no record of him in my old address books, but I did have that carton of Ronnie's labeled *memorabilia*, in his large looping writing. It was still shoved behind the wing chair in my living room. I pulled it out, took a deep breath, and opened the box.

Inside was a series of photo albums titled *Luna by Star Lite*, each with a number. The top one was *number 14*. There were big glossy photos of drag shows and fund-raisers like Fashion Cares, parties in bars and Pride Day floats, all labeled with handwritten comments and captions. Glori Daze, aka Duane Kelley, was featured in many of the drag shots. Glori was the first drag queen I had ever known. I still remember taking Ronnie to see his show at the Manatee in the early days when he was performing with Craig Russell, watching Ronnie's delight in the glitter and joie de vivre, the outrageous over-the-top wit and chatty bitchiness. The whole dangerous glamour of an underground subculture pulled at him. It was like a second coming out for Ronnie, and Glori had been a great help getting him started along the road to his somewhat-dubious fame. Soon after Ronnie's formal entry into the drag world, Glori got his big break and began the first of many tours across the US with a drag show, pulling down big bucks for a lot of years, or so I'd heard. He had even made a few movies, which was why everyone was so pleased that he would be the star of this year's Wilde Nights.

I flipped though the pages, seeing images of a man I hadn't known: Ronnie Lipinsky, slight and elegant in a tux, presiding at dinner parties, pouring wine, proposing a toast. Ronnie as Luna La Dame, curvaceous in a striking red dress and long blond hair, lighting the huge candles in front of his Wall of Death, lounging on the couch with another guy in drag I didn't recognize, dancing at a Trillium Monarchist Society Ball in a net formal with a train. As I turned the pages, I saw familiar faces everywhere, grown older, tighter, eyes more cautious and wary. Some had gone the other way and thrown over all caution. I saw men I had known slowly dying as the pictures flipped by. And finally I came to the bottom of the box.

Under all the glitter and glitz was a scuffed, old school scribbler, with the crest of Shatterly Hall on the front and Ronnie's name and the words *Private Journal* written in his ornate looping script. I went into the kitchen to get some coffee and added a shot of Baileys.

I took my mug outside to the small square of garden in the back. I sipped it as I watered the few flowers in pots along the edge of the patio, wondering why I was going out of my way to rake up details from a past that had been the most painful period of my life. When I came back to Toronto last fall, I knew I would meet Ronnie again, but a lot of years had gone by and time heals all wounds, they say. Long ago I had gotten over him. But do we ever really get over our first love? I felt slightly guilty about Laura when I admitted that Ronnie had, indeed, been my first genuine passion. But when he and I met again after all those years, everything was warm and easy between us. I knew he was ill, and quite naturally joined his support group, visiting him, picking up prescriptions, giving him lifts to doctors' appointments and lunch dates, drives in the country, to the ballet and the theater. I thought I had truly grown up at last, but when I was pulled so suddenly and completely back into our shared past, I had misgivings. My whole view of that past had been shattered with the discovery of that body in his trunk. Had I lost my head over a murderer? This question nagged at me, the need to know that I was not wrong in my estimation of his character, so strong I was shaken. How could I have been so misled? The fact that countless people have fallen for someone who turned out to be capable of murder made no difference. I had lost my heart to an open, loving boy who had sought refuge here to escape the violence of the Vietnam War. How could someone like this have turned to murder? Or had he been driven to it by forces I knew nothing about? I had left town. I had fled. Had I abandoned him? In some twisted, strange way was I responsible? And is this, perhaps, why he had named me as executor?

I turned off the water and wound up the hose. I had found no pictures of Al in the later photo albums. I would have to open Ronnie's notebook diary if I wanted more information.

September — 1964

Miz Lard-Ass wants us to keep a journal for English. Sure. Like we'd write anything we really thought about for her to read, to drag her owl eyes over and gloat that now she really knows us. Oh yeah. So then I thought of Uncle Earl, who always kept two sets of books on account of the IRS was always on his tail, or so he said. So that's what I'll do — keep a double set of journals. I'll write a few pages of pap for L-A and then I'll write what I really think. Here in the Scrapbook of My Life, where no one but me will ever see. And I'll put in pictures, too, with the camera Mom gave me last year.

This place isn't much like what I thought it would be. I knew I wouldn't be going to a public school like back home, because I'm not a citizen, but this place? At least they don't make us wear ugly uniforms and people aren't stuck-up or anything. After all, most of them have messed up big-time along the way.

The kids call this school The Shaft, or Shits Hall, depending on who's talking. The real name is Shatterly Hall, which sounds grand but it's really a dump — just this humongous old house that needs a whole lot of repairs that no one seems interested in making. Part of the ceiling in the second-floor hall is falling down. You have to eat your lunch in the classroom, because there's no student cafeteria or anything. No one can sit in the back of Mr. Dunn-Barton's class because the pipes leak, but I don't care. I like to sit in the front row anyway, get up close and personal, and watch his cute ass when he turns to write on the blackboard. And I love the way he talks, sort of English. Real classy. But you have to wonder what do they do with all the fees we're paying here. They're higher than some of the regular private schools even.

Jeez! I never thought I'd say this, but thank God for old Uncle Bunny!

I don't really mind this place, but it's a lot different than school back home in the States. First of all, there's an extra grade tacked on to high school, like we need more of this shit. It's a make-work project for teachers, is what I think. I have to take French and there are these things called "matriculation exams" everyone in Ontario has to do and the staff gets all bent out of shape about it. What Shits Hall is, really, is a cram school. Most of the kids have been kicked out of other private schools and they've all got their own personal timetables so they can pick up credits in different grades all at the same time. This one girl, Monica Heising, says she's been kicked out of five different places, so this is her last chance. Like she should get a prize or something. I like her a lot.

Everything's so new, and that's good, but it's bad too, because there's no place to go to relax, you know, and not have to be thinking, yeah, this is different so I've gotta keep learning stuff. It's a strain. I'd love to tell Harry about it, to phone him up and just talk and tell him what's new…and then I get real down, 'cause I can't do that anymore. Shit.

But I've got a great place to live — a groovy room up under the roof in an old house not far from the subway. Someone painted the slanted ceiling in swirling colors of lime green and mauve and bright neon pink, like they were on acid at the time or something. I love it. There's a double bed, which is kind of useless so far, but I'm working on it, and a big desk that just fits in an alcove in front of the window. I made a bookcase out of some boards and bricks I found while checking out the back lanes where people leave garbage. I found a chair, too, that's not too bad.

There's a college girl in the other room on this floor, and we share a bathroom, which is fine as long as her or her long-haired greasy boyfriend aren't in there barfing out their guts, which they do a lot. College seems to be real hard on the stomach. There's another American downstairs, a draft dodger like me, but a real one — like he waited to actually get called up before he skipped out. His name's Tucker Freemont. He's a pot-smoking, guitar-playing hippie who never wears shoes, but he's somebody to talk to now and then. And he's got a TV set, so I can watch *The Avengers*. Too bad there's only a few shows left. Tucker likes *Gunsmoke*. Odious — a bunch of skinny-assed cowpokes don't do it for me, man. Anyway, he's moving to Rochdale College soon with all the other hippie druggies, so I'll probably never see him again. Just as well. I don't want to get sidetracked from The Plan by too much free acid, before I get out of Shits Hall.

Sex, on the other hand…. I could do with some of that.

CHAPTER SIX

"Ohmigod, Michael, how are you holding up, sweetie? Is this a nightmare or what?" Glori Daze enveloped me in a powdery embrace the moment I walked into the room. She must have been lying in wait, one ear on the buzz of conversation, the other on the creaking stairs outside the auditorium of the 519 Community Centre where the rehearsals for Wilde Nights were lurching along. It was two o'clock on a Sunday afternoon, still early in the day for this crowd.

"Welcome home, Glori," I said, extricating myself from the extravagant bosom. "You look wonderful."

"Fucking great homecoming this is," she snarled, flinging the diaphanous crimson shawl over one shoulder. "I can't believe this crap! Tell me I'm dreaming?"

"I'd love to, but unfortunately you aren't."

"Christ on a sequined cross! Why can't they let poor Luna rest in peace?"

"They can hardly ignore a body found on the premises," I remarked.

She drew back and looked at me more closely. "Honey, you don't look so good," she said. "Remember, this craziness has nothing to do with you."

"Tell that to the reporters parked on my front lawn," I said, heading determinedly toward the piano through the chaos of chattering queens in various stages of drag.

They were, for the most part, a clashing rainbow of sparkle and glint in home-sewn dresses and gowns, false eyelashes and heavy makeup. Those who had not used the occasion to go all out wore short tight skirts from Value Village or Goodwill, with brightly colored tops. All ages were represented, from the twentysomethings like Ellis to my generation, to pushing fifty really hard, like Glori. I guessed that the majority were under thirty-five. All were in the high heels needed to rehearse the dance numbers.

Ellis, in a blond wig and turquoise sequins, was working his recent contact with gruesome death for all it was worth, the center of a circle of admirers. What was he saying about those brief moments of chocking dust and horrified recognition? I wondered what it had done for his sex life.

As I sat down at the piano, I realized there were far more people here than needed for the numbers slotted for this afternoon's rehearsal. Not only that, but they were on time, something almost unheard of, according to Logan, who had been helping out long before I came on the scene. This could be because of the return of the now-famous Glori, but I suspected it was more about getting closer to the gory details of the skeleton in Ronnie's closet, through Ellis, me, and Jaym, who I now saw perched on the speaker in one corner of the room. He looked pale and in need of sleep. Where Ellis had bloomed as a result of his macabre experience, Jaym had withered, and I liked him the better for it.

I was sorting through the untidy pile of music when Ellis pranced up. "Miss Mope is really bringing me down," she said, indicating Jaym with a jerk of her blond head. "Shit, I'm so nervous! And it's not even my big scene today."

"You hide it well. Did you —"

We both turned as a shrill voice pulled all eyes to a tall, skinny figure in an acid green dress, absurdly high heels, and a bad wig. The dead black of the hair drained the haunted face beneath it of all color.

"Euww, she's not from planet fashion, is she?" Ellis murmured.

"…and I know I missed the first few rehearsals and all," the apparition shrilled, "but it's okay, really. Luna said I could just come in late and it'd be fine. I got my music right here." She pulled open a big handbag with a flashy clasp, balancing the weight of the thing on a skinny knee as she bent over, pawing through it with jerky movements. A compact clattered to the floor, followed by a lipstick and two bottles of pills. Jaym stepped forward, scooped up the stuff, and handed it back. All around us, the talk had died down to the sibilant hiss of whispers.

The skinny queen smiled. "Me and Luna, we go way back," she said and giggled.

"That's nice," Jaym said and dropped the stuff in her gaping purse.

"Who the hell *is* it?" Ellis muttered, staring.

I shrugged. I had no idea. I noticed Bob Keyes, the choreographer, slipping though the group toward her.

A loud clapping made everyone turn toward the improvised stage as Stan Wynkowski, a big solid guy in charge of rehearsals, shambled up to the microphone. A ragged silence fell. I still hadn't figured out how this show was actually being put together, or who was in charge of what. So far I had seen only bits and pieces of it, since I was one of three or four accompanists who volunteered time and patience to get this show up and running by the fall. It was a huge effort, and I had seen little to give me faith it would all come together this side of paradise. I could certainly understand why it was not an annual event.

Stan began by welcoming Glori back home with enough hyperbole to satisfy the biggest ego. As Glori preened beside him, I noticed the skinny queen in the acid green dress had found her music and now held it clenched in one beringed hand as she made her way to the platform. Bob tried to catch her arm, but she shook him off.

"Remember me?" she cried shrilly. "I'm Bianca Bombe, star of the Velvet Box Review." She held out one hand to Stan, the great rings flashing in the sunlight. Sweat gleamed on her forehead.

"Oh puleeze," said Glori.

"Me and Luna, we go way back," Bianca said, ignoring Glori. Her wide smile split her pale face with a gash of cruel color.

"Of course I remember you," said Stan, taking her hand gallantly. Bob moved up on Bianca's other side. "I remember when you and Luna La Dame and Glori Daze all appeared together back in the '70s. Great show."

"I'm going to do some of the same numbers here," Bianca said. "In your dreams," snarled Glori. "Bianca, you were washed up and thrown out with the rags twenty years ago."

"*I'm* not the one who was paid to leave town!" shrieked Bianca. "Luna and me stayed right here and founded the Trillium Court and —"

"Because no one wanted you anywhere else!" shouted Glori.

"Liar!"

"Ladies, ladies, that's enough." Stan's voice easily cut through the shrieks. "Bianca, this show is already cast, but I'll take your name down for the next one. Look, I'll make a note in the official production book right now." He flipped over a few pages on his clipboard and flourished his pen, then began to write. "We need stars like you, Bianca, for the next show. See?"

She watched his moving hand as if mesmerized by the letters flowing from it.

"The star," she said, nodding. "That's right."

"That'll be a first," said Glori.

Without warning, Bianca leapt forward with a scream. "Bitch!" Her purse flailed, her long, bony fingers reached for Glori's carefully made-up face. Glori grabbed the black wig just as Bianca's heel caught on the raised platform and she toppled backward. "Bitch!" she cried again. Tears streaked her makeup. Bob was struggling to lift her up as Stan bent over to help. Jaym patted Bianca's arm, his eyes pained. He took the wig from Glori's hands and put it back on Bianca's nearly bald head. It sat there uneasily, slipping to one side as she struggled to her feet.

Stan and Bob exchanged glances. "We'll call you a taxi," Stan said, steering her toward the door.

"*Was* she a star?" Ellis asked, looking at me.

I shrugged, watching the little group lurch its way into the hall. The steady hum of conversation had broken out again, growing louder as the doors closed behind Bianca and her entourage. Bianca Bombe. The person I remembered by that name had nothing to do with this wreck. She was vibrant and sexy, a loud, laughing vixen who loved practical jokes. She couldn't dance worth a damn, but her personality made you forget this while she was on stage. She must have been around Ronnie's age, which would make her about forty-two. She looked a lot older. *"Me and Luna, we go way back."* They had just begun to hang out together when I left.

"Ready when you are, Michael." Stan's voice pulled me back to the present. Glori was ready to launch into her first number. Her dusky, gravelly voice, roughened with decades of smoking and booze, brought back a few memories, too. She was still a good female impersonator, lip-synching her way through the traditional canon with flair. She could be down and dirty and funny as hell, but she lacked Ronnie's sly wit and originality, and I had often wondered why Ronnie had never left town to make his fortune as Glori had. After my recent discovery, however, it was beginning to make more sense.

Glori was duly applauded when she stepped down, but I thought the effort and the fight with Bianca had really taken it out of her. The thundering chaos that followed as the whole company lumbered into a dance number trying to follow Bob's agile steps was painful. Whoever thought all gay men can dance should have been there. I was glad when it was over and I could pack up my music and get out in into the fresh air — or as fresh as it gets in Toronto in June.

"Thanks, Michael, you're a doll," breathed Bob, rushing over before I could escape. He never forgot the niceties, and I appreciated that. I didn't appreciate the light kiss on the cheek. I hardly knew the man. I heard Ellis stifle a laugh as he watched my futile effort to escape.

"Any more of that and you don't get a lift home," I told him as we clattered down the stairs.

"It's okay, Michael. Jaym and me are going to grab a bite to eat with some of the girls, and then we're going to the 501.

Speaking of bars, I saw you at Woody's the other night. I didn't know you played pool."

"I didn't see you there. Why didn't you come over?"

"Well, you were — oh how will I put this? — real engrossed." He grinned. "See you later. Come on, Jaym."

They swayed off down the street, big hair, sequins, and huge earrings reminding me of giant Barbies who had been on a long-delayed binge. I had meant to drop in on Logan, but the rehearsal had left me drained. I ransomed my car from the lot down the street and went home instead, parking in the lane behind Mrs. Goldstein's place and hopping the fence into my yard, just in case some intrepid reporter was still hanging about on my front lawn.

I was still ignoring the answering machine. People I hadn't heard from in years kept leaving messages of concern and suggesting get-togethers over coffee, drinks, a light supper at their place. They were even sending me e-mail, to my address at the Gay Blade BBS, which I also ignored.

I let the silence of the old house settle around me. I loved this place, my refuge. It was smaller, more intimate than the huge apartment I had lived in when teaching at Montmorency University. I no longer craved the space, or all the furniture I had collected for a while, trying to re-create the atmosphere I had grown up with and been denied by "disgracing the family" when I left my wife for Ronnie. At the time I wasn't aware of what I was doing as I haunted antique stores, but I could see it now, and I didn't need these props anymore. I had kept what I really loved: my father's sword, the old high-backed wing chair, the harvest table, the pine blanket chest I now used as a coffee table, three huge paintings I had bought in England, and the spinet harpsichord. Everything else was sold at auction. All I needed now were my books and the tiny garden out back, which I was slowly transforming into a place of rest and tranquility where there would be the constant sound of water spilling from a fountain into a small pool. I had to admit my simplifying process did not include the kitchen, which I had modernized completely, using up most of the money I had made from the furniture auction.

I spent the evening sitting in the sunporch at the back, ignoring the constant ringing of the phone as I plowed through rewrites for my book. I was so completely immersed in my task that it took a while to realize there was someone at the front door. I considered ignoring it, but surely it was too late for reporters. Whoever it was persisted.

"You win," I said, opening the door and frowning into the dimness. I had forgotten to replace the lightbulb again.

"Does that mean you lose?"

I straightened my shoulders. That voice was familiar. Young. Sexy. As I processed this information I recognized him as the twentysomething guy from Woody's a few nights before. "Ryan, isn't it?"

"Yeah. You gave me your card, right? Well, here I am."

I didn't know what to say.

"You said you need some work done in your garden? And some painting around the house?"

"It probably could do with some work," I hedged. I was not prepared for this. Part of me was still back in ancient Greece, which was not a good idea, in the circumstances.

"I came by earlier but you weren't home," he said, shifting his feet. "I'm real good with my hands."

"No doubt," I murmured, glad for the dimness as I felt the heat in my face.

"I can do a bit of carpentry and that," Ryan went on earnestly. "And paint too. And I grew up on a farm so I know about growing things." He moved forward into what little light there was and looked straight at me.

I shouldn't have looked into those hazel eyes. I saw the knowledge grow there, and I felt foolish standing protectively in the open door. We both knew that if I were going to send him on his way, I would have done it by now. What had ever possessed me to give him my card?

"I don't have no place to go."

I stepped back and waved him into the hall. He didn't need any coaxing. He scooped up his backpack and bounced into the house, grinning literally from ear to ear. His pleasure was infectious. His ass, in the tight jeans, was divine.

"You want some coffee? It's fresh."

"Cool. Hey, man, you wanna catch the phone?"

"No."

He followed me silently to the kitchen. I could feel him watching as I reached for another mug, cut a few slices of pound cake, and set them on the table. I poured the coffee, and he added generous portions of sugar and cream. His hands were large and oddly delicate. An expensive gold link bracelet glinted on one wrist. He ate with concentration, slurping the coffee noisily as he looked around, assessing my brand-new kitchen with all its gadgets and appliances.

"Nice bracelet," I said.

"My mom gave it to me," he said, his mouth full.

"So, tell me something about yourself." I wasn't sure what game we were playing. The whole scene was unreal to me, the lateness of the hour, the persistent phone calls, his unexpected appearance in my private space, the way we avoided the real questions.

"I hate it when people talk like that! Like, I mean, what're you supposed to say?" He glanced at the phone. "Do you, like, hate the phone or something?"

"Not at all. I just don't feel like answering tonight. Tell me, why are you on the street?"

The kid looked hurt. "Hey, you gave me your fucking card."

"And now you're here and I asked you a question." I sat back and waited for him to spill the shabby story of his unhappy home life. It took longer than I expected, but there was nothing unusual about it when it finally came.

"So when my friend Brad split to the city to get a job, I came too," he finished.

"You have a job?"

"For a while I worked in a service station filling in for some guy who was off sick, and me and Brad shared a place. But then the job ran out and so did my money and then Brad's fucking girlfriend moved in, see, and they threw all my stuff out back in the rain. Some friend, eh?"

"Ever have any trouble with the law?"

"Look, man, even if I had a record as long as my arm, which I don't, I'd be dumb to tell you about it, wouldn't I?"

"Good point."

He dropped his lashes for a moment, then gave me a frank look. Man to man. No more beating around the bush. "The place I was at kicked me out, like they do everyone after three weeks. I can't take those shelters, man. Last time I got beat up by some guys and then they took my Docs right off my feet." He paused, took a sip of coffee. "I thought maybe I could work for room and board. There must be lots to do around this old place, and with me around you wouldn't have to hire anyone else."

The phone rang again. *I must be losing my tiny mind,* I thought to myself. One night I go to a gay bar for the first time in years, and look what happens! I unplugged the phone.

We didn't talk much after that. I just sat back and watched him finish off the rest of the cake. He didn't seem to mind. Perhaps he was used to being looked at.

His hunger satisfied, he leaned back in his chair and stretched out his legs. His tight jeans clung to his lithe body, the color washed out around the creases of his groin and fly as if worn off by a lover's hand. I poured us both more coffee, thinking as I did so that it was a good thing I had switched to decaffeinated.

Gradually it was understood between us that he would move into the little room on the second floor, over the garage. It was a mess, full of cast-off things and junk from the previous owner I had meant to sort through and never had. That could be his first job. And then there was the garden.

"It needs a lot of work," I said. "I'm putting in a reflecting pool and a small waterfall. All that needs to be dug out and concrete poured."

"Sure. I can do that."

"Good."

When I led him up the back stairs to the room, he looked around with pleasure as if the place was the royal suite at the King Edward.

"Cool," he said. "I can fix this place up good."

"Easy, Ryan. We're taking this one day at time, okay?"

"Yeah, sure."

I felt a disturbing warmth in my loins as I watched him. I cleared my throat. "Sleep well. I'll see you tomorrow."

The last I saw of him that night he was sitting cross-legged in the middle of the narrow bed as he sorted through the few possessions in his backpack. For a second, I flashed back to another room under a sloping roof — Ronnie Lipinksy sitting cross-legged on the bed while we shared a joint and planned a future that would never come to pass.

I ran downstairs, cleaned up the kitchen, and went for a long walk.

CHAPTER SEVEN

Ryan's presence filled every corner of the house. As I lay in bed awake, staring into the darkness, I was aware of him. As I sat in the kitchen drinking an early morning cup of coffee, my mind's eye pictured him tousled in sleep, his body twisted in the sheets. Even when I couldn't hear him, I knew he was there. When he was up and working on some task I set, every creak and rattle penetrated my consciousness, a continual distraction, pulling my mind away from Ronnie's grim secret. You've lived alone too long, I told myself. Maybe it was good to have someone around for a while to shake me out of the deep rut I was in, to fill my mind with life, keeping death at bay.

He was a good worker, as long as he was supervised. If I left him on his own too long, he would drift off into inactivity, as if his battery was running down. I would find him staring off into space or lying in the grass, smoking, looking up at the clouds. I kept him busy, working on the garden. He dug a new flower bed in the front and planted the perennials we brought home from the nursery. He sawed up an old tree limb that had come down in a storm a few weeks ago and tied it into the requisite bundles so it would be taken away by the city. He cleaned the gutters on the roof, pulled down the old ivy, trimmed the back hedge. I was always catching sight of him as he worked, sweat glistening on his arms, his legs, his sun-streaked hair damp and curling around his face. His energy was unfailing. It crackled in the air, unnerving me in ways that were alarming.

Julie snapped pictures of him while he worked, her expensive camera clicking and whirring. "Relax," she told me. "Go with the flow." She laughed and told me Jeff, her boyfriend, was getting jealous. I suspect she meant this as some sort of compliment, but I found it irritating. She hadn't found any trace of Al Vecchio yet, even though I had unearthed the right spelling, and the newspapers hadn't come up with anything really new.

Of course they were still pursuing me, still parked outside, lying in wait, leaving notes on my car, when they finally found it out back, and phoning constantly. I had turned all the phones off now, leaving the machine to answer.

My appointment with the lawyer was for Wednesday. By some strange coincidence, Ronnie had chosen Archy Marcus, who had been an old friend of my father, as his lawyer. It was a small, very traditional, very WASP firm with offices in an old house in the upscale Yorkville area. I left Ryan toiling in the back alley, digging out the old paving stones so he could pour sand underneath and lay the new ones that had been piled there for weeks. Reporters wouldn't get anywhere with him. He didn't know anything.

Pam Marcus and I had grown up together. She had lived down the street from me, and since our parents were friends, we were often thrown into each other's company. It was a mixed blessing having her as the lawyer in charge of Ronnie's estate. She was tall and slim, with a long, intelligent face and very bright dark eyes. Her hair was swept up on her head, making her look even taller, and she wore gold earrings and a rope of pear could have paid someone's mortgage. Behind the sophistication, I still saw the skinny tomboy kid in braces and a navy blue balaclava, always wanting to join the boys.

"Look, Mikey, I inherited this mess when my uncle died," she was saying now, looking me in the eye in the disconcerting way she had always had. "Frankly, I don't give a hoot in hell what you do. You want to back out, fine. All the more money for me, and let me tell you, with taxes the way they are now and Mother refusing to move, even though the house is falling down around our ears, I could use it. So don't get me wrong when I say I think you're making a big mistake."

"Pam, I want out. I don't want to be dragged back into Ronnie's shit."

"Makes sense to me. But hear me out, Mikey."

"No one has called me Mikey since kindergarten."

"God, you're touchy. Some people never change. Okay, okay. So I understand where you're coming from and everything, Mike —er, Michael — but look at it this way. You know the people involved in this. I don't know them from Adam, and frankly, I don't understand any of it: the courts, the balls, the Wilde Nights. God! It might as well be Chinese! But that's okay. I can do it, not a problem."

"What's your point?" For someone so direct, she was taking a long time to get to the heart of the matter.

"My point is that it would be simpler for you to do it. And look, the story will be off the front page in no time. It already is, as a matter of fact. The *Globe* has it on page three already. Soon it will disappear. New massacres. Some big politico sued for paternity. New grist for the media mills."

"Pam, why don't you really want to do this?"

"Fuck," she said, startling me. She took a deep breath and leaned back in her chair. Her face looked pinched and strained. She looked tired, worn down by hard work and disappointment. She was still not a partner in the firm started by her uncle. I had heard a rumor she had almost lost her job a few years ago when the old man died.

We looked at each other over the piles of files and papers, the two untidy baskets of correspondence, the pink pile of phone messages jammed on a spike.

"I don't have the time," she said at last. "Look at this mess! I'd be behind even if I stayed at this desk twenty-four hours a day, seven days a week. Not so long ago I had time for long lunches with a friend now and then and the occasional visit to the spa. Now I come here at seven thirty and leave around eight, and I still have to take stuff home. They need to hire more people, but they won't as long as —" She stopped and took a long breath. "Downsizing," she said and gave a sudden bark of laughter. She reached for her cigarettes, then slipped them back into her bag. "And another thing," she went on. "Even if you give up being executor, you'll still be connected to the case. It's your story that's interesting, and the reporters won't give up just because you're no longer executor. Am I right? So you might as well get paid for it, I say."

"Well, the damage is already done, I suppose," I said after a pause. "What more can they say?"

"Good man! That's the spirit! Bash on, regardless!" The color had come back to her cheeks. I felt defeated. How had she managed this? I had been so sure when I came in here. "I was always on your side," she said as I was leaving. "Laura was Miss Priss even in school." She kissed the air near me and closed the door.

My side. I guess a lot of people say things like that. Me, I was just trying to get along, move along in my life, and lately that was getting more and more complicated.

Logan thought it was amusing, how I had been neatly trapped by pity.

"She was all crisp efficiency when this started," I said.

"She was getting it off her desk," Logan said. His cracked lips gleamed with medicated gel, and his eyes were too bright, but he was very aware and interested. I felt guilty for not visiting in several days.

When I explained about Ryan, he laughed, a startling, rough sound that grated on my ears. "Michael, you're getting old. Women walk over you, boys move into your house. Watch out for the silver."

"God, he can have it. Heavy, old, ornate stuff that's a bitch to clean."

"And you use it all the time, right?"

I shrugged.

He adjusted himself on the bed, his breath rasping as he changed position. "So did you know your Ronnie was involved with the mob?"

"What?" I stared at him, knowing he was going for shock value, knowing he had succeeded, but not wanting it obvious. I took a big breath. "He hasn't been *mine* for twenty-five years," I said testily, "and he was certainly *not* a mafioso. I expect they wouldn't want to claim him, either," I added, as an afterthought.

"What about the Krays?"

"Don't be ridiculous. Anyway, they weren't Mafia."

"I take it you haven't seen the paper today."

"I thought it was off the front page."

"Of the *Globe*, maybe. The others…. Anyway, the big news is that the corpse was shot in the back of the head with a .32."

"That's not news. We already knew he was shot."

"In the back of the head, Michael. Execution-style, and that spells mob. Big bad guys with no necks and black shirts."

"Oh shit."

"That too."

"But that's ridiculous! If the corpse is as old as they say, that means Ronnie was just eighteen or nineteen. Twenty, max!"

"And he did some drugs, right?"

"It was the '60s, Logan. Even I did some drugs!"

"I hear you. Was Ronnie dealing?"

"I don't know. He was going a bit wonky there for a while before I left. But no, not in '65. Whatever it was he was into, I'm sure he was just experimenting. He was a kid. Everyone was into it."

"A bit wonky," Logan mused.

"Maybe Al was the one in the mob," I suggested, feeling a slight tingle of delight at the thought. Danger, at a safe distance. "Maybe that's why he was executed."

"And why Ronnie kept him all these years in his trunk?"

I shrugged. "That's a problem, I admit."

"The main problem is that we need the chronology to figure this out. We don't know exactly how long that thing was in the trunk. Once we do, we can start to narrow down our suspects."

"Narrow down our suspects," I repeated, incredulously. "What is this? You auditioning for Hercule Poirot now?"

"There's not a hell of a lot to take my mind away from these closing-in walls," he said bitterly. "These sickly hospital smells, the ooze of my own putrefaction always seeping into my brain. I need a distraction."

"Fine. I give you what my friend Lew calls cosily *The Mummy Guy*. He's all yours."

"I need details."

"You just said yourself you can't start until we know how old the thing is. Julie is tracking down Al Vecchio for me, so we can start to do a 'last seen by so and so' scenario."

A nurse swept in, looking most un-nurselike in a purple pantsuit, her long blonde hair in a French braid down her back. "It's that time again," she said, with a false heartiness that set my teeth on edge.

"Oh boy," Logan sang back. "Time for *us* to have our scrubba-dub."

I didn't envy his nurses as I gathered my things and left, promising to fill him in as soon as I had some info.

Ryan was stretched out in a deck chair sound asleep when I got back. His body was streaked with grime and sweat, and a gash on his leg looked new. The flagstones were laid all the way to the back gate.

Julie yodeled from the front door. She must have been watching for me, she got downstairs so fast.

"Julie, you're the only one I ever knew who actually says *yoo-hoo*."

"Big wow," said Julie. "Hey, hey, listen up. I've got some good news and some bad news."

"Shoot."

"Good news is — I found the guy. I found him!"

"Great! What's the bad news?"

"He's alive."

"I'm sure he wouldn't think that was bad."

"Good for him. Bad for us. Now we don't know who the corpse is."

"Right."

"I've got his home address, business address, phone number, fax number, you name it. Here." She thrust the paper at me. "He lives in London, Ontario. Sells cars."

"Why does that not surprise me? Thanks, Julie."

"So who's the next suspect? Anyone else I can run down for you?"

"I'll see what I can dig up," I said, thinking of all those scrapbooks and photo albums I had only skimmed.

When I had opened that box, memories escaped like smoke, carrying sharp pinpricks of guilt and longing and betrayal. But smoke thins, I told myself, dissipates in the air and is soon gone. Those memories have been preserved too long. It was time to let the light in before they mummified like the body in Ronnie's trunk. There must be something in all that information that would be useful. Why else would Ronnie have insisted I take it away?

(excerpts)
October 4, 1964

....When I started having Evil Money dreams, I finally drew up a budget like Dad made me do when I got into grade 9 and he raised my allowance. I hate to admit it, but it works! It's still depressing. And I'm so fucking sick of Kraft Dinner!

On the bright side, Dunn-Barton is going to help me with French. Monica says his first name is Michael. She heard him and his wife talking in the parking lot the other day. How can he have a wife? If he's not a fucking homo, neither am I! I swear I can feel him looking at me. He wants me. I know it! He blushes sometimes when I look at him, like I've caught him masturbating or something. I wish. God he's sexy!

Which is more than I can say for this new guy who arrived today. He's all apple-cheeked and round-eyed behind his glasses. He wears a suit and tie like a junior exec or something and he has bad asthma. Five minutes after sitting down in math class he started wheezing and gasping and had to leave. When I went outside to see how he was, he was smoking a joint out in the alley behind the garages. Some scam! At first I felt like a fool for feeling sorry for him, but he said grass helps asthma. Oh yeah! And at least he shared. As we smoked, he told me his family isn't rich. Both his parents are working so he can come here. He's had to miss so much school because of his breathing problems, so he's trying to catch up fast because his parents want him to go to college. Funny how we all try so hard to please our parents. But what do *we* want to do? How often does any parent ask?

Sometimes I think about what I miss most about the old place I used to call home. I guess, maybe, I miss Deb. I was surprised how good it was talking to her the other day when I called. And walking home with Harry, going the long way so we can score cigarettes and sodas from his uncle's variety store, then opening my front door to the smells of Mom's honey cake, curling around me like a big hug. I wonder if D-B likes honey cake? If he even knows what it is? I wonder how big he is under those expensive trousers. Yeah, sure. Like I'll ever get the chance to find out.

November 14, 1964...

...Everything is copasetic! I'm in love! I'm mad about M.A.D. And it's taken two months, one week, and two days for me to know – I mean KNOW – he's mad for me too! Yesterday was Tuesday, and Dunn-Barton gave me a lift home with my science project. He's done this before a few times in bad weather and once when I had a lot of new text books to haul back, but this time he helped carry the stuff up to the third floor. Thank God I'd cleaned up my room on the weekend!

We put the project back together on my desk and then he sat on the bed to talk. I sat down beside him and the next thing I know I just feel us getting closer and closer. The air between us was charged like sparks jumping back and forth between two batteries! Suddenly I couldn't stop myself. I leaned over and kissed him, right on the mouth. And he kissed me back! I heard him moan, a small sound that slipped out of him without him even knowing and I just threw my arms around him and pulled him down on the bed. He was all over me. But when I tried to pull at his pants, he pushed me away and jumped off the bed like a scalded cat. He stuttered and stammered, his face red and his gorgeous eyes full of panic. He was afraid. Of me, of himself, of all the emotion swimming around in my small psychedelic room, pushing down on us from the slanted ceiling. Maybe he thinks I'll turn him in or something. I'd rather tear my skin off with red hot pincers, like that old saint in the book of martyrs Mary Margaret

McGee showed me once in grade school. I tried to tell him how I feel about him, how I'd never want to hurt him, how I'd wait if he needed to think or whatever. I don't even know what all I said, but he kept backing away, gesturing in the air with his hands as if trying to keep me away.

I burst into tears. I couldn't help it. And that was the best thing I could have done, 'cause he took me in his arms and rocked back and forth in the middle of the room, him crooning over me like I was a wounded pigeon or something. And I hung on tight and breathed in the solid smell of him, memorizing the strength in his arms and the comforting sexy feel of him against me. But then he pulled away and practically ran out the door and down to his car.

I know he'll be back. He has to come back. If he doesn't, I'll just kill myself!

November 19, 1964

…I hate weekends now! I can't see Michael, can't look at him in class or catch a glimpse of him in the halls or watch him talking to someone in the parking lot. This is awful. For the first time since coming here I feel really alone. Scared he'll never come around. It's been hard before, sure, fucking damn hard, but not like this. Before, I felt like all I had to do was hang on and follow The Plan and it would be okay in the end. Now, I don't know anymore. I feel like I'm losing my way, alone in this foreign city where no one really knows who I am. Or gives a flying fuck.

All week Michael ignored me. He was very formal, not joking around in class or anything, like usual. Everyone noticed. Monica is asking questions. Then on Thursday, when we had our French tutoring session scheduled, I thought he was going to cancel out, but he didn't. He sat there across his big teacher desk and drilled me on verbs and tenses and vocabulary. He read out passages from *Maria Chapdelaine* and asked me questions. He made me go through one of those dopey oral question and answer conversation things that are so dumb. Like anyone really talks like that. Exactly an hour later, he gathered up his books and said he had to go.

By this time, there was no one left but the janitor. We don't have any sports or after-class activities and everyone gets the hell out of here as fast as they can. Why hang around this dump? I jumped up and followed him and grabbed for his arm just inside the door. He spun around and glared at me. It was scary.

"Don't touch me," he said, so quiet and intense the words just went right through me. "This can't happen. It's illegal."

"But —"

"I'm your teacher. I'm married. Get someone your own age."

He turned away and I jumped in front of him, desperate to stop him from walking away. "How old are you?" I said, like that mattered.

"Twenty-two, but that's hardly the point."

Twenty-two. "Only five years difference," I said. "That's nothing."

"Ronnie, you're not listening. I'm married. End of story. This conversation is over." And he walked down the hall, nearly ran down the stairs and out to his car.

I went into Lard Ass's room and looked out the window and watched him. He sat in his car for a long time, his forehead on the steering wheel. Then he burned rubber out of there with a squeal of tires and I was all alone.

God, how I hate the weekends! It was so bad I dropped down to Freemont's and smoked some weed while we watched *Gunsmoke*. It helped a little. I told Tucker all about Michael. He only grunted a few times and said "Whatever turns you on, man." Big help he is. But at least he always has a good supply of grass and sometimes mushrooms too. And he doesn't care enough to try to hurt me and Michael…if there ever is a me and Michael….

...November 21, 1964

...I had the nightmare again. This time I woke myself up by falling out of bed, and for a minute I didn't know where the fuck I was. It was hard to breathe. I was naked on all fours panting like a dog with my head hanging down. I couldn't move. Couldn't get away from the pain. I was so scared I was shaking all over. Uncle Bunny talked about deep breathing exercises after it happened, but I was too mad and grossed out to make it work. But last night I really tried and it helped. It really did. Then I put on my sneakers and went out and began to run though the dark warm streets and it felt great. It didn't smell like a big city or Main Street USA. I could feel the air on my scalp and the blood pumping though my whole body and it didn't matter that there was no one there running beside me. Maybe I'll start running every night, get a schedule or something. It might help me sleep.

Or maybe Uncle Bunny will appear at my door and then I can show him how fast I can really run! Oh sure. Like Dad says: You always have to pay the piper.

Michael could make the bad dreams go away. Oh please! Let Michael give me good warm dreams to fill up my head so there's no room for these fucking terrors! I'm so sick of this! I just want what everyone else wants, right? A little love? Someone to care? What the fuck's wrong with that?

...November 29, 1964

...Monica found me. I hadn't been in school in days. I thought I had a bad cold, but it just got worse and worse and I was so tired I couldn't be bothered going downstairs to the kitchen to get anything to eat. I slept and went in and out of weird dreams. I hurt all over, and the coughing made it hard to breathe. Then one day there was Monica, forcing me to get dressed and into her car, and she took me to the doctor. Her doctor. She told him I was her cousin visiting from the US. He said I had pneumonia and gave me antibiotics. Then Monica brought me home and changed my bed and made me soup. Well, it was from a can but it tasted okay.

Next time I woke up it was getting dark outside and the rain sliced at the window and gleamed on the fire escape outside, making it look shiny and new. I think it was the next day, but I don't know. Someone was sitting on my bed, holding my hand. I thought I was hallucinating again, but it was Michael. For real.

"Don't die," he said.

"Stay," I said. "I won't die if you stay."

It sounds real corny writing it down, but not at the time.

Every day after school he comes over with homework and goes over the lessons with me. Of course, this doesn't really change anything. He's still married, still my teacher.

I never knew loving somebody could be this hard. It's like standing at the edge of the Grand Canyon, with the wind tearing at you all the time, and the deep darkness calling to you, wanting you to make one false step. Just one. And I could ruin his life. And maybe mine. But I want him so bad! Love makes you selfish, I guess. I don't care about his wife. About anyone. Just us. To see the light in his eyes when he looks at me. They seem to get larger and deeper as I look into them. But I don't want to be selfish. I want to be adult and mature — but then yesterday everything changed, just like that.

I was up and feeling much better, trying to fix up some bead curtains I picked up a while ago real cheap at some store on Queen Street. I had the Rolling Stones on loud on the stereo ("Can't get No Satisfaction" — yeah, I can relate to that!) so I didn't hear the knock on the door. When Michael came in, I was startled and I just fell into his arms. Literally. We stood like that for a long time, his arms around me, my head in his warm neck, the Stones pulsing all around us. I licked his sweet, salty skin and he laughed and we fell on the bed and....

I feel funny writing about it. It's so private, so different from anything I've ever experienced before. He's so tentative, gentle, and passionate, all at the same time. I don't think he's ever been with a guy before. Someday I'll ask him, but not now. Everything is too fragile now. God, don't let me ever hurt him! He's going to try to spend Saturday afternoon with me. So for now, life is good. After all I've done, do I dare to hope?

…

December 3, 1964

…I can't believe it! He's going to do it! He's leaving his wife after Christmas, and he's getting his own place. We can be together in 1965, but he won't let me move in till I graduate in June. If he can risk so much for me, I can wait! I can do anything now!

CHAPTER EIGHT

I had been back in Toronto since August, 1989, and for ten months I had managed to avoid speaking more than a few strained words to my sister. So it was not surprising that I was struck almost speechless to hear her voice when the answering machine clicked in, so startled that I actually picked up the phone and said hello. Trish chatted on, apparently unaware that there was anything at all bizarre about the one-sided conversation. When she ran out of breath, there was dead air on the wire.

"Well, Trish," I said. "Nice of you to keep in touch like this."

"We're out of town a lot," she said. "We have the country house now, you know."

"A cottage isn't good enough for you?"

More dead air.

"Michael, I need to borrow Dad's presentation tray," she said.

So that was the reason for the call. "Why?"

"We're hosting the garden party for the Dharman Foundation this year, and —"

"But, Trish, you're rolling in silver trays!"

"I want that one."

"Ah. You want the name. The engraving. The 'presented by, in appreciation of' sort of thing." This was greeted by more dead air. I was enjoying myself. "Okay, so you want me to bring the tray early? Details, please. Day? Time?"

"Michael, it's not a party. It's business." Her voice was getting tight.

"Oh, so you don't want me, just the tray."

"This is *business*, Michael! The last thing we want is a stand-in for that monster who murdered some guy and kept his body in a box for thirty years!"

"I'm surprised you could bring yourself to even call me. How much did you have to drink to work up the courage?"

"Look, I'm not the one who disgraced the family, who was almost arrested and thrown in jail for ten years for buggering a minor."

"No, that was me. The one you want a favor from. Have I got that right?" I could hear her breathing hard on the other end.

"You know as well as I do that tray should have been mine. Dad promised me!"

"The tray, the sword, and the painting are the only things I got from the estate, Trish. You got almost everything. That isn't enough?"

"You got Granny's silver."

"Christ. That's got nothing to do with Dad."

"Look, I was here. Where the hell were you when he was so out of it he didn't know where he was most of the time? When we had to call the police to bring him back from the hospital where he kept going, thinking it was time to operate on patients who'd been dead for decades!"

"If someone had cared to let me know some of this at the time, I would have been here."

"So you say. But when were you *ever* here when you were needed? When I lost my baby? When Mom had her heart attack? When your father —"

"Did you call me? I always made sure you knew my number. You chose—" I stopped, distracted by the thumping of feet on the back stairs. Ryan burst into the room. "Shit." I felt a steady pulse beating at my temple.

"Look, if you don't want to lend us the tray, fine. As you pointed out, we do have others."

"Trish —" I glanced at Ryan, hopping from foot to foot in the doorway. Now all I wanted to do was get rid of Trish and her endless litany of complaint. "Fine. You can have it, but remember, I want it back."

"Of course. I'll let you know when someone can pick it up." She hung up with a clatter.

"Come in," I said to Ryan, arranging the piles of paper on my desk.

Ryan ambled in and flung himself into a chair. He leaned back against the cushions and stretched out his legs. Even then he wasn't still, and his taut body twitched with impatience. The tight, faded jeans set off his slim, lean build to perfection.

"Well, Ryan, how's it going?" I asked, switching on my answering machine again. I felt nervous. Keyed up from my encounter with Trish. Ryan brought something into the room I wasn't ready to deal with.

The boy jiggled one sneakered foot. "Okay, I guess." He studied the poster behind my head, advertising an exhibition of the Group of Seven at the National Gallery in Ottawa. "I was just wondering when I get a day off, like."

"Are you tired of being cooped up with an old man?"

"You're not old." He smiled but didn't meet my eye.

"Thanks. You've made my day."

"Seriously, any day you want is okay with me, Mike."

"It's Michael. Tell me, what would you do with a day off?"

"Hang out with my friends. Go to a movie. See what's happening."

"Sounds exciting."

He got to his feet abruptly. "Go ahead. Laugh. Doesn't matter to me." He paced over to the window and looked out, shifting from one foot to the other.

"So, you need money." I had meant to discuss this with him, but so far it hadn't come up. He seemed happy with the things I gave him: a small TV for his room, a portable CD player, a bicycle I had picked up at a garage sale.

He turned on a sweet, melting smile that gave me a tangible jolt. "I was thinking…like maybe you could give me a bit of pocket money. I mean, instead of all that other stuff. I'll give it all back, if you want."

When I didn't say anything, the smile turned anxious, drifting into uncertainty at the corners. Lowering those wonderful hazel eyes, he said quietly, "That didn't sound very good, did it? It makes me look real ungrateful for you taking me in and all, and I'm not. Honest. It's just that I don't have any money, Michael. And I've been bustin' my ass around here. I mean, like, I've done everything you wanted, right?"

I couldn't help the laugh that exploded from me as he said this. He looked startled, and his face flushed with anger and the effort to hold it back. "I haven't been very demanding yet," I said. At that, he rolled his eyes to the ceiling and hit his forehead with his open palm.

"Jeeezus!" he exclaimed softly and folded into a chair.

The stillness stretched out in the sun-drenched air as I watched him, sprawled sideways, one hand over his eyes, his foot tapping out a private rhythm on the thick carpet. I felt a cloud of sadness drift over me, winding around my thoughts, and for the moment I was mortally sick of it all, seeing the endless repetitious patterns spinning out before me into my future. It was the same old story, choreographed in advance, fascinating in its infinite variations, but basically always the same. I was tired of games, of pretending there was nothing going on. I longed to be able to ask him what he was thinking about and to know he would tell me. I wished we could skip the next few stages and get to the good part, where words and actions start to mean something, if only in a limited way. I wanted to touch… But neither one of us was ready for that. Maybe we never would be.

I cleared my throat. "Let's negotiate a fair fee over dinner in a restaurant," I suggested expansively. His reaction was not what I expected.

"Why can't we stay here?"

"But I thought you wanted to get out of the house."

Not with you, his look said. It was like a slap in the face. "I'm kinda tired."

"A minute ago, you were climbing the walls to get out. What happened?"

"I've been working my ass off around here! That yard-digging shit is hard work! I've got a right to be tired!" He jumped to his feet.

"Stop acting like a bloody prima donna!" I lashed out, losing my temper entirely. "I'm not a fool!"

"No! You're a lousy, skinflint miser, that's what you are! You won't even pay me a fair wage, and you said yourself I'm a good worker."

"You're also a good eater. Have you any idea of the amount of food you've gone through in less than a week? Not to mention the breakage."

"I said I'd pay for the fucking stuff, didn't I? But how am I supposed to do that if you won't give me any wages?"

I shook my head at him in wonder. "I've met some hustlers in my time, boy, but you take the prize. What do you think I am? A philanthropist?"

"I know what you are."

"Watch it."

By this time, we were glaring at each other. I had forgotten what had set off this whole thing, but I suspected it had little to do with what we were now shouting about. One more thing to lay at Trish's door. If she hadn't called and pushed all my buttons, would things have blown so out of proportion now?

Ryan looked close to tears. "You're crazy, Michael, you know that? I thought you were so nice, but you're just a crazy old skinflint pervert whose ex-lover was a murderer and whose own family won't have anything to do with him!"

That sobered me. It also made me cruel. "All right," I said. "Let's talk about family, since you brought up the subject. Specifically, your family. To be even more precise, your mother, who loves you so much she gave you that expensive gold bracelet you're always wearing, presumably before she kicked you out of the house. Do you really think anyone's going to believe that pathetic lie?"

"You bastard! So what if she didn't give it to me?"

"Did you steal it?"

"It was a present! Chris gave it to me!"

"And just what did you have to do for it?"

"You fucking bastard! She's my girlfriend!"

"Ryan —"

"Shut up! For Crissakes, shut your goddamned fucking mouth!" He glared at me, his eyes shiny with unshed tears.

I felt surprisingly cold and detached, with a heavy sadness at the pit of my stomach as I watched him fling himself at the stairs at a dead run. "I take it dinner's out," I called after him, wondering why the hell I said these things. To give him plenty of time to dry his unmanly tears, I sorted through the welter of notes and memos piled on my desk and separated them into their appropriate folders. I could hear him crashing around upstairs. Rock music blared defiantly from his room. The sudden silence ten minutes later was followed by a shattering slam. By the time I made it to the front hall, there was no sign of him but the door was vibrating indignantly.

I sat on the hall chair, my hands dangling between my knees, and wondered how it had all blown out of proportion so fast. What poison from my past had seeped into the atmosphere with that unexpected call from Trish to make me so coolly cruel? Ryan was right. I owed him something.

A knock on the door and I sprang from my perch with relief, ready to hand over the keys of the kingdom to make myself feel better. I flung open the door. "Look, I overreacted, and I'm —"

Julie stood there, the morning sun lighting her hair on fire. She thrust the paper into my hands. "Hey, have you seen the front page? They've identified the mummy! Isn't that cool? God, I can't believe it! After all this time and everything. Hey, are you okay? You look kinda…hinky."

"No, no. I'm fine. But I haven't read the paper yet. Who is he?"

"Some small-time gangster from New York. His name's Rey Montana, and he has a record. That's how come they had his prints on file. So it was the Mafia after all. Who knew, eh?"

"But — Let me see that."

"I'm running late, but I wanted to make sure you knew. Catch you later."

I took the paper back to the solarium and read it through. Julie had exaggerated. Not that the truth needed anything to make it more unbelievable than it was to me. Rey Montana had a record of minor break-ins and several arrests for soliciting and prostitution. He was last seen in New York at a party for his nephew on the third of April, 1965. His aunt had reported him missing several weeks later, but he had never been heard of again. Until now.

I stared into the tiny bit of garden still untouched by Ryan's spade, watching a morning dove dip and peck at the bird feeder. April 1965. I was still living in my fool's paradise. Still planning for Ronnie to move in with me after school was over in June, when he would be eighteen and I wouldn't be his teacher anymore. Was Ronnie already having second thoughts? When did he begin experimenting with drugs? He would disappear for days at a time, leaving me frantic with worry. When he came back, he clung to me and cried and promised never to leave. But he had already left. And now I knew why. Or part of the reason.

And now Ryan was gone too.

After a while, I got up and went to the cupboard under the stairs. I checked the shoulder bag that hung there and discovered, somewhat predictably, that I was eighty-five dollars poorer. There should be some kind of insurance against this sort of thing, I thought. I could see the ad in my mind: "**Has a cute hustler ripped you off lately? Now fight back with CON-ALERT, a whole new concept in insurance to suit your modern alternative lifestyle.**" I was lucky there hadn't been more cash in my wallet. Anyway, Ryan wouldn't be hungry for a few days, and I had had some good work done around the house at a bargain rate. It could have been a lot worse. He could have broken my heart.

Like Ronnie.

CHAPTER NINE

For the next few days, everywhere I went, people asked me about Rey Montana. I found it insulting that they expected me to know intimate details about this person who had a record in New York City. I was amazed that I appeared to be looked on as some sort of '60s radical, when all I did back then was fall in love. To me, this had been a life-changing event, but it was private, and I resented like hell that my life was once again a topic of public speculation. My recent encounter with Ryan didn't help my emotional equilibrium, but at least I hadn't had another scathing phone call from Trish.

"I'm sick of it, Logan," I said, spilling out my frustration onto a captive audience. "Sick of it!"

"Drowning in the past," Logan said, wafting a hand in the air. His rictus of a grin twisted his face into a parody of humor. "Come on, Michael. You can't really blame them. It's an intriguing story, even *you* have to admit. And you were there, right? Who else can we ask?"

I leaned back in my chair, struck by the question. "I've been looking through the old diary he started in school," I said slowly, the names scrolling across my mind in Ronnie's carefully embellished handwriting.

"That must be illuminating."

"Not really. Mostly it reminds me how very young he was." I paused, feeling a wave of cool sadness touch my heart. "He mentions Monica Heising a lot. I'd forgotten about her."

"The activist? You knew her?"

"Back then she was just one of my students. Her parents were at their wits' end with her as I recall from the emotional parent-teacher interviews. She was brilliant, stubborn, and erratic. She was probably on drugs a lot of the time, but she was a great pal of Ronnie's."

"Didn't she run as an NDP candidate a few years ago? You should talk to her."

"Why? I don't want to be pulled into this even more!"

"Michael, do you really believe Ronnie killed that man?"

I stared at the window, not sure how to answer.

"You're reading his diaries," he went on. "You knew him then. Very well."

"Apparently not." I thought of the strange erotic passages in his embellished handwriting, the nightmares, mentions of rough sex and S and M. Just hints, but I had no idea he had any knowledge of what was then a very closed world. Overactive imagination? Fantasy driven by teenaged hormones, like the explicit purple passages about me that made me blush even now?

"Do you honestly think he could shoot a man in the back of the head? Think about it. How could that kind of action be in the heat of emotion? And another thing — where would a seventeen-year-old get a gun back then?"

"From some other draft dodger?"

"They were armed?"

"Well, not as a rule, but some of them were deserters and probably had guns. And some were just…strange."

"And anyway, I thought you said he pulled away from them quite soon after you two got together."

"Look, when Ronnie came here he was just seventeen, too young to be called up, so he wasn't technically a draft dodger. He turned eighteen in February."

"But he knew a lot of them, right? And he pulled away from that crowd after you two —"

"God, Logan, I can't remember exactly when anything happened back then! It was a long time ago. I tried to forget, you know?"

We were silent awhile. The gray afternoon angled in through the venetian blinds. The low, mechanical hiss of some machine came from behind the curtains surrounding Logan's new roommate. I imagined it forcing blood through the shriveled shell of his body.

"It was a difficult time for me," I said at last, breaking the silence. "My whole life was turned upside down by Ronnie, and I mean that literally. My marriage cracked and shattered, and after that my family disowned me, terrified of scandal, and most of my friends stopped calling. I know it wasn't his fault. What I felt for him was the knife that cut me adrift, and I didn't care, Logan. I was happy for the first time in my life and it made me cruel and selfish and delirious with freedom. And then he left me and I was totally alone. Can't you see why I tried to forget?"

"You survived," Logan said.

And so did Laura, I thought, by retreating into the past. "Oh sure," I said. No wife. No home. No family. No friends.

"Perhaps it would be healthy to do a little digging. Therapy," he added, watching me, his head angled back to relieve the strain on his burned neck.

"Oh, so now you want to play Freud."

"Never. Anyone but the F man."

I smiled. "Fine. I'll humor you." I cleared my throat and settled back more comfortably in the chair. "Glori Daze knew Ronnie back then. She was performing at the Manatee, and I introduced them. She took Ronnie under her wing, as it were. When I saw Ronnie on stage for the first time a few months later, I was sure he would eclipse Glori, and soon. I always wondered why he didn't go on tour, the way she did."

"So when do they think Montana was killed?"

"It's still vague. But since he was last seen on April 3, 1965, they assume he was killed sometime between April and September of that year."

"Maybe we can narrow it down," he said, picking thoughtfully at a bandage on his wrist. "You said earlier Ronnie went a bit wonky. Maybe you could get more specific. For instance, you could make a time chart from the diary. Would that work?"

I was drawn in, in spite of myself, thinking back to Ronnie's growing erratic behavior, his emotional outbursts and equally inexplicable calms. At the time I had put this down to experimentation with drugs. But maybe there was another reason he began to push me away. "The entries are sporadic," I said, "but they're always dated. It's a place to start."

"And you could track down this Monica Heising too," he went on, his eyes alight with an enthusiasm I hadn't seen for months.

"Maybe I'll bring her in for you to interrogate," I said sarcastically.

Logan thought that was a great idea. I threw up my hands. "What the hell," I said. "I can't seem to avoid it, anyway. And you know, you're right, what you said a few minutes ago. I can't see Ronnie shooting a man in the back of the head."

When I arrived back home, Llewellyn ab Hugh was hunched over with both hands shielding his eyes, peering in my front window.

"Is that a new rug I spy in there?" he asked smoothly, turning to face me as I arrived beside him.

"No, it's not. And you better be careful the neighbors don't call the police, seeing you casing the joint like that."

"Ooo, I love a man in a uniform," cooed Lew. Sometimes I wondered what I had ever seen in him. "Anyway, they'll probably think you've hired me to defend your crumbling reputation."

I unlocked the door and led the way to the living room.

"The young Adonis not home?" Lew asked, looking around as if expecting to find Ryan lurking in some dark corner or possibly under a table.

"He's gone."

"Oh, too bad. What happened?"

"Something to drink? Scotch? Vodka? Coffee?"

"I suspect this might be a scotch moment," he said, sinking into my sofa. "What happened?"

"Water? Ice?"

"Your memory going?"

"It's been a while since you honored me with your presence." I splashed water over the scotch, added ice, and handed him the drink. I mixed my own and sat down in the wing chair, wondering how soon I could ask him to leave. Not that I didn't like Lew, exactly, but he made me nervous. He seemed to appear whenever I felt vulnerable, or perhaps he just brought out this feeling in me.

"Great scotch," Lew commented, flipping his ponytail over one shoulder. His eyes were the same color as the drink, I noticed. "So what happened to the boy toy?"

"Lew, he was just staying here a few days while doing some much-needed chores around the house. He's gone. End of story."

"Any chance he'll be back?"

"I sincerely doubt it."

"I see." He grinned at me over his glass. "So you let loose that killer tongue of yours."

I looked up, startled. "It's none of your business."

"Too bad. And I never got a look at him. Did he look anything like Ronnie at that age?"

"What?" I tried not to react to his words, but I felt their force like a blow, and my hand jerked, almost spilling my drink. They were both slim, lithe, blond. "No," I said, "they didn't look one bit alike."

"Didn't mean to hit a nerve," Lew said. "It was just an educated guess."

"Perhaps there's such a thing as being overeducated." I got up and selected a CD, slipped it into the player, switched it on. Harp music wafted out from the speakers.

"Thank God it's not those dreadful monks," Lew said. "For a while there you couldn't go anywhere without feeling as if you'd slipped into a medieval cathedral with everyone in full chant." He shuddered dramatically. "Any word on the mummy-guy?"

"Apart from knowing his name, nothing, as far as I know. But I'm not privy to police reports."

"Pity. I used to date a guy on the force. Maybe I'll give him a friendly little call."

"Lew —"

"Don't bother to thank me. I'll let you know if I find out anything useful." He glanced around the room as if looking for something. "Still not smoking, I see."

"I gave it up years ago, Lew. You should too."

"Don't lecture me. I'm not one of your students. These days us smokers are becoming an oppressed minority. Do you know they won't even let me smoke in my own office anymore?"

"Shocking."

"Did your houseboy smoke? You probably wouldn't let him, poor thing. I suppose it's a good thing he left, him being so much like Ronnie and all, he might have done you in at any time. Ever think of that?"

"Shut up, Lew. Stop trying to stir things up."

"Oh hon, you don't need me for that!" He laughed.

"Ronnie didn't do in anybody," I said, surprising myself with the intensity of my conviction.

"They could hardly arrest him even if he did," Lew pointed out. "And let me say I think your defense of your old lover is quite touching. When my sins rise up to accuse me, I hope you'll be on hand to leap to my defense."

"You have skeletons in your closet?"

"Don't we all?"

"After that initial excitement in the '60s, my life became pretty dull."

"Montreal was anything but dull, as I recall," he said.

"Hotter for you, I suspect," I said.

"A hit! A palpable hit!" he cried, recoiling into a corner of the chesterfield as if mortally wounded.

"What I meant was, you had a lot more action than I did."

Mollified, he sat up again and sipped his drink.

"How well did you know Ronnie back in '65?" I asked suddenly. "Were you ever at his place?"

He looked at me speculatively, as if trying to decide what trap I was laying for him. "He wasn't really my type," he said at last. "I remember meeting him with you now and then. And I remember when he started performing I saw him a few times. After you two split up, I heard he got into an abusive relationship, as we say these days. Then…didn't he have a thing with Phil Starkman? And then I think I heard something about joining a commune or something."

"You're joking. When was this?"

"I kid you not. But I really don't remember when, Michael. You should talk to Glori Daze and that other queen who was around then. She performed with Ronnie as a sort of queen tag team event for a while when Ronnie came back. What was her name…? Binaca, that's it. Binaca Labamba or something."

"Bianca Bombe."

"Right." He finished his drink and stood up. "I'd love to stick around and chew the fat about the old days, but I have an appointment with my plastic surgeon." He blew me a kiss and was gone.

I suspected he was really off to the gym to battle Father Time. For some reason he never wanted to admit he did any strenuous exercise. An image thing, I suppose. So far he was doing pretty well. I suppose being in shape is useful when you're defending major crime bosses. As I watched him drive away in his white Jag, I noticed the vanity plates. QCQ. Queen's Council Queer? Good old Lew. A TV news truck from a local station rumbled up and parked in front of my house, half on the sidewalk. I closed the drapes and turned off the phones. Again.

CHAPTER TEN

Monica Heising was not hard to find. She left a trail everywhere she went, and she seemed to have been a lot of places, from the Right to Privacy committee to Planned Parenthood to a home for teenage mothers. I started with the local NDP Party office and found out she had left them after a flare-up about some policy or other regarding Native women. Then I tried the alumni office of the University of Toronto and got better results, an address in North Toronto. The phone number was unlisted so I got into my car and drove up there one afternoon later that week.

Monica's neighborhood was filled with similar two-story houses with a small porch out front and garage at the end of a shared driveway. Fenced backyards could be glimpsed from the street and kid's bikes and brightly colored plastic toys lay about on the lawns. Monica's house had a fire engine red door. A friendly golden lab-ish dog wagged his tail as I walked up the steps. I hoped Monica would be as approachable. A sign on the door said the bell was out of order, so I knocked. Loudly.

"Okay, okay, I hear you!" The door was flung open and there she was. She had gained a lot of weight but the eyes were the same; the hair, though gray, still cascaded down her back as it had back in the '60s, and her face was surprisingly youthful. "Oh my gawd," she said. "What a blast from the past!"

"You recognize me?" I was amazed.

"Fuck, yes! After all the commotion in the papers about Ronnie, of course I do! Besides, you're the only teacher I ever had who was fired over something as exciting as an affair with my best friend. Come on in!"

I followed her and the dog into a house humming with activity. The dining room table had been extended to its full length and all around it sat chattering women, stuffing envelopes, peeling stamps, and sticking them into place, an efficient and noisy assembly line. They were all ages, though mostly younger than Monica, all dressed casually in shorts and T-shirts. Sun streamed in the dining room window, which was filled with plants in varying stages of ill health.

"Ladies, this is my old high school history teacher, Michael."

"Hi, Michael," they chorused.

I felt as if I were in an AA meeting. I nodded stiffly.

"Michael was the first person I ever knew who struck a blow for gay lib," she went on. "God, that impressed the hell out of me! You were a real role model, Michael."

I shook my head, stunned at this sudden testimonial. "Monica, I —"

She waved a hand at me dismissively. "Oh go ahead and belittle it, but I was there, remember? And I knew it was against the law back then. So don't shake your head at me!" She laughed, the same laugh that used to disrupt my classes on numerous occasions. Even then, I didn't really mind. "We're getting a mailing out for the latest fundraising appeal for Allegra House. Most of these people live there, or have lived there somewhere along the way, when they needed it. Let's go upstairs. I left the printer spewing out more letters."

She thumped up the carpeted stairs in front of me, talking all the way, her Birkenstock sandals slapping her bare feet smartly. She made me feel as if I had been slothful my entire life and I had only a little time to make up for my past unsatisfactory performance.

The small hall was made smaller with cardboard boxes of stationery piled in one corner. Ahead, her office overflowed with paper and files. Bits and pieces of computer equipment crowded shelves, cheek to cheek with books and boxes of labels and envelopes. A stack of banker boxes leaned perilously in one corner. On the end of the desk, her printer spewed forth a jumbled pile of letters. Monica collected them as she talked.

"Damn machines are a godsend when they work. McDuff, get out of here. Go! Nothing to eat here." The dog hung his head and slouched out to the hall, where he lay down, head between his paws, and looked up at her soulfully.

"Christ," muttered Monica, refilling the printer with paper. "To look at him you'd think I clobbered him regularly."

"Somehow I doubt that," I said, smiling.

She laughed and pushed the hair away from her face. "Damned air conditioner isn't working very well. Or maybe it's just me," she added, wiping her forehead. "Millie! Come get the rest of these letters!" she bellowed down the stairs. A young woman in jeans cutoffs and a tiny T-shirt ran up, gathered the papers in her arms, and disappeared again without a word.

"Poor thing has had three abortions," Monica said, shaking her head. "So many people afraid of the Pill these days. Okay, let's say we take a break. It's cooler out front."

I followed as she led the way through what appeared to be her bedroom, stopping en route to get two Coronas from a bar fridge used as a bedside table, and then going out sliding doors to a deck on top of the front porch. The dog followed, sniffing all around the area before skittering down stairs to the back garden, his toenails clicking against the painted wood.

Monica flung herself into one of the deck chairs and put her feet up on a big empty flowerpot. "Shits Hall," she said with a smile. "I actually liked that place, can you imagine? I guess there are no places like that anymore."

"I don't expect so. Don't need cram schools when there aren't any provincial matriculation exams to worry about anymore."

"There were some damned good teachers in that place, though. Remember old Harcourt? What a dynamite teacher! I don't understand why he stayed there."

"He didn't have an Ontario teaching certificate. None of us did, though some had pretty impressive credentials from other places. Harcourt had taught for years in England and didn't want to go back to school at his age."

"I don't blame him. What could they teach him? And there was Ms. Lard Ass, as we called her. Poor Miss Bates. She was potty over you, you know. We used to watch her waylaying you in the parking lot, on the stairs, in the hall. You had no clue, did you?"

"Miss Bates?" I said, perplexed. I remembered her as being breathy and disorganized, her briefcase always overflowing with papers to mark. But if she was "potty" over me, it was the first I knew of it.

Monica laughed and took a long drink of her beer. "You were so young, and you looked it, too. We all adored you, but you only had eyes for Ronnie. Once we figured that out, we gave up trying to get noticed. Except Miss Bates. She never clued in. Even when they fired you for fraternizing with the enemy."

"Monica, I think you exaggerate."

"Me?" She grinned, the same grin that used to annoy me so much in class — knowing, impudent, teasing. Suddenly her smile disappeared, her face dimming as if a light had gone off. "Christ, what a mess," she said. She gestured vaguely at the house, but I knew what she meant.

"I was lucky they did nothing more than fire me, Monica. I could have gone to jail."

"Are you kidding? Bring everything out in the open and have parents pulling their kids out of the school? No chance." She took another pull of her ale. "Poor Ronnie," she murmured.

"Monica, what's your theory about this Rey Montana thing?" I asked.

She looked into her glass thoughtfully. "Frankly, at first I thought you'd done it."

"What!"

"You asked." She shrugged. "Maybe you came in one night and found him with some guy, got jealous, and shot him."

"And where did I get the gun?"

"Tucker Freemont."

"That draft dodger guy who lived in Rochdale?"

"The very same. He had a gun. I saw it."

"Where did he get it?"

"No idea. I hate guns. So did Ronnie. He was with me that day. We'd gone to score some weed, as they say, and Rochdale was the place to go then, as you no doubt remember. Anyway, when Tucker showed us the thing, I thought Ronnie would throw up or pass out or both. We just got the hell out of there."

"When was this?"

"I don't know. Sometime just before he went to that commune, I think. So that's where I figured you got the gun. Besides, you were the only one I could think of with guts enough to pull off such a stunt."

"Thanks. Any more testimonials from you and I'll end up in jail."

"Only thing I know for sure is that Ronnie couldn't have done it."

"I could, but he couldn't."

"You're more macho," she said and grinned.

"Well, I agree with you in one thing; Ronnie couldn't have done it. Which begs the question of how the damn thing got into the trunk."

"That's why I thought it might have been you," she said. "He was trying to shield you."

"Oh, and I just walked off and left him to deal with it."

"A really bad trip?"

I laughed. "God, Monica, you certainly have a wild notion of how colorful I was back then!"

"Well, Ronnie thought you were pretty terrific." She sighed. "Remember when you threw me out of class for braiding his hair? He used to sit in front of me, remember?"

"As I recall, I threw you out of class on a regular basis. You never would shut up." I smiled, the memories suddenly sharp and clear as yesterday.

"Haven't changed much, in that respect."

"In any respect," I said, and I meant it.

"Sure, what's seventy pounds and some gray hair?" She paused and looked down over the railing at the dog, who was digging busily in the backyard. "Damn dog," she muttered affectionately. "So, Michael, what are you up to these days?"

I gave her a brief sketch of my teaching gig at the university, the book I was working on, and went on to mention the Wilde Nights rehearsal.

"God, yes! I went to the first one and sat front row center. Ronnie threw me a rose. I went last year too. He was getting quite sick then, but he did one terrific, show-stopping number and still brought the house down. Did you see it?"

I nodded.

"I'm glad he had you at the end, Michael. I'm no good with sickness. But you, his first love, you were there, at the beginning, and the end. That was important to him."

I felt a sudden surge of unwanted emotion. I took a drink of beer and cleared my throat. It was just an accident, I wanted to say. I didn't plan it that way. "I didn't realize you were such a sentimentalist," I said dryly.

"When you two broke up, he just fell apart," Monica went on, ignoring me. "He got real wild. I vividly remember my birthday in June '65. My parents had a garden party for me. Well, it was mainly for the relatives, but they bribed me to come, and I invited Ronnie. Well, let me tell you, he sure caused a sensation, showing up after midnight, stoned out of his mind, dressed in nothing but green paint and a feather boa. He said he was Ms. Photosynthesis. I thought my grandmother would have a heart attack! It was glorious!"

She looked out over the railing, her smile slowly fading. "He flunked half his subjects, did you know? After you left, he started hanging out with Tucker at Rochdale, dropping acid and doing mushrooms and God knows what else. Then he suddenly packed his bags and took off to a commune in Quebec."

"I heard he'd done something like that. It doesn't sound like him at all."

"That's what I thought, but he did. He still kept his old room, though, so I guess he knew it was only temporary. He was gone all summer, all fall. I went to visit him there once." She shivered.

"What was it like?"

"A dump. And I got the impression Ronnie was not popular there for some reason. Weird vibes. Anyway, he came back around Christmas."

"How big was this place? Who were they?"

"Apparently there had been about fifteen people there at one point. When I arrived, there were about eight or nine, more women than men, I think. Three of the guys were Americans."

"Oh? Any Latinos?"

"Michael, my memory isn't what it used to be. And anyway —" She stopped. "Oh," she said. "You mean one of them could be…."

"Rey Montana. Just a thought. Right time period. Right age. I don't suppose you remember any names?"

"As I recall, they all had those made-up hippie names. I doubt any of them used what was on their birth certificates."

"Strange period."

"Ronnie would never talk about it. By the time he came back, they must have been freezing to death at the old commune. I remember inviting him to my place Christmas Day. He'd lost a lot of weight. He looked totally wasted and about five years older. Anyway, in January he went back to Shits Hall and worked like hell. This time he made it. He missed you so much."

I shook my head.

"He did. But he refused to write or call, even though he found out where you were from the university."

"That's how I found you," I said. "The alumni office." We were both quiet awhile, listening to the kids playing in the street below, the women downstairs laughing and talking. "What about you? Married? Children?"

"Oh me. Yup, I got married at nineteen to a totally unsuitable man from South Africa. Ronnie was my bridesmaid. It was a perfectly weird and lovely wedding out in the country at my crazy aunt's old cottage. We had a kid. I went to university. I marched in protests, organized sit-ins. The usual." She laughed. "Then he died."

"Oh Monica, I'm sorry."

"So was I. Anyway, I got through it. I had Andy, my son, to look after. Ronnie used to babysit for me. He was great with Andy. Then I got married again at twenty-nine. But I divorced him three years later. I didn't have any luck with men. And now I don't have time for them." She finished off her beer and got to her feet. "Speaking of time, I'd better get back to work."

"Thanks for seeing me, Monica."

"Anytime, Michael. Just drop by, and we'll talk about the old days."

"As long as you don't bring up my murderous past," I said, following her down the stairs.

"Forgive and forget, that's my motto these days," she said. "Before you go, maybe you could spare a few dollars for Allegra House," she said, one hand on the handle of the front door. Her gray eyes danced as I pulled out my check book.

"Somehow I didn't expect to get out of here scot-free," I said, making out a check for a hundred dollars and handing it over.

"Hey, thanks. And come back anytime!"

"Can't afford it," I said, laughing as I made my way to my car.

"Next visit is free," she called, waving as I got into the car. "I promise!"

As I drove back downtown, I kept thinking of the Monica Murder Theory, starring me as I had never been. Was it possible anyone else could jump to the conclusion that I had done it? It was a sobering thought I fervently hoped would not occur to the police. Her reasoning about Ronnie shielding me, however, led me to wonder. Could he have been protecting someone else?

And who were those shadowy people out at the commune? Those people he would never talk about? Could one of them have wound up in Ronnie's trunk with a bullet in his head?

CHAPTER ELEVEN

"This here's a weed, Mr. Dunn-Barton. It'll have to come down." The workman hitched up his faded green pants and scowled up at the graceful branches arching against the gray sky. "These Norway Maples are nothing but trouble."

"It looks fine to me," I said. "If it were gone, there wouldn't be any shade at all at the front."

"You can always plant a proper tree here. Give you shade in no time and still let the grass grow proper."

"All I want it a little trimming so the branches don't hit the upstairs windows." Just a bit off the side, I thought, and suppressed a grin.

"These here weed trees, they got no root system, see," the man went on earnestly, gesturing toward the ground. "Come a storm and she'll topple right into your living room. Clip your chimney too. Take down the wires."

"The tree was here when I bought the house," I said, distancing myself from the evil weed. "It did fine last winter."

"One more ice storm and splat, bam, she's gone." The tree man shook his head sadly. He shoved his cap farther back and wiped the beads of perspiration from his forehead.

I pushed my hands deeper into my pockets. "Look, I appreciate all this advice, but all I want you to do is to trim the damn tree back."

"Make her grow even faster," murmured the tree man.

"Fine. Just trim it. Thanks."

"She's your tree."

I turned and walked away. I hoped I wouldn't have nightmares about the tree crashing through the living room windows every time there was a thunderstorm.

Inside, the house was cool, dark, and silent, for a change. I checked through the mail and tossed out the ads and offers of unlimited platinum Visas and MasterCards.

The furor in the papers had died down again. The headlines now screamed about the latest sex scandal in the lives of some libidinous politician, and Ronnie and Rey Montana's mummified corpse were old news, leaving my front lawn free of vultures. Even the police had lost interest, returning the keys with the polite comment that the apartment was no longer an official crime scene and I was free to return there anytime I wished. In short, no one cared anymore. Perhaps that was what frustrated me the most.

Outside, the unfinished garden that was supposed to be a refuge of tranquility in my life lay raw and broken, baking in the oppressive heat. I grabbed my car keys and headed for the garage. I was meeting Stan Wynkowski at Ronnie's apartment to sort through the costumes and makeup and things he thought might be useful for Wilde Nights.

The air was thick, dripping with humidity. The radio broadcast dire smog warnings and the danger of heat prostration. I was reluctant to get out of my air-conditioned car.

Ronnie's old house was close and silent. This time I didn't hesitate at the purple door but pulled it open and went inside at once, making for the air conditioner. I should leave it on permanently, I thought, since I was going to be spending some time here for a while, sorting through Ronnie's personal effects, boxing up the few things he had left instructions were to go to certain friends. If I settled down to the job, it shouldn't take more than a week. I wanted to clear things out and put the house on the market.

Ronnie's desk was in perfect order, just as his business papers and investments had been. I found no surprises there, thank God. Everything was labeled, with contact names and phone numbers attached. I spent about half an hour writing checks for friends and charities listed by Ronnie in amounts ranging from five hundred to five thousand dollars, and had just worked my way to the bottom when I heard feet pounding up the stairs. Stan had brought company.

"I guess now we know why Ronnie never moved," said Stan, coming into the living room.

"I could have gone on a lot longer without finding out," another voice said. It was Glori Daze, aka Duane, carrying a stack of folded cardboard boxes. "Hi, Michael, how's it going?"

"Slowly," I said. "Getting the dresses sorted out will help."

"That's what we're here for." Duane flung the boxes on the floor by the door and went into the small front room that Ronnie had turned into his closet. "Sweet Jesus," he muttered. "I remember teaching him to sew."

He and Stan began inspecting the costumes piece by piece, subjecting each one to some unspoken scale of worth. Some were pushed to the back on the second row, but most were tagged with a red label for transport to the Wilde Nights wardrobe department, which I suspected was in Stan's basement. While they sorted, I finished my notes and checked though all the files on Ronnie's computer before reformatting the hard drive. The computer was going to Fife House Hospice, along with his extensive CD collection.

I was packing that into boxes when Duane took a break. He came into the living room and wandered over to the Wall of Death. "Fucking morbid," he muttered, shaking his head as he inspected the pictures. "Whoa. Great thundering Jaysus, Michael, here's a pic of you! Are you dead and didn't tell us?"

"You must be mistaken," I said, a little stiffly. I wasn't in the mood for corpse humor.

"See for yourself. Unless my aging eyes deceive me, which they might, that's you standing in front of the school you used to teach at."

Unwillingly, I pushed my chair back and went over to look. He was right. The picture was faded, but easily recognizable.

Stan joined us. "Christ," he said, "there's Bianca Bombe, that poor thing who crashed the rehearsal the other day. She was cute in those days, yes?"

"That no-talent cow?" Duane sputtered. "You call that —"

"Zip it, Duane. She may as well be dead. I hear she just got out of the Clark. Leave her be."

"That explains it," Duane said, but he still sounded surprisingly bitter. "She was always loony tunes."

"Well, it doesn't explain me," I said. "And it doesn't explain that these photos weren't here earlier, when I first started coming around to help out last winter."

"Well, I hear poor Ronnie was getting really strange near the end," Duane said. "Look, there's the Manatee! And that's Neon Lites! Now *she* had talent."

"And she's very dead," Stan pointed out.

"Maybe it's people who were only dead in the sense of out of Ronnie's life?" suggested Duane. "What store is that? Look there's another pic of the place."

"Duane, we'll be here all day if we try to figure out the key to this thing," Stan objected, glancing at his watch. "I've only got another hour before I have to pick up Bob at the airport."

"I'll help you get them packed up," I said, "as soon as I check out the cupboard in the bedroom." I wanted something to distract me from the Wall of Death and my part in the puzzle. When had Ronnie added me to his mad gallery? I was glad to have company while I finished my checking of drawers and cupboards. Tomorrow I'd start the cataloguing of items to be sold.

Duane and Stan threw themselves into the packing while I rummaged through things in the bedroom. I wanted to get out of there fast, since this was the only room that held any real memories for me. In 1965 Ronnie ate, slept, and studied in this room. We made love here, talked all night here, and sat outside on the fire escape wrapped in each other's arms, waiting for the sun to come up. And the brightly painted trunk set against the wall, holding candles stuck in Chianti bottles and a bronze incense burner. I shuddered.

There were no surprises in the dresser drawers, or on the shelves. I pulled back the bed and knelt down to see if there was still a door there, leading to the cupboard that ran under the eaves. The small wooden knob had been painted over and it turned with great difficulty, but the door opened, dragging on the hardwood floor as I forced it back. Heat and dust wafted out, making me cough. It was dark, but from the small part I could see, there was nothing there. I pulled out the flashlight I had brought with me and shone it inside. Nothing on the left but dust and what looked like a few two-by-fours. On the right were a couple of shoe boxes. I was almost disappointed at the ordinariness of the find. I coughed again as I opened the first one. Old letters. In Ronnie's handwriting. I realized I had been holding my breath. Why? Can't hide a skeleton in a shoe box. I popped the lid of the second one and glanced inside. A notebook with the name Uncle Bunny, on the outside in Ronnie's ornate childish writing I remembered from school, a hand more scrawling than his later neat notes. Inside it seemed to be a ledger of some sort with the date 1970 written across the front. I flipped the notebook aside and stared at what was underneath. Neat packages of crisp green US one-hundred-dollar bills stared back.

"Are you almost finished?" called Duane. "We could do with some help here."

"Coming." I stuffed the money, notebook, and letters into the box, slammed the door back into place, and pushed the bed against the wall. A casual observer wouldn't have known the crawl space existed. I doubted that Duane knew, and he had been a constant visitor for a time. But I remembered. Is that why Ronnie was so insistent I be his executor?

Ten minutes later, the money, ledger, and letters safely stowed in a GAP shopping bag I had grabbed from a cupboard, I helped load Stan's van with the boxes. Then I tossed my shopping bag into the front seat of my car and headed for home. The bag on the seat beside me would not be ignored. I was aware of the dust on the outside of the boxes, the smell of age, the aura of money. Several thousand dollars, at least. It was its mysterious source that kept nagging me. Why did Ronnie hide it? Why did he put his uncle's name on it and not send it? And where had he gotten so much money in the first place back then?

Halfway home, I pulled into the left lane and turned the car toward the hospital. I didn't want to go back to the house with all these questions buzzing at me. Maybe Logan could see something here that I couldn't.

But when I told him about it, he frowned. "This is getting worse and worse," he said. "First thing I think of is drugs."

"He wasn't a dealer, Logan."

"How do you know? You didn't think he had a corpse in his trunk, either."

I had to admit I didn't really know that much about the man who had changed my life so drastically. Had I been completely blinded by my own emotions? I wondered what Monica would say about this find — apart from wanting it donated to Allegra House, that is.

Logan coughed. He looked exhausted, his skin grayish and shiny with sweat. I wondered how he could be hot with the air-conditioning whirring away so efficiently.

"So where is this swag?" he asked, looking around.

"It was too dirty to bring in here. Germs from the '60s, doncha know. Might give you hallucinations."

"Might be an improvement. Any letters addressed to this uncle in the other shoe box?"

"From my quick look in the parking lot, no. It looks like a few letters to his family that were returned unopened, and some to his sister at another address."

"Aha! So at least you now know where they are."

"Were. People move around a lot these days."

"Worth checking out, no?" One corner of his mouth quirked up, but his heart wasn't in it today.

"My neighbor croaked," he said, noticing me looking around.

I shivered, remembering the creaking whoosh of the machinery that was all I ever heard from the other bed. I didn't know what to say.

"I think it was good," Logan said, "but that's just me."

There was an awkward silence. My mind had gone completely blank. "Have you seen Ella lately?" I asked. His sister was one of the few who still came to visit.

"She's up at a friend's cottage. By the time she gets back, I might be out of here."

"Really?"

"No, but I like to fool myself it's possible. I should be out in another month, though."

"That's good news."

Logan sighed and turned his head away to the window.

"I better go."

"Maybe you're right about him," Logan said suddenly. "Maybe he wasn't a dealer. Maybe he was just laundering money."

"Lovely," I said. "Just laundering money for his uncle? Well, then, that's just dandy. As long as he keeps it in the family."

CHAPTER TWELVE

Rain streaked the plate glass window of De Groote's and blurred the cars crowding up Church Street. The headlights glowed dim in the early afternoon dullness. People under umbrellas stopped to look at the cuts of meat and marinating goodies displayed invitingly in the window. I took my chops and kabobs and stir-fry chicken from the cute blond behind the counter, noting his strong hands and the fine gold hairs on his wrists, then I pushed my way though the Saturday crowd to the door.

Outside, a tall, scrawny drag queen huddled under a striped golf umbrella was peering at me. "I know you!" she exclaimed, one long beringed finger pointing at my chest. "Yes! I know you!"

"Hello, Bianca." I shifted my parcels and took her hand. She was wearing a hideous orange print dress that draggled to the ground and clung to her skinny legs in the rain.

She looked pleased that I knew her name. Her long, bony fingers continued to clutch my hand. The door opened behind me and a large woman nudged my back.

"Let's go across to Papa Peaches," I suggested. "Have you had lunch yet? I'm starving. We could have a bite to eat and catch up." I had been wanting to talk to her anyway. It seemed a perfect time. "I'm buying. What do you say?"

Her face brightened at once, a wide smile showing yellowed teeth. "That would be nice, dear. I think I have the time." She shifted her handbag to the other shoulder and took my arm, moving the umbrella over my head as we started across the street.

Once inside the restaurant, Bianca wanted to sit in front, right in the window. She took out some Kleenex and blotted her face. "I hate the rain," she said. "I must look a fright."

"Everyone gets wet in the rain," I said inanely. I smiled at the waiter, an attractive Asian guy with a colorful bead choker around his neck. I ordered a Bloody Mary for me and a margarita for Bianca.

"How did you know?" she asked, raising her tweezed eyebrows.

"Just a guess."

"Nice to be on the same wavelength with someone," she said. "You know that Stan Whatsisname, at the Wilde Nights thing, he doesn't know from nothing. You gotta tell him, honey. Tell him he needs to put me in the show this year. You can do it, I know you can."

"Bianca, you have an exaggerated idea of my importance in the show. I have no influence. I'm just one of many accompanists helping out with rehearsals."

"Luna told me — me and Luna go way back, you know — she told me I could be in the show when I got — I mean, this year. So this Stan person should listen to her."

"Luna's dead, Bianca."

She just looked at me. Our drinks came, and she took a long pull at the margarita. "I miss her."

"So do I." The words surprised me. "Tell me when you met Luna?"

She smiled, softening the harsh lines of her angular face. Her shoulders dropped as she relaxed with me, with the alcohol. She smoothed back her draggled hair with one hand. "When I first met Luna, he was still in school. He was in love with his history teacher, some guy named Marc or something. They went everywhere together, and one night I met them in the Manatee. He was just Ronnie back then, hadn't gotten into drag or anything, but I saw he was a natural, right from the beginning. The real thing. Not like that no-talent slut Glori Daze." She spat out Glori's name as if it were poison and took another long pull at her drink. I ordered her another.

"Anyways, she took to drag right away, like I said, and we were soon doing an act together."

"Wait a moment. Slow down. Did you visit Ronnie? Go to his place often?"

"Oh yeah, sure. He lived in this rooming house on the third floor. He had a tiny room with a slanting roof, painted all groovy colors. I remember it smelled real bad up there, dead raccoons or something he said, but he burned incense and smoked a lot of pot, so I guess he didn't care. There was this bitch who lived downstairs who went to the police about the smell, I remember that. We fixed her real good."

"What did you do?"

"Me and Luna, we filled out all these cards, see? All these forms ordering magazines and books and that, in her name, with her address. She must have been flooded with the stuff." She laughed, a sharp cackle that turned heads in the restaurant. "Anyways, she moved soon after that, so I guess it worked."

I ordered chicken Santa Barbara, and Bianca, giving in to my urging, finally ordered steak. While we waited for the food, Bianca maundered on about the Velvet Box Review and the Trillium Monarchist Society and the early court balls she and Luna went to. Luna was crowned empress several years in a row. According to my reckoning that must have been in the late '80s, since the society hadn't been around earlier, but I wasn't sure. My knowledge of the court system was scant, and it was all mixed up in Bianca's mind. That wasn't what I was interested in anyway.

When our food came, we ate for a while in silence. Bianca was shoveling it in as if she hadn't eaten a good meal for a while. Then she slowed down, a faraway look on her haggard face. "I remember the first time Luna got really dressed up, in a red tulle gown I loaned her. In those days I had a wardrobe to die for. Anyways, Luna had to shorten it a lot, 'cause she was just a little thing. I was taking her to Bobby Mason's Queen's Birthday Ball — you know, on the Queen's official birthday, May twenty-fourth? But Luna wasn't any good with a needle back then, so she'd used scotch tape and pins to hold up the lining. She couldn't sit down all night, afraid of getting stuck with a pin! She was in a real state that night anyway. I guess all the excitement…. She was real upset about —"

"About what?"

Her eyes suddenly went scared, losing focus. She felt around for her purse, pulled it onto her knees, and rooted around. I watched as she pulled out a bottle of pills, tipped a few into her hand and took them, washing them down with the margarita.

"What was Luna so upset about?" I asked.

Bianca started eating again.

"When did Luna get upset?"

"I never said nothing." Bianca took another drink. "We sang on stage, did you know? We did a duet and then Luna danced and we danced together. It was grand." She began to hum, keeping time by waving her fork in the air.

I reached over and took her hand for a moment. "Do you remember when Ronnie broke up with the history teacher?"

She paused, a piece of steak halfway to her lips. She looked up at the ceiling, as if seeking inspiration up there. "That was a bad time," she said. She ate the piece of steak, chewing thoughtfully. "Ronnie got real weird. I don't know why that teacher walked out the way he did, just when he was needed most."

"Walked out? What do you mean?"

She shrugged and adjusted the bangles on one skinny wrist. "Well, it looked that way to *moi*. And Ronnie was crying his eyes out and smoking up and you name it. It was the worst time to break up with someone. Good steak. Want a bite?"

"No, thanks. But I didn't —"

"And another thing I just remembered." She pointed her fork at me accusingly. Did she suddenly grasp who I was? "Losing his boyfriend opened the door to that dreadful violent man — what was his name? He used to beat on Luna somethin' fierce. It was awful."

I swallowed, remembering the times Ronnie had called me for help. I remembered taking him to the hospital, the crowded, noisy waiting room, the brisk attendants and nurses, the lies I put down on the forms to make sure he was covered by my insurance. "Going out with Al Vecchio was his choice," I said.

"Shows what you know," Bianca muttered darkly, spearing the last of the steak.

"What do you mean?"

"Honey, Luna had her reasons, okay? 'Nuff said. I ain't telling no tales out of school."

"Ronnie owed him money, right?"

"I didn't say that."

"But he had a good allowance from his family. Why would he need money?"

She dabbed at her thin lips with her napkin. "I gotta powder my nose."

I watched her go, weaving slightly between the tables, her large purse hugged under one arm. I wondered which restroom she would use. I wondered why Ronnie had needed money so badly he put up with being a punching bag for Al Vecchio. Why hadn't he come to me?

I waited fifteen minutes before it occurred to me to check.

"Her? She's gone," said the waiter. "She went out the side door. Didn't you know?"

I paid the bill and left. The rain has faded to a fine mist, and the sun was poking through now and then to glint on the slick street and dripping awnings. I hurried along the lane to the parking lot and headed home, stopping at the Harbord Bakery to pick up a few bagels and some Chelsea buns.

As I turned into my street, I saw Julie on my front porch, laughing and talking animatedly with a young man. When he turned toward her, I recognized Ryan. I slowed the car even more and watched as Julie tried to unlock the door while holding several plastic grocery bags. As one began to slip, Ryan caught it deftly, moving close to her and laughing into her eyes. I felt a hot anger sweep through me and accelerated into the alley behind the house and around to my garage. I barely stopped to close the door before rushing through the upheaval in my garden, through the house to the front. Ryan was just disappearing upstairs to Julie's.

I caught her door in one hand. "Ryan," I said.

He turned around, one foot on the step ahead of him, and looked me in the eyes. Then he glanced away. "I thought you weren't home," he said.

"Hi, Michael." Julie spun around and grinned at me. "Ryan didn't have his key so I invited him up to my place to wait."

"Thanks, Julie." I stood aside, holding my front door open pointedly. Ryan handed the parcel to Julie and slipped down the steps and into my apartment.

Ryan turned around and began backing away, his hands out in front of him as if in supplication. "Look, Michael —"

"What are you doing here?"

"I'm sorry. I'm real sorry."

"And?"

"I shouldn't have taken your money, but I was just so mad —"

"I owed you the money. Nevertheless, you had no right —"

"I know, I know. I was just so mad and… Shit!" He was looking over my shoulder. "What the fuck you think you're doing?"

Everything happened at once. He sprang past me to the front door. I spun around as someone called my name, and a flash exploded almost in my face.

"This is private property!" Ryan shouted. "Get the hell out before we call the cops!" He slammed the front door in the guy's face and slipped the chain in place. "Getting so's you're not safe in your own house," he muttered.

"Who the hell was that?"

"Photographer with the *Rainbow Rag*," he said. "I recognized him from Boot's Patio. He's always hanging around there."

"Thanks. Guess you spoiled that picture for him. I thought I'd closed the door."

"Guess it didn't catch."

I walked into the kitchen, shaken, and pulled two Coronas out of the fridge. I led the way to the solarium and sat down in the wicker armchair.

Ryan flung himself into the other armchair, his lean body still thrumming with tension. He had a shadow mustache on his upper lip. A muscle jumped in one cheek. He took a long pull at his beer, then raised his hazel eyes and looked right at me again. I felt the strength of that look, the calculated heat he threw my way. "I owe you a lot," he said. He reached into the back pocket of his tight jeans, squirmed around a bit as he pulled out his wallet, then leaned forward to hand me a card. A credit card. *My* credit card. "I didn't use it," he said. "Not once."

"Big of you," I said, taking it. The plastic was warm from his body. "Is this why you came back?"

He nodded. "And I want to know…I don't want you mad at me anymore."

"Look, I'm not your father." I felt the tension twist tighter in the air.

"I know, I know. I just want to, like, start again, okay?"

"I have to be able to trust anyone who lives in my house, Ryan." We both drank in silence for a while. I saw the shadows in his eyes, the tension in his body, the nervous tapping of one foot. I wondered what he had been doing while he was away, how he had been living. He wasn't wearing the gold bracelet.

Ryan suddenly slid forward, off his chair and onto his knees in front of me, one hand on my thigh. "I'm real sorry," he said, gazing up at me.

I wasn't sure anymore who was in whose debt. Did it matter? He had saved me from getting my face splashed all over the gay news. Were they doing an article on me? Was it for their notorious Around Town spread? "I need you to finish the garden," I said, looking through the window at the desolation outside. "And maybe some painting," I added. "After that, I can't say. I'll pay you a regular wage, and you can have your old room back. But Ryan, this is the last time. Shape up and fly right, or you're out." My father's expression made me wince inside, but I could see it impressed Ryan.

He sat back on his heels and nodded solemnly. We talked out a few details. I resisted the urge to take his hand off my thigh. I got up instead. "When you need a key, take the spare from the brass bowl in the hall. It can't be copied, and I want it returned when you come in, okay?"

"Got it." Ryan stood up too. His eyes glowed. His whole body seemed to uncoil. He had what he wanted. Did I?

After he had gone upstairs, I took the old shoe box full of Ronnie's money and hid it in my bedroom closet. Tomorrow I would put it in my safety deposit box.

CHAPTER THIRTEEN

Next morning found me on the 401, heading west to London. I had stopped at the bank first, to put the pile of US bills into my safety deposit box, and I had given Ryan detailed instructions about the garden. It was heavy work and should keep him busy all day. I was reasonably sure he would stick to it, since he was still acting apologetic and anxious. With Ryan back in the house, I was feeling restless and jumpy again. I had to get out. But I admit waiting till Julie left for her temp job.

The air was clear today, washed by the recent rain. Asphalt steamed. Clouds still rolled dark and threatening in the east, but as I drove, the sun came out. This had once been a familiar route for me. When I was young, there had been many trips to the Stratford Festival to get our annual dose of Shakespeare with my family, and as I grew older, I kept up the tradition.

As I drove, it was the family trips I remembered, the muted bickering in the back seat between me and Trish, the lofty discussions between my parents, who tried to ignore us. Hildy used to pack a sumptuous picnic lunch that we were never allowed to poke into until we arrived. We would have it by the outdoor pool at our motel or on the grass by the Avon river. My mother's carefully tended eyebrows always arched in surprise by what Hildy had chosen — the ham and deviled eggs, the European sparkling cider, the cubes of cheese and thick slices of home-baked bread and mouthwatering strudel — even though it was always the same every year. I think Trish would have been just as happy to stay in the pool all the time, it was such a novelty for us, but of course that was not allowed. Later on, when I was in university, there were memories of friends, apprentices with the company who carried spears and lugged dead bodies offstage, or worked in the props department or making costumes. There were cast parties and people sleeping haphazardly on the floor in tiny basement apartments or third-floor aeries with ugly Danish furniture and lava lights, a feeling of adventure and camaraderie with people who were almost total strangers. I had wanted to bring Ronnie here. I had even bought the tickets, but everything exploded in my face before we got there.

At any rate, it was to London I was headed this time. I used to know a few people who taught at Western University and longed for the bright lights and gay streets of Toronto for most of the year. But I had lost touch with them, and now my only purpose in coming here was to search out Al Vecchio.

The drive seemed longer than I remembered, perhaps because I was alone. I listened to CDs of world music that I had bought to share with Logan. The pipes of pan, the jumbled rhythms were unfamiliar, taking me away from my small claustrophobic world as I listened. At last I came to the turnoff at Hightower Road and swung the car north. This was a section of malls, of fast-food joints, and motels, with a strip of small bungalows now and then. It was not a part of the city I was very familiar with.

The gaudy triangular flags flying along the front of the car dealership came up fast on the left. It took a few moments to ease over to the left lane, make a turn, and edge back. I glanced at my watch as I drove onto the lot. Ten to twelve. Good timing.

So far I had been relying on Julie's research. From now on, I was on my own. As I got out of the car, I saw a salesman heading my way, swinging out the door with a wide smile on his round face. He was too young to be Al, too fair.

"Anything I can help you with today, sir?" he chirped. "Looking for a second car for the wife? Or something a little more sporty?"

"I'm looking for Al Vecchio," I said.

"Sure. He's in the office. I'll take you through."

As I followed him through the glass doors and down a narrow hall past several open doors of empty cubicles, he told me his name was Walt Loomis, and he was Al's brother-in-law. "No shit," I murmured.

He knocked at the door at the end of the hall and opened it without waiting for a reply. "Hey, Al. Someone here to see you." He gave me a pleasant grin and headed back down the hall.

This cubicle was larger than the rest, with a window looking out on the back parking lot and walls paneled in the ubiquitous fake wood. Cheap photos of a soccer team the dealership sponsored decorated the walls, along with several awards for best salesman, best dealership, service to the community, and the like. Al was getting to his feet from behind a large metal desk covered with forms and several plastic baskets overflowing with paper. I remembered Al as stocky and solid, with melting dark eyes and bright red fleshy lips. He had put on a lot of pounds. Even his nose was spreading, covered with the telltale tiny lines of the heavy drinker. Now he looked more like an extra in *The Godfather*.

"Come on in. Sit down. What can I help you with today?" Al was struggling into his jacket. Sweat stained his underarms. "Want a cup of coffee?"

"No, thanks."

"Know what you mean. Trying to quit myself." He laughed. His smile was all professional salesman. He finally got into his jacket and perched one fat thigh on the desk. "So, what can I do for you?"

"It's been a long time, Al."

"I know you?"

"Not since the '60s."

I watched his smile melt, his eyes grow still and watchful. "You've got the advantage of me here, pal. My memory's not that good these days."

"I'm sure you remember Ronnie Lipinsky."

Al stood up and looked at the door. He closed it. "Who the fuck are you?"

"Michael Dunn-Barton. I met you back when I was with Ronnie. I'd like to talk to you."

"Why, for God's sake? What's the point of dredging up that nonsense now?"

"'Nonsense'?"

"Look, Michael, I'm a different person now. I've got a wife, kids, a good business —"

"Al, all I want is a little of your time."

"It was the '60s! We all went a little crazy."

"Look, I'm talking to everyone who knew Ronnie then, trying to piece things together."

"You a journalist? TV or something?"

"No. This is personal. Just for my own peace of mind, Al. Come on. Let me take you to lunch."

He ran a pudgy hand over his flushed, sweaty face, his eyes darting around the room as if seeking escape.

"Or we could talk here," I went on, pulling a chair in front of his desk.

"Time for lunch anyway," he said quickly. "Let's go."

We went in my car, with Al giving directions and in between times talking nonstop about what a great car the Mercedes was, how good this particular model was, what kind of mileage it got and on and on. I tuned him out, just letting him talk until we were in the restaurant, a big place in the middle of a large parking lot, with rough barn board paneling on the walls, hung with farm implements and copper pots and old-fashioned ads for chocolate and oatmeal and whiskey. The music was loud and all the wait staff wore jeans and red and white checked shirts with red kerchiefs around their necks and big name tags. Our waitress bounced up and announced her name was Karin, accent on the last syllable, and she was going to be our server today.

"Goody," I said.

She recited the specials, took our drink orders, and bounced away, unperturbed by my surliness or Al's heavy-handed flirting.

"So what are you into these days?" Al asked, rubbing his hands as if he was cold.

"Well, I haven't changed much, Al. I'm still into boys, same as before."

"Christ! Do you have to talk like that?"

"You asked me a question, I answered it. If you don't like the answer, I can't help that." I felt so much anger against Al I wanted to hit him. Barring that, I would hurt him other ways.

Our drinks came and Al finished his rye and ginger in three gulps and ordered another. "What do you want?" he said, eyeing me across the table like a cornered animal.

His second drink came. I waited until Karin had bounced away. "1965," I said. "I want your memories of Ronnie in 1965."

"Fuck, you were there. Haven't you got your own memories?"

"He left me and went to you."

"You care about that now? Christ!" He wiped his face again and loosened his tie.

I stirred my Bloody Mary with the celery stick, then bit off the end and chewed it.

"I'd never met anyone like Ronnie before," he said, looking over my shoulder into his memories. "I was really hot for him. I was officially going with a Loretto Abbey girl named Carmela, but after I met Ronnie it was all just going through the motions with her, know what I mean?"

"I never went out with a Catholic girl," I said.

"No, you were married."

"Touché. Still, I did see you in a gay bar now and then, as I recall."

"Yeah. I was…conflicted."

I laughed. "So that's why you were so violent."

Al sighed, took another drink, and signaled the waitress for a refill. I wondered if he ever hit his wife. The muscles had gone to fat, his gut hung over his belt, but he looked as if he could still pack quite a wallop. Still, the fight seemed to have gone out of him. Maybe he had poured it all away into a bottle.

"Okay, so I read the papers. I know why you're here. But I don't know nothing about the corpse."

"At first I thought it might be you," I said, more to get a rise out of him than anything else.

"You *what?* You thought I killed someone?"

"No, no. I thought Ronnie had killed you."

Al threw back his head and roared with laughter till the tears poured down his cheeks.

"That's the funniest thing — Ronnie wasn't much of a fighter, ya know. God, I don't remember you having such a sense of humor."

"I must have improved."

Lunch arrived, and Al dived into his steak and fries. I forced myself to begin the hot chicken salad.

After a few minutes, Al said, "So, what do you want to know? I can't promise how accurate my memories are, but I'll give it a shot."

"That's all I ask. When was your first date with Ronnie?"

"Why does that matter?"

"What month? Do you remember?"

Al put down his fork. "Yeah, as a matter of fact, I do. I had been dropping into this gay bar on Church Street to play pool and that for several weeks. I was hoping to meet a certain guy who had picked me up a few times there, but he never came in again. So anyway, I just hung out and played pool. I felt sort of invisible, you know? It was a secret part of my life, totally separate from anything else. And it gave me a charge of adrenaline every time I was there, doing something forbidden. A rush. But it was sort of seeping into my life with Carmela, you know? Anyway, it all kind of blew up just before her graduation dance, so that would be May, around the middle of May. Somebody had given me Ronnie's number, and I was calling him all the time but he wouldn't bite. Then suddenly, right out of the blue, he said okay, come over. I couldn't believe my luck. I canceled a date with Carmela for him. I thought he wanted some weed, you know? So we smoked up and then we went to bed. He was wild." He took another drink. "And another thing —I remember the smell. Ronnie said a raccoon got stuck in the crawl space and died. Anyway, after that, Carmela told me to get lost." He shrugged.

"Okay, now we're getting somewhere," I said, though I had lost any appetite I may have had. I remembered the raccoon smell. That was about the time we were getting rocky, and I didn't know why. "You remember your first fight?"

"Sure do. It was the second or third time I was with him. He got a phone call, then threw me out. Said you were coming over so I had to go. I was mad as hell. I hit him. He tried to kick me in the balls. He had spunk, I'll say that for him."

I smiled. But I wondered why Ronnie needed Al, when I was still there? "Did you ever lend him money?"

"Me? Are you kidding? I was a stock boy in my uncle's hardware store. I barely made minimum wage. Every penny went onto my back and into my car. I loved that car more than anything."

"But you scored weed for Ronnie."

"Yeah. That's the third thing I spent money on. It wasn't that much, though, back then. It was a way to get chicks. Or guys," he added, with a glance at me.

"Did you ever move in with Ronnie?"

"You're kidding, right?"

"Why would I be?"

"Look, pal, I was just fooling around then. Just experimenting, trying it on, you know? I'm not into guys."

"Just Ronnie."

"We were kids. And he was a bit of a slut, anyway."

"What?"

"You know, pal, I think you're conveniently forgetting a few things about that guy. Really. I wondered a few times if he was selling his ass, but I never had any proof. He always seemed to have money and didn't have a job back then, so…"

"His parents were —"

"Oh come on. He didn't have that money look, you know what I mean? You should. You've got it." He tossed back the rest of his drink. "You want to know what finished it for me? That little cocksucker almost got me arrested!"

"How did that happen? You hit him in front of witnesses?"

"He kissed me, right on Yonge Street! After that, I never called him again. Okay, go ahead and laugh, but it was no laughing matter back then. I could have landed in jail. My dad would have killed me! Look, I gotta go."

"Do you remember Rey Montana?"

He stared at me, his eyes hard and angry. "You prick. You think I had anything to do with this you're crazier than Ronnie was."

"It's a logical question. You were there. So was he."

"And so were you, remember?"

"Montana probably showed up in June or July. Maybe even later. By then I was out of the picture."

Al shrugged. "I can't help you, Michael. It was just a fling for me, you know? Nothing serious. And as for that Montana guy." He shook his head. "Sorry, I don't remember him at all."

"It was a long shot."

"One other thing I remember." He grimaced. "Around the first of July, long weekend, it was. I had a hell of a time getting out of some family outing. Ronnie talked me into taking him to some party on the island. Hanlon's Point, I think it was. Next thing I know he had his swimsuit half off and was pulling me into the bushes. High as a kite and not giving a damn. He was nutso and getting worse by the minute! I took off like a bat out of hell, I tell you. You know, you've got rose-colored glasses about that guy, Michael."

"He never was a closet case," I said.

"Whatever. Look, I gotta go. I can't take too much time away from that place or they'll give it away from under me, know what I mean?" He laughed, a false-hearty salesman's laugh, and started to dig for his wallet.

"My treat," I said, pulling out some bills.

"Can't say it's been a pleasure," he said, as Karin rushed off to get change.

"Every piece of the puzzle counts," I said. "Thanks. I didn't mean to come down on you like a ton of bricks."

"You were always a hard-ass, Michael."

I was so surprised he was almost to the door before I caught up to him.

CHAPTER FOURTEEN

We settled into a routine, Ryan and I. I felt better knowing we had laid down some guidelines, however vague, and that there was a time limit hinted at on his stay. He worked outside after breakfast, while I worked at the table in the solarium, doing course outlines, making phone calls, writing letters about Ronnie's estate and notes about the book. I admit that my eyes often strayed to the garden, to Ryan's naked shoulders straining and sweaty in the sun, to the hair plastered to his forehead, to his arms corded with unexpected muscle. I knew I wasn't the only one. I was aware of Julie on the floor above me and was glad only one of her windows overlooked the garden. He was a pleasant distraction, a secret vice I enjoyed, even though I felt a little like a voyeur at the keyhole of my own bedroom.

Logan phoned to let me know he was coming home on Friday. I was amazed but pleased for him. I know how he longed to get outside those hospital walls. He had been in and out of the burn unit for so long now, but this time, he said, would be it. I hoped he wasn't being overly optimistic. His sister was cleaning the apartment and stocking the cupboards, so there wasn't anything for me to do but pick him up on Friday morning. I told him about my visit to London. I didn't tell him about Ryan's return. Was that because he was straight and I didn't want to make myself a stereotype in his eyes? Or because I wanted to keep Ryan to myself?

But it seemed I couldn't keep him a secret for long. Lew seemed to sense that Ryan was back. He called a few days after he arrived.

"I was just thinking of dropping over," Lew said, after a few moments of idle chatter.

"Not now," I said irritably.

"Look, hon, I'm going to meet him one way or another, so let's be civilized. Thursday, eight p.m., my place. Dinner with all the trimmings."

"You can do all the trimmings that fast?"

"I'm a fast boy, Michael. Always was."

"True enough." I sighed. He was right. He would just persist until he wore me down or caught me unawares. I would rather get it over with. "Okay, you win. See you there."

"You remember the address?"

"I remember." I hung up and joined Ryan on the patio.

"Looking good," I said, walking over the paving stones, testing their balance and the way they settled under my weight. I ignored the cigarette butts strewn about.

Ryan thrust his shovel into the ever-diminishing pile of sand and mopped his forehead. "Yeah, it's working pretty good. Should be finished the stones in another day." He pulled out a crumpled pack of Players and lit one. He inhaled deeply and blew a jet of smoke over his shoulder.

I sat down on one of the wrought-iron chairs shoved in a corner of the tiny patio. "We've been invited to a friend's place for dinner. His name's Llewellyn ab Hugh. But Ryan, you don't have to go if you don't want to. I won't mind."

"That the lawyer guy who's in the paper all the time about those gangster cases and shit?"

"The very same."

"Cool! Yeah, man, sure I want to go. Why not?"

I sighed.

"So how come you know him?"

"We went to school together. Okay, dinner's on for tomorrow at eight." I looked at him consideringly. "You want to go shopping this afternoon?"

He laughed and cocked his head. "You buying?"

Well, he can hardly afford good clothes on what I pay him, I thought defensively. I blamed Lew for this, for turning me into a daddy, though I had to admit I had helped.

♦ ♦ ♦

Thursday evening, as we drove to Lew's fashionable condo in an ex-slum near the waterfront, I was absurdly nervous. I knew Lew and the razor-sharp mind he tried to hide behind all that flamboyance, and I dreaded being the object of his dissection. Ryan kept glancing down at himself appreciatively when he thought I wasn't looking. The new stonewashed 501s were tight-fitting, and they showed off all his assets in ways that made my mouth water.

Ryan was impressed with Lew's gilded, portly doorman. He shot me a quick grin, then swaggered to the elevator, his thumbs hooked into his belt loops. I caught a glimpse of us in the plate glass mirror just before the doors closed and smiled at the picture of the conservative middle-aged man in the navy blazer with requisite brass buttons and the boy who was trying to look like a hustler. Maybe the clothes were too new. Is that why he didn't quite make it? Or was I fooling myself?

Ryan seemed overawed by the showy splendour of his surroundings. "I guess lawyers really got it made, eh?" he whispered in the wide, broad-loomed hall outside penthouse nine.

"True," I agreed, "but think of having to talk to criminals all day long. Not very appealing, is it?"

"Who cares! I'd talk to anyone for all this!"

When Lew opened his door and I heard the murmur of voices behind him, I felt a hot flush of anger. Too late it occurred to me I ought to have rehearsed Ryan in the finer points of etiquette, like keeping your mouth closed while eating. *If Lew serves lobster in the shell, I'll never forgive him*, I thought as I followed him into the living room.

Lew was into his jungle period. The whole place was done in different shades of green and brown with a lot of ferns and wicker furniture. Huge murals of lions and tigers decorated the walls and fierce African sculptures lurked on teak shelves among the ivory and brass.

Ryan was enchanted, gazing around in unabashed curiosity. "Cool," he murmured in awe. "Awesome." He totally ignored the three other men in the room, who were watching him with quiet amusement. I recognized them all and shook hands, murmuring the usual platitudes.

"I thank you, and my decorator thanks you," said Lew. "I wish all my guests were this appreciative."

Ryan smiled uncertainly. He paid attention as Lew made the introductions, repeating each name softly. He shook hands and smiled with diffident, boyish charm. When Lew left to get the drinks, I followed and cornered him in front of the fridge.

"You didn't mention you were planning a circus," I said coolly.

"Circus? What circus? I'm having a few old friends over for dinner. Pass the lemon juice."

I banged the bottle down on the counter beside him. "I didn't bring Ryan here to provide amusement for you and your gossiping friends."

"Our friends. It's all in the family, Michael."

"Since when is Glori Daze an old friend of yours?"

"Since when do you get to critique the guest list? Anyway, I thought you liked Duane." He gave me a quick grin. "And you know my partner, Tony."

"When did lovers start being partners?" I asked irritably.

"Keep up, baby. Bob Keyes is a friend of Duane's. I think he has something to do with that Wilde Nights thing, so you know him too, right?"

"He's the choreographer."

"Right. Here's your drink. Take this one to the boy and relax, for God's sake."

When I got back to the living room, Bob had taken Glori, aka Duane, off to view the latest artistic acquisition. That left Ryan with Tony. Tony was short and blond and muscular and wore a large diamond earring. He was working hard at keeping the conversation going.

Ryan wasn't helping. As he listened, he stared at the golden hairs on Tony's chest, visible in the wide V-neck of his fashionable Italian sweater. He had more there than on his head.

"So you're working at Michael's for a while," Tony was saying between sips at his drink. "There must be lots to do around that old place."

"Yeah. Keeps me busy."

"I bet Michael's a real martinet sometimes," Tony went on with a wink at me.

Ryan frowned in thought. "He's an okay guy," he said at last.

When the others joined us, the conversation drifted into plays and opera, but I was tense, noticing the veiled glances in my direction. Finally Duane asked the question they'd all been thinking about.

"Anything new?" He leaned forward, his pink face beaming, blue eyes bright with interest. He looked younger when not in drag, I decided.

"Nothing," I said. "Look, I don't have any pals in the cop shop, guys. Give me a break. Let's get back to Rex Harrison."

"Not so fast," Lew said, holding up a long, pale hand in a gesture I'd seen him make on TV. "We know you've been nosing around, Michael, so give. What have you learned?"

There was utter stillness in the room. The CD had even stopped playing. I stared at my hands, feeling anger and disgust at myself for walking into this in the first place. Ryan smiled sympathetically.

"What is this? Truth or dare? You really want to go there, Lew?"

"Ooooh," said Duane appreciatively. "Gotcha."

"Why should he tell you anything, if he doesn't want to?" Ryan said suddenly. "He's sick of everyone asking about that crap. I thought you were his friends."

There was a moment of stunned silence.

"Bravo," Tony said.

"Indeed." Lew shot me a wicked grin. "And on that note, shall we adjourn to the dining room?"

I sat beside Ryan, ignoring the place cards. I knew how judgmental Lew could be, and I felt fiercely protective of my young companion. In some strange way, Ryan had become an ally. While Tony was serving the soup, I moved Ryan's elbows off the table, then, without thinking, reached over, unrolled his serviette and placed it on his lap. He twisted around to look at my face, and there was a disturbing glint in his eye.

"What's up?"

"You'll love the soup," I remarked heartily, trying to sidetrack him.

"I love a lot of things," he said and reached over for my serviette. Knocking my hands away, he insisted on spreading it out on my lap, expertly groping my crotch as he did so. He'd never touched me before. I felt my face flame scarlet as my cock responded under his hand. "There," he said with a melting smile. "We're ready for anything."

"Togetherness is so rare these days," Lew remarked from the head of the table.

I was afraid to say anything. Ryan had already turned his attention to the soup, which he was eating with a dessert spoon.

I don't remember a great deal about the meal. The conversation stayed civilized, if you don't count some lethal gossip about a few of our leading citizens in the arts world. At least no one mentioned Ronnie, though I felt his name in the air around me all evening. I drank more than usual and tried not to notice when Ryan sampled the gravy using the tip of his knife or picked his teeth thoughtfully between courses.

It was a relief when dinner was over and we moved back to the living room for brandy. Bob and I were soon embroiled in a heated debate about censorship and the Mapplethorpe exhibition that was causing such a stir in Cincinnati, and it was a while before I noticed that Lew and Ryan were among the missing.

I found them in the den. They didn't see me push the door open. Lew was talking softly. Ryan was sitting close beside him on the suede couch, one hand moving up and down Lew's thigh. I couldn't hear what he was saying, but after a moment,

Ryan slid to the floor between Lew's knees. I felt bolted to the spot. My blood rushed into my head. Gulping, I loosened my tie and watched Ryan take Lew's pale cock in his hands and roll on a condom. Then he opened his mouth and gave him an expert blowjob.

Lew closed his eyes and leaned back into the cushions. His mouth opened slightly as his breath came in gasps. His head began to roll back and forth, and he reached out blindly for Ryan, fastening his fingers in the boy's sun-streaked hair. I wanted to leave, but there was no way I could move. I was condemned to stand there, my heart thumping in my ears, my hands sweaty. My mind tried to tell me there was no reason I should feel betrayed. My heart couldn't hear.

Then it was over. Ryan peeled off the condom and tied it, tossed it casually in the wastebasket. Lew moved his head and saw me and held my eyes for a moment. Had he known I was there all along? He slid some money into Ryan's hand, zipped up his fly. Without saying a word, he got up and walked past me out of the room. I knew he would never mention this moment.

Ryan got to his feet and smiled, a brilliant, studied smile that said nothing at all out of the way had happened here. If I had seen something, it must have been my imagination. I watched him unbutton his shirt a few more notches, slide his hand inside, and scratch his chest thoughtfully. He looked up at me through his lashes.

"I want to go home," he said softly, gliding over to stand close beside me. "Don't you want to leave?"

I was so hot for him now, I didn't care what he had just done! I nodded.

Lew, ever the thoughtful host, called us a taxi. On the way home, Ryan kept sliding against me every time we went around a corner. He was almost purring. By the time we got home, I didn't care what his motivation was. In my anxiety to get into the house, I over tipped the amused taxi driver. I knew I was making a fool of myself. It didn't matter.

Nothing mattered when I finally stood in the front hall with my blazer sliding unheeded to the floor and Ryan put his strong arms around me and pressed his mouth firmly against mine. I tasted wine and chocolate. His breath intoxicated me, sent me spinning, gasping for air. I flung my arms around him and clasped his lithe body against me hard, trying to squeeze out anything that came between us. My heart knocked hard against my ribs as if trying to touch his. The taste of him, the feel of him, the smell of the new leather of his jacket, all combined to drive me out of my usual painful reticence.

"Take off your clothes," I gasped.

"Not here. Upstairs." He slid out of my arms and took my hand and pulled me up the stairs to my bedroom. "I always wanted to make it in a four-poster like yours," he said. "Wait here."

I was helpless, confused. I hadn't had sex for a long time. I was under the spell of his lithe young body and sun-streaked hair, and wide, innocent eyes that hid a world of knowledge I would never have. I began to get undressed. Mesmerized. High on my own fantasy.

In a moment he was back, carrying the silver candelabra from the dining room. I felt like a child, standing naked beside my bed, watching him light the candles, switch off the light.

The golden flames leapt and danced as Ryan took off his clothes and flung them out of the way with an abandon this room had never seen. His body was smooth, almost hairless, as I'd guessed it would be. His nipples were cinnamon. The sun had already left his skin like golden honey. There was a clear line of a brief bathing suit low on his hips.

I reached out for him. I think I said something, but it made no sense, a sound of inarticulate need. As our bodies touched, he pushed me onto the bed. We tangled together. It was like trying to hold on to a dancing candle flame. He was hot and constantly shifting. I rolled over, pinning him beneath me, holding his slender wrists on either side of his head. He laughed up at me, and I covered his mouth with mine. I drank in his essence, his breath, tasting him, touching the roof of his mouth with my tongue. He was quiet now, letting me explore him. He began to return my kisses. Then he slid out of my grasp and wriggled down to suck my right nipple.

I cried out. I could smell the sun in his hair, the wind. Youth. I wasn't thinking anymore, letting him bring my body back to tingling life with his tongue, his lips, his teeth. I heard the rip of the foil package. Ryan was waiting with a condom. I flashed to that picture I knew I would always remember: Ryan kneeling between Lew's legs. I blinked hard, banishing the image.

"Fuck me," whispered Ryan.

I did.

The boy held his breath, then expelled it in a long, keening sigh as I sank into him. I wanted to hold on to that moment, hold on to Ryan, never let him go. I felt tears behind my eyes and blinked, seeing his sweat-slicked face waver before my eyes. Then I collapsed on top of him, my heart pounding.

"You okay?"

I nodded feebly. "It's been a while," I said, when I got my breath.

He laughed softly. "You're something else."

"Yeah. Sure."

"I mean it." He pushed me off him and propped himself on one elbow. "I don't get it," he said, looking down at me. "Why don't you just…let go?"

I shook my head and smiled. How could I explain almost half a century of control to a kid like Ryan? I had let go once, twenty-five years ago. I was still paying. "Maybe I need a teacher," I said.

He laughed and snuggled against me. "Okay, you got one. When's the next class?"

"Give me a minute to recuperate." I watched the candle flames dance and glisten on his smooth chest. I began to stroke his hair. "Did Lew turn you on?"

"Not like this."

"So it was just a job, blowing him, I mean?"

He shook his head. "Nah. That was a freebie."

"Ryan, I saw money change hands."

He smiled, obviously amused at the old-fashioned expression. "That wasn't for the blowjob. He said the money was to see you got a good time. Hell, I would have done it for free, but why tell him?"

I kept stroking his hair, forcing my breath in and out, in and out. One of these days, I may kill Lew. But at least for a short time I hadn't thought about Ronnie. Ronnie, whose image hung like a ghost over the evening. Would I ever be free of him?

CHAPTER FIFTEEN

I woke up with a hangover at three thirteen. Ryan was fast asleep, snoring gently, his face buried in the crook of his arm, one leg outside the sheet. I got up cautiously and crept downstairs. I took some Tylenol and got a drink of ginger ale from the fridge. I was wide awake now. I could smell Ryan on my skin, on my hands. I got Ronnie's shoe box of letters off the shelf and sat down in the solarium to sort through them. This was a task I had been putting off, but thanks to Ryan, I was ready to think about Ronnie again, and more clearly than I had been doing lately.

There were six letters to his parents in the box. None was addressed to Albany. All had been sent back, unopened, with *return to sender* scrawled on them in the same tight, slanted handwriting. If his parents hadn't been paying his bills at school as he had told me, who had? Uncle Bunny? Or was there a glimmer of truth in Al's malicious allegation? I'd never heard of the place in the address, but it was in New York State. Why had he lied? The other packet of letters was from his sister, from a different address in the same town. I wondered if she was still there. Julie would know how to find out. So would my librarian friend on the Gay Blade. I went to my computer and logged on to the BBS. There were quite a few people online, even at this hour. No matter when I logged on, there was always someone there, reading files, chatting, sending e-mail. I sent a long detailed message to WondRBoy, asking him to find the Lipinskys for me, asking him to keep this private, and logged off. I knew there would be an answer for me by noon. He was always fast and very reliable. Debra Lipinsky could be married and divorced several times over by now, which was why I suggested he look for the parents. They were more liable to stay put.

I pulled out the letterhead I had done up for correspondence about Ronnie's estate and wrote them a letter, stating that their son had died and I needed to discuss some things with them. I had been a friend of Ronnie's. I would like to come down there, if I could. It struck me as an odd sort of letter, but I didn't care. The pile of money in my safety deposit box was haunting me. I wanted it to go where it should go, but how? I needed family help to track down Uncle Bunny. As soon as I got the address, I would send it.

I pulled on some shorts and a sweatshirt and ambled down the street. I was more relaxed than I had been for some time. Sex does that, I reminded myself, with a smile. What to do with Ryan now, I wouldn't think about. Just let things take their course, for once. At the corner I paused and looked up at the dark windows of Logan's place. On Friday I would bring him home. I was glad to be able to do something concrete for him at last.

My headache was gone by the time I got home. I went upstairs, stripped off my clothes, and climbed into bed beside Ryan, fitting my body to his. In minutes, I was fast asleep.

"Now I see why you're acting so chipper," Logan said, as he settled into his adjustable hospital bed by the window of his front room. "How come you forgot to tell me about him?"

"Drink your vitamins."

Ryan had helped get Logan upstairs. He had carried up the bags and wheelchair and other such things, then waved and jogged off to the corner store for cigarettes.

"You're blushing." Logan was enjoying himself. "That good, is he?" he cackled merrily at my embarrassment. "It's good to have a fling now and then. Relax."

"If I was any more relaxed, I wouldn't move for an entire day," I said, laughing.

"How's the great Ronnie caper coming along?"

I told him about Ronnie's parents' returned mail, about my online friend who had found they still lived at the same address, and the letter to the Lipinskys that I had sent off by courier.

"Uncle Bunny doesn't have to be a relative," he pointed out.

"I thought of that. In my day, we weren't allowed to call adults by their first name. I had a lot of honorary aunts and uncles. Ronnie could too. He was only a few years younger than me, after all."

"My point, exactly."

"But real or honorary, his family would know this Bunny person."

"Great name. Could be a musician." Logan lay back on his pillows. He had had some color, but was now looking a bit drained.

"Look, I'd better let you rest. If you need anything, just call. Ellen got a long cord for your phone so it'll stretch to the table. She'll be by later, and your nurse is coming tomorrow morning."

"For fuck's sake, stop fussing, Michael! I'll be fine. It'll be great to be on my own for a while."

"Right." I paused, wanting to touch him but afraid to trespass. "See you later."

Ryan was taking the rest of the day off. I had a meeting with the real estate agent. Ever since my name appeared in the papers as Ronnie's executor, I had been plagued by calls from real estate people begging to list the house. Some had sent flyers and notices by mail, or just thrust something through the mail slot. I hadn't responded to any of them. When the time came, I called Mary Fratacelli, the agent I'd bought my house from, and set up a meeting. I told her I appreciated the fact that she hadn't called to badger me, although I suppose that showed a lack of selling push on her part.

I met Mary outside Ronnie's house at eleven thirty. She was a small nervous woman, with many rings on her hands, several heavy bracelets, and chains around her neck. Her suit was a bright fuchsia number with big shoulder pads, and her brassy red hair frizzed around her face. She looked anxious before she saw me. It occurred to me this might be the biggest sale of her career. The place would go for a lot of money.

"Thanks for calling me about this." she said, bearing down on me with outstretched arms. She was one of those women who seemed to think they had a license to kiss gay men. I got out the key.

"I like dealing with people I know," I said, "and you did a good job for me with my place."

"Thanks, I try. This is a great location. Should go in a flash. Is it in good shape inside? Outside looks pretty good, though the porch could do with a coat of paint. The grounds are well maintained."

"Ronnie had a yard guy who came around on a regular basis to look after the lawn and the flowers." I opened the door and stood back, waiting for her to go in.

She looked around the small foyer. "It could do with a coat of paint in here too," she said.

"I'll see to it. The first two floors are rented. A longtime tenant on the first floor and a couple who teach at University of Toronto Schools on the second. They both said it was okay to go in."

She poked in every corner and cranny, insisted on going down to the basement and poking around the laundry room, and finally followed me to Ronnie's apartment. She looked around without saying anything.

"Maybe I should have this place painted too," I suggested. "Would that make it seem more...marketable?"

She nodded. "This is too weird."

"And the furniture should be out soon. I have a guy coming over to assess a few of the good pieces."

"You know what? Let's just leave it all here. Having the place furnished makes it show better."

"Fine. I can do all that after it's sold. I'll tell him it stays here for a while."

"That would be good." She was making notes in a leatherbound notebook, pausing to tap her teeth with the thin gold pen as she thought. She turned and named a figure even higher than I had thought of. "Asking price," she said. "We may have to come down a tich, but not much."

"In spite of the corpse in the attic?"

"In this area, a whole family of corpses wouldn't make any difference. Trust me. There's a big demand and hardly any supply. We can name our own ticket."

"You're very optimistic."

"Just a realist." She dropped her notebook into her briefcase and pulled out some papers. "We can get this started right now," she said, sitting down at Ronnie's rolltop desk and spreading out the papers.

"I'll run all this by my lawyer and pop the papers into the mail to you," I said.

She nodded, gathered them up and shoved them into an envelope. "Here you go. Let's get this baby on the market ASAP, shall we?"

"Will do." I thought of her commission, a hefty sum she was obviously itching to get her hands on. I thought of all that money going to the hospices named by Ronnie in his will. "ASAP," I said.

I turned down her offer of a lift and walked home. It was less humid today, and the exercise would do me good. I had been lazy lately, skipping my usual thrice-weekly swim at the Hart House pool and driving everywhere. As I walked, I vowed to get out the old bicycle in my garage and use it. Last year I had walked to classes and back, even when the weather turned cold. *You're getting soft and self-indulgent*, I chided myself. *Time to shape up.* I heard my father's voice: *Shape up and fly right. Yes, sir!*

The phone was ringing when I walked in the door, with the peculiar urgency of a call you are just about to miss. I grabbed the phone and flung myself into a chair, panting slightly.

"Hello."

"Hello? My name is Debra Shopiro. I'm Ronnie Lipinsky's sister."

I took a deep breath. I remembered the snapshot on Ronnie's wall — a pretty, round-cheeked girl with warm, dark eyes and lustrous hair. "Thank you for calling. I'm Michael Dunn-Barton."

"Yes. You know, my parents are both sick, and I was here when your letter arrived. When I saw the Toronto return address, I opened it. I don't know how much you know about us?"

"Not much," I admitted. "Ronnie always told me his fees were paid by his parents, so it wasn't until now that I find out they weren't communicating."

"Fees? Didn't he go to a public school? That's what he told me."

"No. It was a nontraditional school, but it was private. I taught there."

"I know. He told me about you."

There was a pause. What had Ronnie said about me? What version of our life did he write about?

"Look, I think it would be good if we could meet and talk, like you said. I'd like my parents to get this last chance to forgive and forget. They shouldn't take such bitterness to the grave."

"I'm sorry your parents are ill."

"They're old and they never looked after themselves," she said irritably. "Mom's had a hip replacement and Dad's had a stroke. I'm trying to get them into a nursing home together, but it ain't easy and the bills are something else." There was a pause. "How did Ronnie die?"

This must be a really small town. Or else she had been on a news fast.

"Complications from AIDS."

She sighed. "Oh God."

"We can call it cancer," I said quickly, thinking of those old people, hanging on, needing to forgive.

"Thanks. When can you come? The sooner the better, I'd say. I have to go back to work soon."

"I can drive down on Tuesday," I said, remembering the Monday night rehearsal.

"Good." She gave me careful instructions how to get to her parents place, where she was staying, and hung up.

I sat staring at the wall. Suddenly I laughed. I remembered Ronnie saying, *"Deb's all right. She taught me all about peroxide for lightening my hair."*

CHAPTER SIXTEEN

I spent the rest of the weekend getting as much work done in the garden as possible before the pool liner arrived. Then I took Ryan over to Ronnie's place where he would be working while I was away. He thought it would be a breeze, compared to the hard labor he had been putting in in the garden. Then we went to the paint store and chose the paint for the foyer and stairwell.

"You sure you know how to do this?" I said to Ryan, eyeing him warily.

"Sure, sure," he said airily. "What's to know?"

My heart sank. "You have to be careful," I said. "You have to make sure everything is covered by the drop cloth. And you have to use the masking tape."

He looked at me and clicked his lighter. Off and on. Off and on. I was losing him. I took a roll of masking tape and began to show him how to put it along the baseboard.

"Wouldn't it be easier to paint the baseboard?" he asked.

"It's hardwood," I said. "It's a selling point."

"No kiddin'!"

The idea that it was worth money seemed to register with him. I felt a little better. When I left, he was halfway up the stairs with the tape, Walkman firmly in place.

My turn at the piano at the Wilde Nights rehearsal came around on Monday night. When I arrived at the 519, Glori Daze bore down on me like the *Queen Mary* steaming into port. She was wearing a sequined top with a tight-fitting black velvet skirt that went almost to the floor and pink platform shoes with ankle straps. The skirt was slit up the front almost to her crotch. She enfolded me to her cushiony bosom with enthusiasm, her perfume wafting over me in suffocating waves.

"Michael, baby, it's so good to see you," she cried, as if she hadn't seen me for years.

I untangled myself from her embrace. "Likewise," I said.

She laughed. "Always cut to the chase," she said. "Thanks for helping with the costumes. By the way, I better warn you. That Bianca broad is looking for you. She's been in here twice since the last rehearsal you were at, looking for, quote, 'that doll who plays the piano', unquote. Watch it, Michael. Don't let her get her hooks in you. She's several slices short of a loaf, you know. Been in and out of the Clark several times, not to mention drug rehab. Nutty as a fruitcake." She adjusted her tits absentmindedly. "I hear you took her to lunch at Papa Peaches."

"I feel sorry for her," I said.

Glori shook her great blonde head sadly. "Poor you, having to listen to all her nonsense. Did she say anything really off the wall?"

"Several times."

She laughed shrilly. "What a nightmare. It's a good thing no one pays any attention to anything she says these days. Later." She blew me a kiss and swayed off to talk to Stan, who had just came in.

I wondered why she was so down on Bianca. The poor thing seemed pretty harmless to me. I remembered she hadn't had much good to say about Glori, either. Was it just jealousy? But what had Glori got to be jealous about? She was the one with the career, strutting her stuff on stage across America, and Canada too, I suppose. I sat down at the piano and pulled my music out of my briefcase.

Ellis came slinking over and slid onto the bench beside me. "Did you hear I've got a duet now? It's with Dawn Valley Parkway. You know her? The reigning empress?"

I shook my head. "Sorry."

Ellis made a noise of disgust. "I wanted to do one with Glori, but she didn't want to share the spotlight. Guess she doesn't want me to show her up for the has-been she is."

"Ellis," I said, "that's cruel."

"Oh, I'm so not like that, Michael. Anyway, it's a big step up for me."

"Congratulations. I'm sure you'll be a hit."

"I'll bring the house down," exclaimed Ellis, never one to hide his light under a bushel. "So anything new on the skeleton in the trunk? Nothing in the papers anymore."

"No," I said.

"Bummer." He ran one hand through his spiky blond hair. He was wearing lipstick and eye makeup and high heels, but otherwise was dressed in jeans and a tight bright orange T-shirt. The effect was unsettling. So was the feeling I got that he wanted to talk about something else. I noticed Jaym watching me intently from the stage, where he was snapping pictures with that expensive camera he often had around his neck. When our eyes met, he blushed and looked away. My mind flashed to Ryan pushing me aside, shoving the photographer out my front door.

"Ellis, does Jaym work for the *Rainbow Rag*?"

"Jaym?"

"As a photographer?"

"He says that's just a hobby, but I don't know. He never talks about his job. One time someone asked, and he changed the subject, like he was embarrassed about it. Who knew?"

I kept waiting for Ellis to slide away, but he just sat there, making the air around us hum with energy. I looked round uneasily, hoping we would begin soon. Most of the principals were here, and we usually started with them first. The chorus was still straggling in, their chatter punctuated by frequent shrieks and loud laughter.

I glanced at my watch, shifted on the bench. Ellis edged closer. Was he making a pass at me?

"Ellis, I'm forty-seven years old. I'm —"

"No shit! You don't look it!" His startled face gave me a lift.

"Probably because I inherited the good-hair gene from my mother's side of the family. What's all this about?"

Ellis looked away. "I gotta talk to you about something. Can I buy you a coffee afterwards?"

"I can't stay long."

"We can just sit in the park, okay? It won't take long. Just ten minutes. Please?"

I nodded just as Stan clapped his hands to get everyone's attention and the chattering died away.

Outside the windows of the auditorium, day faded into darkness as the rehearsal lurched along to the end. I was nervous about Ellis. What could he possibly want to talk to me about? It was almost a relief when the rehearsal was over, and he slipped in beside me going down the staircase to the front door of the 519 Community Centre.

"You go on and find a table, and I'll bring the coffee," he said, heading for the snack room.

I wandered outside. Cawthra Park looked its best in the dusk, the lights glowing softly, hiding the worn-out grass and patches of dried mud, the overflowing garbage and the cigarette butts ground out along the winding paths. Couples lay on the grass or sat talking softly at the square tables scattered about. Two woman sat on a bench, pushing a baby back and forth in a stroller. Their laughter made me smile. Cigarette smoke wound lazily from two men, their bodies close together as they strolled toward the AIDS memorial.

I walked around to the north side of the park and sat down at a table near the street. Ellis joined me a few moments later, juggling coffee, creamers, and Saran-Wrapped squares made of healthy-looking seeds.

"I forgot to ask how you take it," he said, sitting down opposite me.

"Black," I said, peeling off the cardboard top. The coffee smelled strong and dark. I hoped there was enough caffeine to pull me out of the gloom that was settling over me like the deepening night around us. "So what's this all about?"

"Well, I've been thinking about campaigning for Empress of Toronto," he said. "What do you think? Will I get any support?"

"I haven't the faintest idea, Ellis," I said, "but from what I hear, you've got quite a following."

"Yeah, that's true."

"The time you saw me at Woody's a while ago was the first time I've been in a gay bar for years, so I'm the last person to ask. I have no idea how this Toronto Court thing works. Anyway, didn't you say that Dawn Valley Parkway person is the empress now?"

"I'm talking about next year," he said.

I sipped my coffee, watching Ellis fiddle with the creamers, stacking them into a tower, lining them up so the tops all pointed in the same direction. I'd never seen him so nervous.

"Ronnie said he'd back my campaign," Ellis said.

Money. It was about money. I took a deep breath, curiously relieved.

"Ronnie did back you, with those gowns, remember? That's worth a grand, maybe two."

"It takes more than that. Ronnie knew. He was empress for years."

"He paid his own way," I said.

"He had a high-paying job," Ellis shot back.

"What kind of job do you have?"

"Retail," he said sulkily. "It's the pits."

"Look, I don't know what you expect me to do about this," I said, losing patience. "I'm sorry if Ronnie led you to believe there'd be some money for your empress campaign, but there isn't anything written down. I can't do a thing."

Ellis sighed and slumped over the table. "I guess," he said.

"Can't you find someone else? What about Glori?"

Ellis looked at me as if I'd just lost my mind. "She wouldn't agree to doing a duet with me, you think she'd back me for empress? She's a bitch anyway. I hear —" He paused, stirring his coffee.

In spite of myself, I leaned closer. "Don't stop now."

"Well, Dawn says —"

"The empress."

"Yeah, yeah. Dawn says Glori has been supplying that old wreck Bianca with drugs. Is that uncool or what?"

"Maybe she feels sorry for her?"

"Oh, I'm so totally sure of that!"

I laughed and stretched my arms above me head. "Well, Ellis, I can't help you, and I guess Glori won't. So that leaves a fund-raiser."

"Cool!" said Ellis. "Thanks, Michael! You wanna help?"

"No," I said. "I'll make a donation, but that's it, okay?" I stood up and gathered up my coffee cup, creamers, and paper serviettes. "Good luck."

I walked out of the park, strolled south on Church Street to where I had left my car. Glori and Bianca. Was there any truth to a rumor spread by one drag queen about a rival?

"Me and Luna, we go way back…"

I shivered and picked up the pace. I seemed to have inherited a lot of unexpected problems from Ronnie. But Ellis and Bianca were minor irritants compared to Rey Montana, who had inhabited Ronnie's trunk for twenty-five years. I was still no closer to finding out who he was and what the connection could be between them. If there was one.

I got into my car, found a Vivaldi CD, and turned the volume up, trying to drown out my thoughts as I drove home.

CHAPTER SEVENTEEN

Next morning Julie knocked at the door around eight thirty. She knew I wasn't one to sleep in. When I opened the door, she held out a plate of muffins invitingly. "Hey, hey," she said. "Got a minute?"

"Not much more than that," I said, opening the door. "Just made coffee. Where did the muffins come from?"

"I made them." She looked smug.

"*You!* Your hidden talents amaze me."

"Me too. Actually, I do bake from time to time. But I don't advertise it. I don't want my boyfriends getting the idea that I like to cook or be domestic in any way."

"Wise policy," I said. I poured coffee, sat down, and sampled a muffin. "Good. You should do this more often."

"Oh no. It wouldn't have the same effect if I did it on a regular basis."

I laughed and agreed she had a point. "I wanted to thank you for the search job you did on Al Vecchio," I said. "I went down to London a few days ago, and he was right where you said he would be."

"Cool. What did he say?"

I told her about our lunch in the generic steak house, about Al's nervousness and his business and family. "There wasn't anything there from the man I remember, except maybe something in the eyes"

"I guess twenty-five years is a long time," she said thoughtfully.

"For you, a lifetime," I said, laughing as I got up to collect the coffee cups and rinse them out at the sink. "Now I'll have to throw you out. I've got to go."

"You're always throwing me out," she complained good-naturedly. "Where's Ryan?"

"He's doing a painting job for me over at Ronnie's." As she disappeared into her own apartment, I wondered if she had really baked the muffins for Ryan. I was glad he was safely out of the house.

After hours of driving along miles of baking highway, listening to opera CDs, I arrived just before six in the evening. Ronnie's hometown was a nondescript place of strip malls and car dealerships selling John Deere tractors and ride-on mowers, of run-down bungalows with a tiny square of parched, beaten-down grass out front. I passed four churches on my way down Main Street. The high school was a low building right out of the '50s. Ronnie must have gone there. I felt depressed and stiff and achy. I wondered why I had come.

In the back was a small box of stuff of Ronnie's I had picked out to bring along for Debra and her parents. Now I felt embarrassed by it. They were without relevance to this place. I turned the car right along Anderson Street and saw Lipinsky's Cleaners across the street. The sign had been repainted recently, but it was as dated as the high school. A Korean woman stood in the window, ironing shirts.

I pulled up on the asphalt lot in front and turned off the car. From habit, I snagged my jacket from the back seat, got out, and put it on. I slammed the door shut and looked around. The number sixteen was painted on the milky glass panel of the door beside the cleaners. I tried to picture Ronnie going in and out, working in the cleaners after school, but I hadn't known this boy. Maybe if I had, I could have helped him. As I raised my hand to push the bell, the door swung open. The woman who stood in the fading sunlight had an anxious, round face, short, curly brown hair obviously a wig and a heavy body. She wore careful makeup, a dark blue dress with tiny buttons down the front, and matching pumps.

"You must be Michael," she said. "I'm Deb." She held out a surprisingly small hand.

"I'm pleased to meet you after all this time," I said.

"Come on in. Just go upstairs. The door's open. I hope the trip went well?"

"It was fine," I said. "Luckily I have air-conditioning."

The stairs were steep and uncarpeted. At the top, we both paused for breath.

"I gotta get in shape." Deb laughed. "Who am I kidding?" She led the way into the dim living room. Boxes were piled against one wall. There was a large TV in the corner and two recliner chairs upholstered in powder blue in front of it. TV tables stood beside each one. A matching chesterfield stood against one wall. Above it hung a large print of a most improbable flower garden, in a heavy gilt frame. A wedding photo from the '30s hung on another wall, along with a formal family shot of all four of them. Ronnie must have been about eight or nine. He looked so innocent, so full of hope. I turned away.

"Take off your jacket," Deb was saying. "It's cooler in here since I convinced them to get that air conditioner. They're so stubborn, in the end George and I had to get it and bring it in ourselves. George installed it. He's my husband. Iced tea?"

"Thank you. That would be nice."

"It's still not exactly cold, though," she said as she headed for the kitchen down the narrow hall. I could hear her open the fridge, take something out. She must have had everything ready on a tray, because she was back almost at once.

"You look like your mother," I said, glancing at the picture. "Same eyes."

She laughed. "I never see it myself, but that's what people say. I always thought Ronnie looked like a softer version of Dad."

She poured the iced tea and sat down on one of the recliners. I sat on the couch.

"When was the last time you saw him?" I asked.

"He came back here for a visit…let's see, I think it was about ten years ago now. Dad wouldn't let him in. Mom and I met him in the hotel on Main Street. He used to send money, you know. He'd send it to me and tell me to get something they needed with it. For a while I did; then one time I mentioned that they had Ronnie to thank for the new paint job on the car, and Dad went ballistic. Then he walked out the door, down to Beecham's, and sold the car." She shook her head. "Men."

"Deb, could you explain what really happened here? Why he left? I know it doesn't matter now, but I feel…I don't really know him, and I thought I did."

"You think I know him? You were his 'significant other' — is that what they say?"

"You know how he got to Toronto. The story I heard, I realize now was just that. A story."

"Actually, I don't know either." She paused, put down her glass. "Hell, I think we need something stronger than tea." She got to her feet. "They don't keep much to drink around here," she said, heading for a glass-fronted cupboard at the end of the room. "Just peach brandy and Manischewitz and cooking sherry. And rum!" She pulled the bottle from the back of the cupboard in triumph. "Aha! Probably a gift from someone. Never been opened. There's Coke in the fridge." She rushed off. "Diet okay?"

"Fine by me." I loosened my tie. The room was stuffy, the shades pulled down to keep out the sun. I wished she'd let in some light.

When she came back, she had ice and cans of Coke in a small cooler in one hand and the drinks on a tray in the other. "This will keep us going," she said. "Have some banana bread. I just made it this morning."

I dutifully took a slice of the bread, slathered with butter, and ate it. It was good. It reminded me I hadn't eaten for a while.

We ate and drank for a few moments in silence.

"What did he tell you?" she said.

I took a deep breath. "First of all, he said he came from Albany."

She snorted. "Much classier," she said.

"He never actually said, but he led me to believe your dad was paying the school fees and his rent. He talked about his allowance. He always seemed to have enough, barely. I realize now I assumed a lot of things that he never really spelled out."

"Assuming our dad would do what yours would."

"In a way. He told me about his friend Harry. He said he didn't want to fight in a jungle in a country no one had ever heard of before in a war that wasn't even a real war. Just a police action where people got killed. There were quite a few draft dodgers in Toronto. It made sense."

"It was that damn war," she said at last. "Vietnam."

I nodded encouragingly.

"Ronnie was so scared. A guy we knew in school, Ace Klinger — he was ahead of us but everyone knew him, captain of the football team, valedictorian, you know the type — was reported missing in action in '64. That hit us all hard. But Harry was a friend, a guy he'd gone all though school with. Ronnie had nightmares after Harry was killed. But Dad had served in WWII and was all gung-ho. He called Ronnie a coward. Then he called him a lot of other things he probably regretted later. I don't know. They never really got along well."

There was another pause, with only the clink of the ice in our glasses. Deb reached over and pulled out another Coke. I did too. I passed her the bottle of rum.

"You know, I don't think Dad even got out of the States in his war. Maybe that was it. Maybe he felt cheated or something. Who knows? He was all for Uncle Sam. And then Harry Lang got killed in action. Ronnie went into a tailspin."

"Yes. He talked about him sometimes."

She nodded. "Harry was such a sweet kid." Her voice choked up, and she got up and pulled a box of tissues off the coffee table. She carefully blotted her eyes, thinking of the makeup no doubt. "I think it was after that Ronnie began to have nightmares."

I remembered the nightmares. I wondered how bad they got after Rey Montana went to sleep in his trunk, and what he did to stand it. I remembered the drugs near the end.

I added more rum to my drink. "You know, I think I've been discounting that war in thinking back to those days. For us it was just something happening on the news every night. Sure we talked antiwar and marched in a few demonstrations, but it didn't affect us directly. So I was thinking that the main reason he left was probably because he was gay."

"Oh that," said Deb, waving a hand at me. "No one talked about that in those days, least of all Dad, except that one time he blew up at him and called him all those names." She winced, remembering. "It was after that row that Ronnie borrowed all fifty-eight dollars and seventy-nine cents I had saved up, stole another thirty-two dollars from Ma's purse and walked to the highway to hitch a ride out of town."

"Why did he choose Toronto?" I asked.

"No idea."

"Maybe that's where the ride was going."

"Oh no. That time he ended up in New York City."

"He did?"

"He did. He phoned me a few days later, said he was fine and settled in with some guy he'd met."

"Do you remember his name?"

"After all this time? Besides, I didn't ask too many questions. I didn't hear anything for a while; then several months later I got a fat envelope from Toronto with the money I'd lent him, plus five dollars interest." She laughed. "Best investment I ever made. He paid Ma back too."

I thought of all those old US dollar bills in the shoe box in Ronnie's dusty attic cupboard. Had they come from New York?

"Deb, who is Uncle Bunny?"

"No idea. We only had one uncle, Earl, and he died a few years after Ronnie left."

"What about the honorary kind?"

"Oh sure, lots of them, but no Bunny. It's not the kind of nickname any of my family's friends would have. Trust me on that."

I nodded. The room was dark now. Deb reached up and switched on a floor lamp.

"And now we've got a new war to send the kids off to," she said quietly. "That high hell we see every night on CNN."

I thought of the Gulf War coverage that had just started to appear on TV, all at such a distance, at night, the navy sky streaked with bright streamers of death. "War is hell, no matter how you fight it," I said. I glanced at my watch. "It's getting late. I'd better go. I passed a motel on the way in. I can stay there."

"You know what? Why don't you stay here tonight? There's plenty of room. I don't like the idea of you spending the night in that dilapidated place."

"No, no. I don't want to put you out at all."

She waved her hands dismissively. "No bother. The spare room's made up anyway. I was expecting my daughter, but she couldn't make it at the last minute."

I relaxed back into the couch. "Truthfully, I'm so relaxed I'd much rather stay," I said.

"Then it's settled."

"Before I get any more relaxed, I'll just get my bag out of the car," I said, pushing myself to my feet. A few more drinks and I'd never make it back up those stairs.

When I got back, Deb had poured me another drink. I took it and sank back into the welcoming arms of the couch. Deb had taken off her shoes and had her feet up on a brown vinyl hassock that must be a period piece. I handed her the small photo album I had made up to bring. "I thought you or your mother might like to have these," I said awkwardly. I had tried to think of how they might like to see Ronnie — successful, happy, accomplished. It was hard to find pictures that wouldn't need a running commentary, but there were some: Ronnie accepting an award for community work; Ronnie dressed to the nines, at a classy restaurant celebrating with his partners when he became a partner himself. Ronnie in a purple T-shirt, painting the clouds on his bedroom ceiling, laughing into the camera; a candid shot of Ronnie sitting at his desk in his office, shirt sleeves rolled up, concentrating on some paperwork. There was a picture of him with me outside the school in 1965 and several of him and Monica Heising. Deb was dabbing at her eyes.

"He was always so damned photogenic," she said.

I laughed.

"We used to take figure skating lessons, you know? Well, it was supposed to be me taking the lessons, but Mom used to bring Ronnie with her and he wanted to skate so badly, so Mom let him, without telling Dad, needless to say. Ronnie took to it right away, a natural, they said, and first thing you know he was ahead of me. And that was when the shit hit the fan. Ronnie won some sort of a title, and it was in the paper and Dad found out. And that was the end of Ronnie and skating. I'd quit by then anyway. Dad was so mad. Poor Mom. She put up with a lot."

"Don't tell me. He thought skating was for girls."

"And sissies. So it didn't matter that Ronnie had found something to excel at." She shook her head sadly. "For a while I remember the skating coach tried to make Ronnie and me an ice dance couple for the ice show the club was doing. But he was shorter than me, and I felt awkward. We did one waltz together and that was it. I fell center ice and rushed off in tears. Ronnie finished doing a sort of ad lib solo."

"Sounds like him."

"Oh yeah. But he tried to help me. I remember that. It was the skaters' waltz. Wait!" She pushed herself to her feet and padded over to a box filled with old vinyl records. "I've been trying to tape all their old favorites so we can get rid of the stereo. Here it is!" She went to the glass-fronted stereo and laid the record on the turntable, switched it on, poised the needle at the edge of the disk. The ritual brought back memories of Ronnnie's old room and the beat-up record player he had found in a secondhand store. The strains of the skaters' waltz wafted through the dim room. Deb swayed in time, one hand tapping time on the cabinet.

I put down my drink, got to my feet, and touched her shoulder.

She turned, startled.

I bowed. "May I have this dance?"

Her face flushed and her eyes, bright with tears, smiled back at me. I took her hand and waltzed her into the middle of the crowded room, where we twirled and dipped and swayed among the half-filled cartons and remains of her old, forgotten life.

"You're a great dancer," she said, sounding surprised.

"My sister and I took lessons from the dreaded Madam Von Reichenburg. We damn well better be good!"

She laughed. "Ronnie must have had lots of fun with you," she said, and for the first time, her face didn't look sad when she mentioned his name.

"I hope so," I said. I really hope so. At least for a while.

CHAPTER EIGHTEEN

Ronnie's mother wore thick glasses, and her hands were knotted with arthritis. Her hair was still streaked with brown, and she wore it pulled back and fastened in an untidy bun at the back of her neck. She was sitting in what the hospital euphemistically called the sunroom, in a hard plastic chair with metal arms. Her whole face lit up when she saw Deb. I felt my stomach heave unpleasantly, thinking of my own mother, now long gone. Had she ever felt that way about seeing me? Had I ever given her any reason to feel that way?

Deb introduced me and smoothly slipped in Ronnie's death and how he had thought of her and prepared the picture album. I wondered why Ronnie hadn't really done that himself. Had he been so hurt by their denial he couldn't forgive?

His mother took the album and hugged it to her chest, tears spilling over her wrinkled cheeks. "I missed him so much," she said, her voice a whisper in the relentlessly bright room. "I couldn't do anything about it, you know. He had to go his own way. It was for the best."

We stayed for a while, talking about the past. Her mind wandered now and then, and she would forget who I was. Then, "Oh yes, a friend of Ronnie's. Have you seen him lately?"

"Just a while ago," I said after the third time and a look from Deb. We left when the physiotherapist came and took her away.

His father was another story. Heavy and dour, he sat in a wheelchair beside his bed, staring into space. He barely acknowledged Deb and ignored me completely. I wondered how much, if anything, he was taking in. I gave him the silver and pearl money clip I had found among Ronnie's possessions.

"So he's dead," he said at last, his voice phlegmy and hoarse, as if he rarely used it. "Was it that homosexual disease?"

I saw Deb's startled look. "He died of cancer," I said.

He nodded, turning the money clip over and over in his old hands without looking at it. I glanced at Deb for a cue. She opened her mouth to say something when Mr. Lipinsky said, "Ron snuck out of my house like a thief in the night. He never said good-bye or explained what he was doing or where he was going. He died to me then."

"I thought you should know," I said.

"So fine. You told me. Good-bye."

"Dad, really —"

"Deb, what do I know from Ron's life this past twenty-five years? What do I care? I'm a sick old man who wants to die in peace."

"I'll be back later, Dad." She pecked his cheek and we left. Deb apologized all the way to the parking lot.

"He's so bitter. Nothing has turned out the way he expected, I guess."

"It rarely does."

"I'm going to have a hard time getting him to move to the home, but I figure if the old place is gone, he won't have any choice. I didn't want to do it that way, but…" She shrugged.

"It's a difficult time for you, isn't it?"

She sighed. "He doesn't realize Mom couldn't even get up the stairs anymore. But that new place costs way more than we expected. I don't know how long we can do it. I'd take them into our house, but George says no way."

"Ronnie left you some money for your parents," I said, the lie rolling off my tongue smooth as butter. "Most of his estate went to charity, but there's a bequest for you to administer for them."

She looked at me open mouthed. "Ronnie had money?"

"He was single, with no dependants, a successful man, and a partner in a big accounting firm. He wasn't a millionaire, but he had money, yes."

"Gosh," she said, sounding like a teenager from the '50s. "He always was good with figures. How much?"

I had been doing rapid calculations in my head, trying to figure out how much I could shave off to ease Deb's burden. I'm sure if he had thought of it this way, he would have done it. Luckily, the way things were spelled out left me with lots of leeway. "I can write you a check right now for thirty thousand dollars," I said. "I'll let you know later if there's any more. Don't count on it, though," I added hastily, seeing more than my commission disappear.

Deb burst into tears. "You've no idea how much I need this!" she said. "With what we can get for the building, that should take us for some time. God bless Ronnie!"

"Amen," I whispered, as I pulled up in front of the cleaners and wrote out the check.

Deb insisted I take a thermos of coffee and some banana bread with me. When I checked the bag later on, I discovered she'd slipped in a bagel and cream cheese, as well. I appreciated the thought.

The drive home was uneventful. My mind was filled with half-remembered things, impressions from long ago. But now I wondered how much I had contributed to Ronnie's reinventing of himself by my reluctance to ask questions. I had really made it easy for him, I thought now, accepting everything at face value, assuming what I thought I saw was the truth. At twenty-two, I was far more naive than he was.

By the time I got back to Toronto, I was swimming in depression. Ryan wasn't home, which was just as well. His presence was rarely soothing. I picked up the mail and noticed one large heavy cream envelope from the Dharman Foundation. Surely Trish hadn't invited me, her despised brother, to her wonderful garden party for the beautiful people! As I scanned the thick square inside, I saw that someone had, and smiled. How ironic. But if not Trish, who? Of course my family had supported the foundation since its inception, and I had contributed every year, the amount coming automatically out of my bank account. It must add up to a substantial sum by now. Perhaps it had just been generated automatically, my largesse having accumulated and spilled over some hidden line that took me into the benefactor category. I tossed the invitation aside and checked my messages. Logan, reminding me to drop over and fill him in. I wasn't sure how ready I was for this. But I didn't want to wander around the house alone, either, my mind restlessly skipping over the shadows of the past, not letting me settle on anything. I picked up the box with the tranquility water fountain in it that I'd bought for Logan as a coming-home present and went down the street to his place.

Logan was sitting up in a padded chair, dressed in loose-fitting olive trousers that looked a little like harem pants and a long-sleeved Indian cotton white shirt open at the throat. His keyboards were on a stand in front of him and he was practicing with the sound off. He looked better than I'd seen him for some time and I told him so.

"You coming on to me, Michael?" he said, his mouth quirked up on one side in his sneer of a smile.

"If I ever do, you won't have to ask," I said. I was in no mood for heavy-handed pleasantries. "How are your hands?"

"Not bad, considering," he said. "Still a little stiff, but I'm working in it."

"Nice flowers." I nodded at the vase standing on the piano. Someone, probably Ellen, had put a paper doily underneath.

"I hate them!" Logan said, with unexpected passion. "Flowers are for sickrooms and gardens. I don't want her to make this into a hospital, but what can you do?"

I picked up the plastic bag I had carried the fountain over in, went to the piano bench, and grabbed the flowers in a stranglehold. Without stopping to think, I stuffed them headfirst into the bag. Then I emptied the vase in the sink in his tiny kitchen and sat down again. "Just blame me."

"I will." Logan nodded once. "A man of action," he said. "I never would have guessed."

"I have hidden depths," I said.

"I guess so. How did your trip go?"

I told him. I left out the part about the check. "I don't know why I went there in the first place," I finished up.

"Sure you do," he said. "You wanted to meet them. To get closer to Ronnie."

"Hell of a lot of good that did," I said bitterly. "I felt closer to him before. I don't know what I found out."

"You found out you fell in love with a fake," he said.

"You have such a way with words," I said. "He wasn't a fake. I don't mind someone reinventing himself. I did it. We all do it to a certain extent."

"*You* did it? I don't think so."

I just looked at him. He shrugged, that peculiar, lopsided shrug he had developed after the fire. "In a way it's like losing him all over again. But now I know it wasn't my fault. That's something, I suppose. All this time I thought it must have been something I did, something I said. There was no explanation. Nothing. Just suddenly he became…different."

"Killing someone will do that to you, I suppose," Logan said, rubbing a thumb over his scarred wrist.

I laughed for the first time that day. "You've gotta admit it's a helluva good excuse for breaking up with someone."

"So what did you find out about Uncle Bunny?"

"Deb didn't recognize the name. They only had one real uncle and none of the honorary ones was called anything like Bunny."

"So Bunny, whoever he is, is not connected to the family. You'll have to look elsewhere."

"The only other concrete thing I found out was that Ronnie didn't come directly to Toronto as I always thought; he went to New York City first. And he went in May, so he was there for a few months."

"Well, well." Logan rolled his shoulders against the back of the chair, twisting to the side to ease his neck. "Now we're cooking."

"I'm not about to rush madly off to NYC on a wild-goose chase."

"Not yet," Logan said. "Not until you have something to chase after. It'll come. Keep digging."

"Easy for you to say," I muttered. I took the fountain out of the box and began to assemble it. Logan looked at it suspiciously.

"It's not flowers," I said.

"Good thing. I have a friend who's death on flowers."

I piled pebbles around the funnel in the bowl, added water, plugged it in.

"I'm tranquil enough," Logan grumbled, but I could tell he was intrigued. When I left him, he was sitting back with his eyes closed, listening to the splash of the water over the pebbles into the bowl.

CHAPTER NINETEEN

I woke up at four a.m. and lay for a while staring at the ceiling. I knew I wasn't going to fall asleep again, so I got up and tiptoed to Ryan's room. He wasn't there. Did he even know I was back? Did he care?

I went downstairs and sat down at the harpsichord to play. It needed tuning but wasn't too far off for a little noodling. I tried some Scarlatti, but my hands were stiff, refusing to flow with the long cascades of notes and precision trills. I thought of Logan, lying in bed hour after hour, squeezing a stress ball to keep his fingers supple. I switched to Mozart, with slightly better results.

Behind me, I heard the door open and a few muttered curses. I kept playing.

"Hey, you're back," said Ryan.

"So are you," I said. I could smell the cigarettes and beer and the sweet hint of marijuana. I kept playing.

"I hate that thing," Ryan said and belched. "Fuck, I'm wrecked I'm going to bed."

"*Bonne nuit.*"

"Whatever." He stumbled off into the shadows. He was obviously planning to take tomorrow off. Then I remembered it was Sunday.

I played for a while longer, then sat in the solarium and read. By the time dawn was lightening the sky, I was drifting off again and went to bed.

I was awakened by the doorbell. Someone was ringing it persistently, peal after peal. I pulled on shorts and a T-shirt, threw water on my face, and went to see who the annoying person was and tell them I was not interested in buying candy to support the local public school.

Ellis stood on the porch, with Jaym, looking embarrassed, a few steps behind him.

"I thought you were an early bird," Ellis said, neatly cutting off my line of attack.

"Come in. I need coffee."

Ellis snickered annoyingly.

"I just got back from a trip," I said, reaching for the coffeemaker. I noticed it was ten forty-seven. "Isn't this a bit early for you, Ellis?"

"Nope. I haven't been to bed," he said. "So I guess it's late for me, right?" He giggled. What had Ronnie ever seen in him? For the first time I wondered if their relationship had been sexual. Somehow I doubted it.

I switched on the coffeemaker. Jaym slid onto a stool and fiddled with the camera around his neck. As I heated up the leftover banana bread from Deb, got out the jam and butter, I noticed his dark eyes studying me. Out of nowhere came the image of him scooping up the contents of Bianca's purse, helping her put them back inside. Jaym, straightening her wig after she fell backward off the platform. I looked at him more closely. He dropped his eyes.

"Hey, Michael, you know, we want to contribute to the Wilde Nights cast party, right? Like, donate some beer and that, but we don't have the gelt. So we had this idea —"

"Ell had this idea," Jaym said.

"Yeah, well, you went along with it, right? So anyway, someone said you, like, make your own wine and that."

I could see where this was going. I didn't like it. "I make a little, yes. For my own consumption."

"Yeah, yeah. So we wondered if you had any room in your basement, like, for our beer? I mean, we could make it and put it in bottles. A friend of mine has all the stuff, but no place to keep it, you know?"

I poured the coffee into mugs and took a long drink. Ellis added sugar and milk. Jaym drank it black.

"I think this is an imposition," Jaym said, standing up.

"Whoa! Hey, Michael hasn't said anything yet. So what do you say, Michael?"

"I don't think so," I said. "When I said I'd contribute to your campaign, I meant one check, at the fund-raiser."

"What?" Jaym looked confused.

"He didn't tell you the beer will be from — what's your stage name, Ellis?"

"Loralei." Ellis flushed. "Might as well start the campaign now, eh? But you wouldn't have to do a thing, Michael. And it would only be two garbage cans, so we wouldn't take up much room."

"Have you ever done this before?" I asked.

"I helped my friend a few times, sure. We can do it, right, Jaym?" Ellis glanced at his watch and took another gulp of coffee. "You know, I hate to drink and run, but I've gotta be somewhere. You and Jaym can talk about it, okay? I'm outta here." He waved and ran for the door.

Jaym put down his mug. "I'm really sorry," he said. "He's always getting me into these jams. I never learn."

I laughed. "He does seem a bit frothy for you," I said.

He shrugged. "I guess I need a bit of froth in my life." He glanced up at me with a quick smile that transformed his face for a moment. "Look, I'll just go. Ellis had no right to ask you this favor. Thanks for the coffee."

"Hold on. There's no reason to dismiss it out of hand. Let's take a look downstairs and see if there's any room."

I led the way downstairs and looked at the three large glass johnnies, two of red, one of white. One of them was Lew's experiment with some fruity concoction, one was a California burgundy, and the other my attempt at a sauterne hybrid. There was plenty of room for a few barrels of beer. The bottling would take up more space, but it could be arranged.

"Do you honestly think Ellis will carry this through?" I asked.

Jaym was examining the label on the closest bottle. He raised his head and looked off into space for a moment. "Honestly, no. I expect I'll be the one doing it. I don't mind," he added. "I don't have anything heavy on right now."

"When would you start?"

"As soon as possible, I guess. There's not that much time till November. If I get my choice, I'll do a lager."

"It's your project if you do the work, so it's your choice. Come on. Let's go upstairs." I led the way back to the kitchen and poured more coffee. "How did you meet Ellis, anyway?"

"He was doing a show at the 519 and I was there. We talked for a while. Then I ended up helping him take his stuff out to the car."

I laughed. "It figures. He needed a roadie."

Jaym flushed, and I wished I'd kept quiet. "I gave him my number and said to phone if he needed help next week. He did, and we began hanging out. He's fun to be with. He always has a group around, laughing and talking — but don't ask me what they talk about." He laughed self-consciously.

"Where do you work?" I asked, handing him a muffin.

Jaym didn't answer at first, chewing the muffin and looking into his coffee cup. Maybe he was unemployed. It had been a tactless question.

"Look, you don't —"

"I'm a trader," Jaym said. "I don't like to mention it, 'cause the stock market's not sexy. A lot of guys don't know about the market, so they think it's boring, or if they do, they ask all kinds of questions I'm not prepared to answer."

"A trader? On the floor?" I said. "I admire anyone who can do that."

"It's exciting. And I'm doing okay," he added, glancing up at me with a quick smile. "Ronnie Lipinsky helped get me started five years ago."

I was filled with questions, but after what he had just said, I pushed them all down and took another look at Jaym, the stock-trading tap dancer. Had Ronnie bankrolled him for a line of credit? Did he pay for his license? Either way, I knew he had been paid back. I had been right about Jaym. He *was* different.

"To get back to this beer project," I said slowly. "If you're doing it, I'd consider it, but I don't want Ellis prancing in and out of here at all hours, with no advance warning."

Jaym nodded. "I told him he should call first."

"If you take over the project, I'll do it. If not, find some place else."

"We'll need more people to do the bottling," he said.

"Set it up in advance."

"And I'd rather not be doing this all alone."

There was silence, while we sipped coffee. "I haven't done beer for a long time," I said. "I'll help, if you like."

Jaym smiled broadly, his whole face lighting with pleasure. He opened his backpack and pulled out a big brown envelope. "I finally finished the roll and developed the pictures I took at Ronnie's place," he said, handing me the envelope. "I did a few experiments in Photoshop. Not sure how they worked, though. If you don't want them, just toss them."

I pulled out the pictures and stared. They were five-by-sevens, all of me, five shots taken that day and four at rehearsals. They were amazing, especially the one of Ronnie and me together, Ronnie looking well and full of life, not the way he had been when I returned.

"I fooled around with Photoshop," Jaym said, turning a ring around and around on his finger. "I thought…"

"I love it," I said quickly. "Thanks so much. I don't have any good, recent pictures of Ronnie. And this…" I shook my head, feeling a strange mixture of emotions I wasn't prepared to deal with just now.

Jaym zipped up his backpack and flung it over one shoulder just as the doorbell rang. I led the way and opened the door to find Trish standing there, her small mouth gathered into its usual tight line.

"Good morning," she said stiffly. She stepped back abruptly when she saw Jaym, her chin lifting with disapproval.

"I'll call about the beer," Jaym said. He stuck out his hand, surprising me again. His shake was firm. Then he was gone, head down as he hurried past Trish.

"You never change, do you?" Trish said. "I've come for the tray."

"You never change, either," I said, holding the door open.

For a moment I thought she wouldn't come in. But she overcame her reluctance and stepped inside. She stood in the doorway of the living room, looking around, taking in every little detail. I saw her estimate the value of the paintings, the harpsichord, the small sculpture of a male dancer on the stand by the window. I left her there while I went into the kitchen to get the tray. When I came back, Ryan was there, wearing tiny red shorts and nothing else, scratching his chest sleepily.

"I thought I heard someone," he said vaguely.

"Jaym was here for a while," I said. "This is my sister, Trish. Trish, meet Ryan."

"Hi," said Ryan, still scratching.

Trish frowned. She didn't want to meet Ryan. She nodded at him, muttered, "Good morning," and reached for the tray.

"You'll have to clean it," I said.

"I don't know why you insist on keeping things you never look after," Trish hissed.

"Because they're mine?" I suggested.

Trish wrapped her arms around the tray as if protecting it from my neglect and headed for the door.

"I want it back right after the event," I called after her.

She didn't answer.

Ryan wandered over and closed the front door, which Trish had left open. "Bitch on wheels, eh?" he said. "Glad I don't have a sister."

I suddenly thought of Debra Shopiro, nee Lipinsky. It takes more than a good, understanding sister, I thought. A lot more.

Ryan looked at the photos I was still holding. "Not bad," he said. He took one, turned it over, and grinned. "Jaym's got his address and phone number on the back," he said.

"All photographers do that," I snapped, taking the glossy back and stuffing it into the envelope.

"Yeah, yeah." Ryan sauntered back to the kitchen. His tight shorts left little to my imagination, but the only feeling this elicited now was one of irritation.

CHAPTER TWENTY

I was fascinated by the picture Jaym had created of me and Ronnie. He had dimmed the background until the crystal mobile behind my head was an unrecognizable sparkle, softening the bright colors in the room. My eyes were looking slightly to the side, the same side Ronnie was looking at. It was eerie, unearthly. It made shivers go up and down my spine, but I couldn't take my eyes off it. A few days later I framed it, using the matte and dark red frame I had left over from my previous efforts at nesting and hung it in the living room, right beside the harpsichord.

Ryan was almost finished in the garden. I called the Annex Nursery people who were going to plant the flowers and stock the fish for the pool. Ryan seemed to have withdrawn the last few days. He had done this once before, leaving my bed for several nights, then reappearing all smiles and eager mouth and hands. I wondered if this time he was worried about the approaching end of our contract and had decided to make me miss him.

The secretary from my department at the university called, reminding me of the meeting next week, the forms that were due and to pick up my mail. I had been so wrapped up in the puzzle of Ronnie that I had forgotten about my mail, almost forgotten my job, except for the new graduate course. I was still reading and making notes about that one. I had a carton of unread articles I was meaning to get through, but it was the carton of Ronnie's memories that called to me. I opened it and looked through it again. There was no diary. I must have left it somewhere. I put the box on the bottom shelf beside the Peloponnesian War articles and turned to the table to clear off the junk mail.

The Dharman invitation.

I turned it around and around, studying it for clues. The envelope was hand addressed, either by volunteers, or they had hired someone with good penmanship to give them that personal touch, as charities often do. I suspected the latter. The writing was too good, but with just that erratic feel about it that made it the real thing. But why was I on the invitation list at all? Who put me there? Certainly not Trish. If I hadn't been certain of that before, I was after her visit.

I went to the phone and called Laura.

"How nice to hear from you, Michael," she said at once, ever the gracious lady.

We chatted a few minutes; then I told her about Trish's visit, leaving out Ryan, but not Jaym and his camera. I could hear her smile as we talked. Then I mentioned the Dharman invitation. "So you see, I know it couldn't have been Trish. She'd have been more likely to cross my name off."

"Trish? Of course it wasn't Trish, dear heart. I put your name on the list."

"You? Why?"

"Because it should be there. Your father was one of the founders, and you're a regular contributor. Why shouldn't it be there?"

"Laura, you're amazing. I never thought of you."

"I imagine you rarely do," she said.

I drew back from the receiver, physically recoiling from the simple truth of her words.

"Are you going?" Laura asked.

"Why should I?"

"I don't know. Just to see Trish in action, perhaps?"

"Laura, you devil." I began to smile. "You mean in reaction, don't you?"

"Why don't we go together?" she went on, as if we did this sort of thing all the time.

"You're an evil woman," I said, "and I love evil women."

"I never much liked Trish," Laura said, "did you?"

"You know there was never any love lost between us," I said.

"Perhaps you should bring your young photographer friend too," Laura went on primly.

My jaw dropped. "You really don't like her, do you?"

"She tries so hard she misses the whole point sometimes, don't you think?" Laura went on. "This is a charity. Perhaps she doesn't know the meaning of the word."

"You're on," I said.

"We *are* still married," she said

"And now I remember why."

She laughed and hung up.

I wondered what Trish had done to Laura recently, or if this went back to their school days at Branksome Hall, and Laura was finally letting loose. I wondered if I would really have the nerve to take Jaym and his camera. What would he think of it all?

Ryan had ordered a pizza earlier and was now sprawled in the garden eating it. Julie sat beside him, her elbows on her knees, hunched over as she talked and smoked. *What could she find to talk about with him?* I wondered. They had nothing at all in common. *No more than he and I,* I reminded myself, but what was between us had nothing to do with words. I warmed up a quiche in the microwave and ate it as I finished one of the never-ending articles on the Spartans.

About an hour later, I drove Ryan over to Ronnie's place to help lug cartons of rubble out of the basement apartment. The place was always bathed in a greenish underwater cast as the long row of narrow windows looked onto the garden and the light was filtered through grass. I thought it was eerie. Ryan pronounced it cool.

The last tenant had been a real packrat. There were papers everywhere, divided into newsprint, circulars, advertising, and magazines. Maybe he had sold it as scrap. Was that possible? There were also piles of old clothes tossed in a corner of the walk-in closet in the hall.

"Gross," said Ryan, shoveling it all into plastic garbage bags.

"When this place is cleaned out, it'll need painting," I said. "Nothing fancy, white will do. Can't rent it like this."

"White is boring," Ryan said.

"Maybe, but it's safer. You want to see a nonboring paint job, come on upstairs to Ronnie's place."

I led the way to the third floor and was ashamed to see I was out of breath when we got there. Ryan was suitably impressed. "Cool," he said, walking through the rooms. "Amazing!"

He touched the mobiles, sending a shiver of sound through the air. He went over to the Wall of Death and studied the pictures there. "Hey, I know this place!" he said, pointing to the one of Ronnie outside some store. "I've been there."

"Where is it? Some friends and I were wondering the other day."

"It's in New York City, man."

"And you've been there?"

"Yeah. When we had that fight, remember? I crashed with some guys I knew and they were going to New York in an old van one of them had, so I went along. It was cool."

"What did you do?"

"The usual. You know. Cruised the bars, went clubbing. What else?"

Of course. "And you went to that shop?"

"Sure. It's like, famous, you know? It's even in the gay guides. Like Stone Pub."

"Stonewall Inn."

"Whatever."

"Why? What's famous about this place?"

"It was a real hangout in the old days, you know? The old queen who owned it put a display in the window of naked guys and it got the place closed down for a while. And they used to have orgies upstairs above the store. Going there was a bit of a downer, ya know? Just an old, junky place now. Dusty statues and shit. Old furniture."

"An antique store."

"Yeah. Boring."

"What's it called?"

"I don't know. The name of some street in the gay village. A guy's name."

"Houston?" I gave it both pronunciations, just in case.

Ryan shook his head. "A first name."

"Christopher Street?"

"Yeah, yeah. Christopher Street Curious, or something."

"Christopher Street Curios, maybe?"

"Whatever." Ryan had lost interest and was now looking at the picture of me and Ronnie in front of Shits Hall.

"Yes, that's me."

Ryan grinned. "Groovy outfit, man."

I took down both pictures of Ronnie outside the store and put them in my shirt pocket. Funny I had found no mention of the store in any of his writings, but he hadn't started the diary until coming to Toronto, so maybe that wasn't so strange.

That night I called Deb and asked her about the store in New York. Ronnie had never mentioned anything to her about it. We talked for a few minutes. She had a good lead on a placement for her parents and had managed to get their names on the accelerated list because of their situation. She sounded in better spirits when I hung up.

Then I called Jaym to leave a message on his machine and was surprised to find him at home.

"I'm taking a mental health day," he said. "I need some downtime."

I asked him about making an enlargement from an old photo. He asked a few questions about the sort of shape the original was in and agreed to give it a try.

"You're not far from me," I said, "I'll drop them off sometime later tonight or tomorrow morning."

"I'll get right on it," he said.

I put the photos in an envelope with Jaym's name and address on it and put it on the table by the front door.

I sat in my rocking chair, gazing out at the garden that was finally taking shape. I had been in London and Amsterdam in the late '60s, and I tended to go back there instead of to New York for my holidays. When I did visit the Big Apple, it was for the opera and ballet and art galleries, often on long weekends. I remember going to A Different Light, the gay bookstore in the Village, but no one had invited me to any orgies above an antique store.

Who did I know who would have this kind of information? I thought of Glori Daze. Maybe. But I couldn't see Duane having the money to get there in the '60s. He wasn't really making money until quite a bit later. I ran a few more names through my mind. And then I thought of Lew.

I stood up abruptly and paced through to the living room, and back again. Lew. Did I want to talk to him? No. Would he know what I wanted to know? Probably. How much did I want to know this?

Then I thought of the gay archives. If the place was famous enough to be in some gay guidebook, as Ryan had said, I might have some luck with them, even though it wasn't in Toronto. I fired up my laptop and logged on to the Gay Blade. In a few hours I had my answer, from several people. As I had suspected, Christopher's Curios was nowhere near as famous as Stonewall Inn, but what Ryan had told me was essentially true. It was *the* party place for boys and men in the '60s. And it had been closed down several times for "obscene displays" involving nude male statues in its window. The owners had taken the case to court and had won. The place was owned by Misha Vishnikov and his partner, whose name was never mentioned anywhere that my online friends knew of. Clever of him, I thought. One of them quoted an article about the place by a gay lib activist, but even the spin he put on it made me wonder about the age of the boys mentioned. Ronnie was seventeen that summer. Misha's age seemed to be midthirties. The "old queen" Ryan had mentioned, perhaps. I grinned. All things are relative.

Ryan was playing MuchMusic loud on the TV in his room, and I could smell smoke, though I suppose he had the window open. On impulse I grabbed my keys and the envelope with the photos, went outside, and walked down the street to Logan's. As I went into his apartment, I noticed the place was beginning to have that sickroom smell, probably from the ointments and lotions he used liberally on so much of his body. He would hate that. I imagine he was so used to the smells, he was no longer aware of them.

"How's it going?" he asked, pulling himself up straighter in his padded chair. A plate of half-eaten vegetables was on the table.

I told him about Christopher's Curios and showed him the pictures.

"You get leads from the most unexpected sources," Logan said, squinting at me in the bright lamplight.

I adjusted the shade and agreed.

"You want to go to New York." It was a statement. I didn't answer. "You don't need my blessing, you know."

I went to his small kitchen and fixed us the green tea he consumed in such quantity. I added lemon and gave him his.

"Fall is creeping inexorably closer," I said.

He grunted.

"I want to know," I said.

"Are you sure this is something you *need* to know?" he asked. "How much can you handle?"

Good question. I shrugged.

Logan slurped at his tea. "Well, if you gotta go, you gotta go," he said. "If this were last year, I'd come with you."

For the first time I realized how tired he looked, and felt guilty. "I'd love that," I said. "When I get back, I'll give you all the details."

"All of them, mind," Logan said sharply. "Every sleazy, titillating bit."

I laughed. "I doubt there'll be much sleaze or titillation," I said. But I wondered. What would I find there? Memories? Shadows? Ghosts? I realized that in that brief span of time, I had made up my mind to go. And Logan had known that when I came in the door.

CHAPTER TWENTY-ONE

Jaym dropped in with the photos two days later. It was early evening, and Ryan was just leaving to go to a movie with some friends. He had even invited me, which I appreciated but would never consider. That way lies feeling your age. Jaym's quiet maturity, on the other hand, made me almost forget his boyish good looks and relative youth.

I showed him the garden, and he got the concept right away.

"This is going to be wonderful," he said, looking around. "I love water gardens. I'd like to have one myself, but I'm afraid I'd forget to do some vital thing and the place would flood or something. I live in a condo. They wouldn't appreciate it."

I laughed. When I had dropped off the photos a few nights ago, I had been surprised by the upscale building he lived in. When I looked at him more closely, though, I realized his clothes were expensive, high-end labels, but they were lived in and he wore them with a casual disregard I found quite attractive. Seeing him always with Ellis had colored how I perceived Jaym. Did he use his drag queen friends as a camouflage? I wondered.

He had done a great job with the photos. Ronnie's young face smiled out at me with the mischievous spontaneity I remembered so well. That smile had really never changed. I glanced at the framed photo of us both on the living room wall. Jaym smiled when he saw it there.

"I'm afraid this one's not quite good enough to frame," he said, misreading my look. "I tried to get rid of some of the age spots, but there are a few things I couldn't do anything about. It's pretty old."

"It looks to me as if you've done quite a lot," I said. "How much do I owe you?"

"Please, Michael. Don't insult me."

"God, you are unusual for your age!" I exclaimed.

He shot me a sudden hard look. "You don't really know me," he said.

"I'd like to."

His face softened at once. "I'm sorry. It's just that….for one thing, I'm older than I look."

"How old?"

He grinned. "I'm thirty-three."

"I thought you were Ellis's age."

"It's useful in some ways. People tend to underestimate me."

I bet, I thought. Floor trader. I can see it now. The tap dancing, well, that was a bit harder to grasp.

As if reading my mind, he said, "Tap dancing is good exercise, you know. Besides, it's fun."

"I don't doubt it!" I would have to be really careful around this man.

I opened a bottle of the Beaujolais I had made last fall. It wasn't bad, and it made our quiet hour sitting in the garden with no light but the two citronella torches a little special. I was totally relaxed when he rose to go.

"Thank you for a pleasant evening," he said, shaking my hand.

"I'm going to New York for a few days," I said. "I'll give you a call when I get back and we can arrange about the beer making."

"Have a good trip," he said and disappeared into the summer night.

I arrived in New York a few days later to the kind of humid, unrelenting heat that seemed worse than anything at home, maybe because of the constant noise and smog and honking of horns. I remember finding this all very stimulating when I was younger. Now I put down my head and headed to the Warwick Hotel on instinct, already longing for the quiet, old-world elegance of the place. This hotel was all dark paneling and quiet efficiency. The rooms here were not cookie-cutter bland, and there were none of the usual tourist type things in the small lobby.

I unpacked, checked my map, and headed down to the street to catch a cab to the West Village. I was in luck. It was air-conditioned. I noticed the cabbie checking me out in the mirror. I guess I didn't look like the usual Christopher Street habitué to him. The cab dipped and wove through the heavy traffic, my driver muttering curses in what sounded like Russian. When we stopped for a red light, two guys to my left jumped out of their cars and began shouting at each other. My cabbie opened his window and joined in. I felt a headache coming on. I would definitely be ready for *Les Sylphides* tonight at Lincoln Center.

I gave the cabbie a big tip, mostly out of relief that we managed to get there in one piece, and walked along the street looking at the numbers. There was a bar that looked cool and inviting. I decided to drop in after finding the store. This part of New York still felt like a community, though not quite as much as I remembered, perhaps because I had no ties here, was not meeting anyone later on in A Different Light or going dancing in one of the clubs after dinner. I had a sudden picture of Jaym here with me, his dark serious eyes taking everything in, making comments. I pushed the picture away quickly.

Christopher's Curios turned out to be smaller than I was expecting. FOUNDED IN 1962, it said on the sign. It must be one of the very few establishments in the area to have survived. That meant an alternative source of cash, I thought. Was the place a front for drugs?

Just like in the photo, the window was made to look Victorian, slightly bowed with small panes of glass. The display was artful and not overdone, with the spotlight on a ceramic Georgian footbath and matching water pitcher of the same era, along with silver platters and a large candelabra beside a substantial plaster cherub, coyly holding a length of blue velvet. Everything was polished and in good condition. The place looked flourishing, although the forest green of the paint could have done with a new coat. The gold letters were fading.

As I entered the shop, an old-fashioned bell tinkled above my head. A willowy young man dressed in a tight-fitting olive top and tight fawn trousers drifted toward me. His head tilted slightly to one side in an inquiring manner.

"You are looking for something particular?" he asked in a nasal voice, his enunciation a bit too careful.

"Would Misha Vishnikov still be here?" I asked.

He looked at me blankly. "I've been here for two years and I never heard of him."

"He used to own the place," I said.

Ms. Willow shrugged his sloping shoulders. He drifted over to a small woman with red hair who sat at a table near the back, doing paperwork. "Ever hear of some guy called Misha…something?"

She looked up as if he had slapped her. "Who wants to know?"

The young man jerked his head in my direction. He turned and frowned at me. I was right behind him. This close I could smell his expensive cologne. And I could see the woman was older than I was. She could have been here awhile.

"Misha is dead," she said, her voice flat.

"I'm sorry. He had a partner…." I let my voice fade out.

"I'm a partner," she said. "What do you want?"

Her apparent hostility was unexpected. I spread my hands in a conciliatory manner. "I'm looking for someone who was here in the '60s," I said.

"Oh God," she said. "Just leave us alone. They're all gone, you know, or old and sick. Just leave us alone." She looked back at her paperwork. Ms. Willow still hovered in the background.

"I came down here from Canada today," I said, "looking for Misha's partner, a man whose name I can't remember, because I'd like to talk to him about a friend of mine who died last month."

"What the hell are you talking about?" she said, looking up, annoyed.

"Want me to get rid of him?" asked Ms. Willow.

I laughed. So did the woman. He pouted.

"Get lost, Evan," she said and got up from behind the desk. "I'm Patsy Waldheim." We shook hands. "Sorry for being so cranky, but we still get journalists and voyeurs sniffing around here and I'm sick of it. I bought into the business about fifteen years ago. I was a friend of Misha's."

"When did he die?"

"About six years ago," she said, sitting down again and motioning me to a chair I hadn't noticed before. "Now, about your friend. Did he work here?"

"Honestly, I don't know." I took out the blown-up photos of Ronnie and put them on the desk.

She took one look and sat up straighter. "What are you trying to find out?" she asked.

I leaned back in my chair, trying to look as nonthreatening as possible. I didn't understand why she was so cagey, but I didn't want to give her any more ammunition. "I met Ronnie in September 1964," I said. "He told me a lot of things, most of which I have just discovered were false. Now I just found out he was here before he came to Toronto, and I'd like to…fill in the blanks, I guess."

"So you're one of those people who always has to know, even if you don't like what you find out?"

"That's right."

"You a lawyer?"

"Teacher."

She nodded, as if I had passed some kind of secret test. "I wasn't around then," she said, "so I can't really help you."

"They used to live upstairs?" I asked.

"Back then, yes, but that was a long time ago."

"And who did Misha live with?" I asked.

There was silence for so long I thought she had forgotten I was there. I cleared my throat. "Patsy?"

"You know, I think you need to talk to Jem." She picked up the phone and talked to someone in a soft voice, asked if he could see me, if she could send me back. "He worked here then," she said. "Talk to him."

She waved me back into the shadows. "Around the corner to your right there's a spiral staircase," she called. "Go on up."

I thanked her and headed for the shadows. Patsy was back at her paperwork before I made it around the desk. The metal rungs of the staircase shivered under my tread. I held on to the iron railing, feeling slightly dizzy as I spun slowly higher. The place had very high ceilings.

As my head emerged into the light, I found myself in a cozy sitting room, surrounded by books. They were in bookcases, piled on the floor, some even displayed in glass cases. Discreet track lighting glowed on polished wood and brass and the dim leather bindings of many of books, most of which were in clear plastic covers.

"Rare books and first editions," said a stocky man with a shining bald head and drooping gray mustache. "Nice to have company," he greeted me, shaking my hand. "I'm Jem."

I gave him my name. "I didn't know the place had anything to do with books."

"A sideline that's threatening to get out of hand." He laughed. "They've always done a trade in rare books. Misha was a real connoisseur. That's why I joined the staff back in the '60s, fresh out of school. Then I left a few years later and moved to San Francisco and worked there for years. Opened my own place. Expanded too fast. Went belly-up. So here I am back where I started. It's a funny old world sometimes."

He led the way between the piles of books to a grouping of sofa and chairs near a surprising stained-glass window of two Greek boys in short tunics holding hands. Jem laughed as he saw my expression.

"Another one of Misha's little artistic efforts," he said. "Not bad, for an amateur, don't you think? At least it's at the back so no one who wasn't invited ever saw it. Tea or something stronger? We have gin and vermouth and tonic, and some brandy around somewhere."

"Gin and tonic sounds great, thanks."

He pottered about, chatting as he prepared the drinks, talking about the books he was cataloging, about how hard it was keeping the humidity right.

"Mold is not our friend," he said, handing me my drink. I was trying to place his age. His skin was pale and lined around the eyes and had lost its elasticity. His waist had spread, but he looked pretty fit. Late '50s, early '60s, I thought, taking a sip of the gin. I hoped I would look that good in ten years or so. He had added just the right hint of lime to my drink.

"Patsy says you're looking for someone who was here in the '60s?" he prompted, sitting down opposite me on the velvet armchair. He crossed his legs at the ankle and leaned back comfortably. "I was here from '64 till, let's see, '66. I followed the love of my life to 'Frisco and proceeded to lose my virginity, my innocence, and my shirt, in that order." He laughed. "Never mind. It was worth it."

"Glad to hear it," I said.

"I was twenty-eight when I came here, and I thought I knew it all. Doesn't everyone at that age?"

"As I recall it's more like seesawing between thinking we know it all and being afraid we know nothing whatsoever."

"Maybe you're right. It's been a while. To the '60s!" He raised his glass. "But it was really the '70s that were more fun for me."

I grimaced. "If you like disco," I said.

"I think there may still be some disco whistles 'round here somewhere."

"Don't go looking on my account!" We both laughed. I pulled out the pictures and showed him.

Jem put on a pair of reading glasses and studied the photos carefully. He shook his head. "I don't know," he said. "Maybe they just had their picture taken outside the store as a souvenir."

"It's possible."

"I wasn't part of the inner circle, so I never came up here to the infamous parties. Frankly, I suspect the whole thing was blown way out of proportion. They loved being the center of attention and speculation. They were perfectly capable of creating their own rumrs to enhance the mystique of the place, just as they did those window displays that got them so much publicity."

"Sounds like a weird PR ploy to me," I said.

"I'm not saying they weren't into boys in a big way. I remember all the young guys always hanging around." He bent over the picture again, frowning in concentration. "I don't know. This guy looks a bit familiar."

He was pointing to Ronnie's friend, the dark boy with the long, straight hair wearing a woven headband. He had dimples and a sort of pixie charm that would make him very attractive.

"I don't remember his name, but he was around for a long time, much longer than most. Wait." He took off his glasses and tapped the picture with them as he gazed into space. "He had a weird name, one of those hippy names like River or Summer. Haven! That's it! He was called Haven. Whatever happened to him?" He put his glasses back on and studied the picture with a faraway look in his eyes. I wondered if he had had more than a few wet dreams about Haven back then himself.

"Ronnie wasn't in New York more than three months, as far I can figure it out. Maybe three and a half. He left home in May and was in school in Toronto in September." Had he registered late? I couldn't remember. Surely I'd remember if he had arrived late!

"Not very long," he said. "Good-looking kid, though. Blond. Carlos may have noticed him. He was partial to smooth, boyish blonds. Maybe you should speak to him."

"Who's Carlos?"

"The silent partner. The boss. Misha's lover."

"I was beginning to think he didn't have a name."

"Oh, he had several. Misha called him Choo, for some reason. His full name was Carlos Maria Teodoro Iglesias y Sepulveda. The boys called him Uncle Bunny."

"What?"

"Uncle Bunny. We called them Bunny's Boys."

CHAPTER TWENTY-TWO

I took a cab back to the hotel. This one was not air-conditioned, and we drove with all the windows open, the roar of the city pounding in along with the dust and grime. As we lurched up Fifth Avenue, my thoughts jumbled together, refusing to sort themselves into any order. Once we arrived, I stumbled into the dim hotel bar to recover from the onslaught of the heat and sudden revelation of Uncle Bunny's identity. I hadn't put the two together in my mind — New York and the mysterious uncle, but it made sense.

I sat at a small round table in a corner of the bar. I wondered what Uncle Bunny would be like. Jem had finally given me his address, after a few phone calls and a consultation with Patsy downstairs. Carlos was eighty-one, I learned, which made him fifty-one when Ronnie was here.

"Don't expect too much," Jem said, as we stood at the door of the shop as I was leaving.

"Does he have Alzheimer's?" I asked.

"No, but he is forgetful at times. When it's convenient, I suspect." Jem smiled. "I just mean it was a long time ago. And your friend may just have met Haven somewhere and someone took their picture in front of the store, like I said. Could be, you know."

I hoped that wasn't the explanation. Somehow I doubted it. There seemed to be real friendship in the pose of the two boys. Had they kept in touch? Could I find Haven and talk to him?

I stopped any further speculation, finished my scotch, and ordered another. I was glad *Les Sylphides* was on the program for tonight. I wasn't up to anything difficult or modern. The rest of the day was for the comforting and familiar. Like this hotel. Like the ballet. And the snack afterward at La Fondue. Tomorrow was Bunny day. I took out my book, a mystery by Peter Robinson, and immersed myself in Yorkshire.

♦ ♦ ♦

Next day the sky hung over the city like dull pewter. The heat was unremitting. My appointment with Carlos was at four p.m., after his siesta. I spent the morning at the MMA and the MOMA, had a late lunch with an academic acquaintance at a local Italian place, and took a taxi to the address Jem had given me. For some reason, I was nervous and was thankful this cabbie was the taciturn type. Maybe he didn't speak English. He looked fiercely foreign and drove with the manic concentration of a Formula One driver on the home stretch. This didn't help my nerves.

Carlos lived in an unpretentious low-rise building not far from the shop. I buzzed number 33 and announced myself to the staticky voice that answered me. Inside, the place looked well cared for. The ancient elevator seemed incongruous in its gilded splendor, but it rose smoothly and without complaint to the third floor. The door to number 33 was opened almost at once by a tall boy with tight blond curls, wearing a loose-fitting black top and the loose, low-riding jeans showing the requisite bit of underwear that seemed popular with black teenagers. He had a red bandana tied around his head. I wondered if this was some new SM code, gang colors, or just a fashion statement.

"Come in. He iss vaiting."

The clothes didn't go with the face and the German accent. I suppressed a smile.

The apartment was large and dim. The young man led me to the back and into a room with half-closed wooden shutters at the windows. The air felt stale and old, as if it hadn't changed for many years. One wall was lined with books and a faded tapestry hung on another. The place was crammed with beautiful pieces, most from the eighteenth and early nineteenth century. Under the window was a gleaming Jacobean oak chest, and a great candelabra that looked as if it must have come from an old church stood on the floor beside it.

It took a minute for my eyes to pick out the still figure of an old man sitting in a high-backed wing chair, the kind you rarely see nowadays. He looked a bit like a gnome as he rose to his feet shakily to greet me. His long face was animated and smiling, his dark eyes bright with interest behind the heavy lenses. He was almost completely bald, and his ears stood out high on his head, making him look even more gnomelike. He was short, but he still held himself well, in spite of the stoop that forced his head forward slightly.

"How do you do," he said, extending his hand. I felt a slight tremor, but his clasp was firm. "This is Max, my grandnephew. He's visiting for a month."

"My name is Michael Dunn-Barton."

"Yes, yes. Sit, sit." He sank back into his chair and arranged his obviously expensive cream-colored jacket to the best advantage. "Max, bring us some Tio Pepe. You like dry sherry? The best. Or we have Malaga wine, and the sweet cream sherry for the faint of heart, as you say."

I opted for the manly Tio Pepe, and Max sauntered off sulkily on his errand.

"And bring biscuits," Carlos called after him. "He has not been well brought up," he confided to me. "Jem tells me you are looking for someone you think I might know. You have a picture, yes? Show me, please."

He spoke quickly, with only a slight accent, but I had to concentrate to follow him, as he seemed to have trouble with his false teeth and spittle flew freely as he talked. That explained the white handkerchief he held in his left hand.

I took out the pictures and handed them to him. He pulled his thick glasses down on his nose and, tipping his head back, peered at them for a long time. Then he took off his glasses and rubbed the bridge of his nose. When he looked at me, his eyes looked bigger, a little lost without the defense of the lenses.

"Jem said he thinks one of the boys is Haven," he said. "Misha loved that boy. I thought he might come to Misha's funeral, you know. A lot of them did, but not Haven. It was a great comfort to see them again, yes, though I confess not to recognizing some. There are so many gone, yes, all the golden boys." He gazed into the dimness, the pictures forgotten in his hand. After a few moments, I cleared my throat.

"Do you recognize the blond one in the picture?" I asked.

He looked at me, startled, as if he had forgotten my existence; then he put the glasses back on and looked again. He looked up suddenly, an impish grin on his wrinkled face. "They called me Uncle Bunny," he said.

Max ambled in with two sherry glasses on a silver tray. An untidy pile of biscotti rested on a paper serviette beside the bottle of Tio Pepe. Carlos looked at the biscuits, shook his head, and shrugged.

When we both had our sherry and the boy had left, I said, "Do you recognize the photo? His name was Ronnie Lipinsky."

"He is dead, yes?"

"Yes."

Carlos sighed. "So many gone, and here I am still. *Ay, que pena.*" He dipped a biscotti into his sherry and sucked on it.

"Ronnie Lipinsky?" I said.

"Patience is a virtue, they say." He leaned back in his chair and grinned at me, his head on one side. "What are you looking for?"

I had prepared for this, had tried to hone the thing to a few sentences. "We were lovers many years ago; then we lost touch. Last year we met again, and when he died last month, he named me executor of his estate. I find a lot of blanks in his life, blanks I'm trying to fill in, just for my own information."

"Surely it is not necessary to go back so many years? Let the dead rest in peace."

"It's the living I'm concerned with," I snapped.

"You know what curiosity did, yes?" He hunched forward and handed the photos back.

I thought of the skeleton in Ronnie's trunk, of the shoe box full of money, the notebook with all the careful entries, Uncle Bunny's name on the front. "I've come a long way," I said. "I missed so much of his life."

He sighed and looked off into space for a moment. I was afraid he was drifting off again when he knocked back the rest of his sherry and struggled out of the chair. "*Bueno*," he said. "Ronnie Lipinsky." He stood a moment, getting his balance, then tottered off to a door I hadn't noticed before behind a velvet hanging and disappeared. I wondered if this was a bathroom, or if Carlos had some letters from Ronnie stashed away somewhere. Maybe he had a whole file of correspondence from the Bunny Boys back there. I finished the sherry. My friendly feelings for Carlos had turned to annoyance. He was manipulative. He was irritating. But he did remember Ronnie, the Ronnie I never knew. In my innocence, I had always assumed I was his first man, just as he was mine. Perhaps that's what was so galling.

The draperies shivered and swayed as Carlos pushed his way back into the sitting room, a dusty folder in his hands. He coughed and wiped his mouth with the handkerchief he was still clutching. Dust streaked across his chin.

"Ronnie, I remember," he said, sinking down into the chair opposite me. "You know, most of the boys, they used nicknames all the time, but not Ronnie. I liked that. He came to some of the parties. What a great little dancer he was!" He smiled.

"These were the parties you had above the store?"

"We had a sort of club, back then. People paid a membership fee to be on the invitation list. It was a way to finance things and keep it private, so the police would leave us alone, which they did for quite a while." He picked up his sherry glass, looked surprised to find it empty. I filled it.

"Thank you. Ronnie was a great subject too. He loved the camera."

"The camera?"

He opened the slim file and eight-by-ten glossies spilled out, the negatives underneath in a plastic sleeve. Ronnie danced nude across the black-and-white paper, his hair flying, eyes sparkling and bright with life. His slim legs pirouetted, arms flung joyously in the air. The light danced with the shadows over his body. In every photo, his pubic hair was shaved.

"Christ," I muttered.

"He was a pretty one," Carlos went on, his hands touching the pictures. I stifled the urge to grab them away from him.

"Who was the photographer?" I asked.

"Me. It was a sort of hobby for me for a long time. And with Ronnie, it came in handy."

"How so?"

Carlos sighed. "*Bueno*, I tell you that Ronnie was the only boy who really surprised me. He caught me completely off guard, as you say, yes?"

I waited, my eyes still glued to the photos spilling across the folder.

"He ran off one night after a session with a member of our club. The man complained that he was not…cooperative, and that was when I found out the guy was into some rough sex. He was banned from our list after that, but meanwhile, Ronnie ran. And yes, he took eight thousand of my dollars with him."

"Christ," I said again. "Did you try to get it back?"

"Haven knew where he went, I'm sure of it, but he wouldn't tell. So I made the money back selling the pictures. It all worked out fine in the end. And Ronnie met you, yes?"

I poured myself another sherry, drank it in silence, listening to the muted roar of the city outside.

"You said most of the boys used nicknames," I said thoughtfully. "What about Haven? Was that a nickname?"

"Oh yes." He thought for a few moments. "Yes," he said, "I remember now because we spoke Spanish together. His name was Rey Montana."

CHAPTER TWENTY-THREE

For days afterward my mind held back the sweet stale scent of Carlos's opulent apartment, releasing it suddenly and without warning at odd times. I would be in my room at home, just before going to bed and the smell would be with me, as strong and powerful as if I had just arrived in the sitting room behind the German rapster. Or I was talking to Rose in her office at the university, and there it was, that unmistakable odor of time and history — Ronnie's secret history, now part of mine, after all these years. Once even in the garage, as I was getting out of the car. Each time I stopped, thrown a little off my stride as if by a physical jolt to the system.

There was a power in that room in New York City, in the image of the old man, his eyes tiny points of inquisitiveness behind the thick lenses, leaning forward in his chair. His long hands, spotted with age, touched and caressed the folder on his lap as he talked. Just as I was about to leave, he said, "Did you love him very much?"

"I never really loved anyone else," I said, turning to look at him. His question and my response were equally surprising.

He swayed, one hand on the curve of the wing chair. "Take them," he said, holding out the folder. "I do not need them now. I have many memories of my other golden boys. This one is yours."

So I took the folder and brought the pictures and the negatives back home to Toronto and felt like crying when I thought of them. Then, a few days later, I got up at three a.m., went downstairs, burned the photos in the fireplace, and buried the ashes in the garden.

The next day, I wrapped up the old shoe box with Ronnie's horde of US dollars inside and addressed it to Debra. Inside I put a note: *I know you'll know what to do with this. Don't ask, don't tell.* I thought for a while and decided not to sign it. She would know who it was from. I was clear on one thing. Ronnie had earned the eight thousand. The rest of it I wasn't going to worry about. His parents could use it.

Ryan slid into and out of my bed. It was curious how I no longer minded. The sex was still welcome, but I was relieved when the boy himself left. Sometimes I heard him creep out the front door afterward, heading out to the bars and after-hours clubs I had no interest in. Sometimes he went back to his own room to smoke up, carefully leaving the window open, thinking this made the smell invisible. Once I thought I heard voices out in the garden and looked out to see Julie in a big T-shirt and nothing else, arguing with Ryan in hard whispers. Ryan shrugged, but he looked worried. I went back to bed. It was time to simplify my life.

Since coming back from New York, I had not gone to see Logan. He had called twice, then stopped. I knew I would have to make up my mind about him soon: what I would say, what I wouldn't say. I didn't want him to think I was abandoning him, as so many of his friends had, but I found myself wanting to protect Ronnie from his probing. Logan had called Ronnie a fake. What would he call him now if he knew the real story?

On Tuesday, the garden was finished. The nursery guys had planted the last of the flowers and miniature trees; the water garden guys had connected the last of the pipes and started the water flowing from the top of the rock garden on one corner, down the small waterfall into the pool beneath. The water lilies had taken hold, and the fish were swimming lazily in their own pool close to the house. The white gravel sparkled, the air was fragrant with the scent of lily of the valley that spread along in the shadows near the house. Logan's the one I had spent hours with talking over the plans, but it was Jaym I thought of first. Jaym, who had been here twice already, slipping in and out without fuss, down to the basement to get a start on the brewing project. But I took a few instant pictures of the garden, from different angles, picked up the bag from the Avery Hall gift shop, and went to see Logan.

It was cooler today, and the apartment seemed fresher. Someone had been in recently and cleaned and dusted. There were no flowers in sight. Logan met me at the door at the top of the stairs, leaning heavily on his silver cane, one shoulder hunched up as if to balance himself in some peculiar way.

"You're back," he said. His eyes were hooded, and I couldn't read his expression.

"I'd forgotten how hellishly hot it gets in New York in August," I said,

"I hear you," he said. He turned and lurched to the padded chair, which was now moved to the window. The bed was farther back against the wall. The grand piano took up the rest of the space.

"You've been housecleaning," I said, sitting down opposite him.

"I hired someone. Ellen was driving me nuts with her solicitousness. In the end, all that sympathy is draining."

"You look good," I said.

"Michael, you're getting old. Your eyesight's going."

I handed him the bag and he opened it, taking out the silk scarf with the piano keys all up and down its length. "Nice," he said. "Thanks."

"You're welcome. I thought you could wear it on your first gig."

Logan didn't answer. He leaned back in his chair carefully and closed his eyes. "How did it go?" he asked.

I leaned back too and stretched out my legs, crossing them at the ankle. "I found the store," I said. "The owner is dead, but there was one guy there who had been at the store in the '60s." I went on to tell him about Jem recognizing Haven.

"And then?" Hogan asked.

I paused and looked out the window at the shifting play of sun and shadow in the leaves.

Logan opened his eyes. "It's not a game anymore, is it?"

"It never was, for me," I said.

"No, I suppose not. You want a drink? You know where it is."

"Thanks." I got up and went to the kitchen, where I poured a weak vodka and tonic for me and got a bottle of water out of the fridge for Logan. When I was sitting down again, I took a drink and sat for a moment considering the glass.

"The only question is this," Logan said, steepling his scarred hands and looking at me over the fingertips. "What has changed because of what you have found out?"

"You're very good at this," I said.

"I'm not emotionally involved," he pointed out.

I pulled out the picture of Ronnie and Haven and showed it to him. "Remember this? I found out who the other boy is. He went by the name of Haven then, but his real name was Rey Montana."

"Jesus, Mary, and Joseph, as my old man used to say. No wonder you look right knackered."

"You've been watching too much Brit TV," I said.

Logan took a drink from his bottle of water. He looked at me, started to speak, then looked away.

"Don't hold back now," I said.

"Most murders are committed by people who know the victim," Logan said. "This new information makes it more understandable."

"Yeah. Ronnie killed a friend. Much more understandable."

"Shut up and listen. Friends know things about each other. Maybe Rey was going to reveal something about Ronnie that he wanted to keep secret. He was reinventing himself back then. You've found that out already. Maybe Rey was going to spill the beans."

I didn't say anything. Logan hadn't come up with anything new to me.

"Are you going to tell the police?"

I snapped my eyes back to him. "What's the point?"

"Right. Let sleeping pigs lie."

"Up the revolution." I finished my drink. I could feel Logan watching me. "I sent the money to Debra," I said.

"Good idea."

I felt his interest, his curiosity, his sharp intellect held back by concern for me and I appreciated it. "I've finished the garden," I said abruptly. I pulled out the photos and showed him.

"Fish and everything," he said, studying them. "You know, Ilse of the SS says I can start on the stairs tomorrow."

"Just let me know when you're ready, and we'll plan a visitation," I said, smiling. I stood up.

"Michael, let it go," he said.

I paused at the top of the stairs, the faint smell of medications suddenly swept aside by the memory of that closed, sweet smell of Carlos's apartment, where my mind would forever see Ronnie at seventeen, dancing naked in the shadows. And I knew I couldn't let it go. I had never really let it go, and now I had to follow to the end, no matter what the price.

I picked up some wild birdseed at the corner store and walked home. Lew was just getting out of his white Jag as I came to my house.

"You can't park there now," I said.

"Watch me. Have you seen the *Rainbow Rag*?" He was dressed in full office drag, wing tips, pinstripes and all. He was carrying an expensive briefcase. A pile of files spilled across the front seat of his car.

"What are you doing here this time of day?" I led the way into the dim coolness of the house and offered him a drink.

"Perrier, if you have it."

I got him a Perrier and mixed myself another weak vodka and tonic. We went out to the garden and sat down. Lew made some appropriate comments about the new look of the place, then pulled a glossy magazine out of his briefcase and flourished it in the air. "Hot off the press," he said. "Have you seen it yet? Check out page twelve."

The *Rainbow Rag* was the slickest and most widely read of the Toronto gay magazines. The ads alone were worth the price. I rarely looked at it, but knew that it was popular. I turned to page twelve. PORTRAIT OF A DEAD QUEEN, by Julie Kates. Several pictures of Ronnie were scattered through it, and one of Ronnie and me outside the school. A quote caught my eye: "We light the candles and Michael reads aloud to me from the *Just So Stories* in his classy voice and calls me O Best Beloved. I play him Janis Joplin records and the Rolling Stones. I love him so much, sometimes I can't breathe." There was only one place she could have gotten that. I was stunned.

"Sorry, honey, I thought you should know. I was sure you had no idea, am I right?"

"That bitch!" I thought of the box of memories carelessly shoved onto the bottom shelf of the bookcase in the living room. I thought of the last time I reached for the diary and didn't find it, thought I'd left it in the bedroom, then forgot about it.

"Looks like you've got some housecleaning to do," he said, getting to his feet. "Look, I hate to hit and run, but I'm due in a meeting in twenty minutes. Can't keep the felons waiting, you know." He paused, kissed me quickly, and rushed out the door to his illegally parked car. No wonder Julie had been lying low lately. And here I thought she was having an affair with Ryan. I thought I was so aware of what was going on around me. How wrong I was! Again.

CHAPTER TWENTY-FOUR

What surprised me was that my anger was almost all directed toward Julie. I thought she had some principles. I knew Ryan didn't have any, but he wouldn't have done anything with Ronnie's diary and pictures unless someone bribed him. Someone like Julie, whose drive to get ahead in journalism was so strong she would do anything for a story. I knew this was the first major piece she had published. I wondered what she had given up for it besides her principles.

I forced myself to read the whole thing all the way through. It was well written, I had to admit that, but it made me cringe to see the slant she had on me. The gist of it was: former private-school boy from patrician Rosedale background falls for pot-smoking US street kid who claims to be a draft dodger. Street kid? I suppose that was preferable to leering teacher seduces innocent young pupil. She could have gone that way easier. But the class thing seemed to fascinate her. Luckily my part in the saga was only at the beginning. I was relieved I hadn't told her anything of what I had discovered since. It was obvious too, she hadn't had any help from Shaw and McGinnis, Ronnie's partners. The dichotomy between the flamboyant drag queen and the sober accountant also fascinated her, but there wasn't much she could do with it. The parts that made me see red were the quotes from Ronnie's diary, his private, raw emotions spread so carelessly across the glossy page. I wondered if I could sue? I made a note to ask Lew that night. I also wondered how the magazine could have printed this without checking about permission.

I called the editor. I started in as soon as I got him on the line. "You don't have permission to use the photos or the quotes for that article on Ronnie Lipinsky," I said. I could hear the tight anger in my voice.

"Who is this, please?" he asked.

"My name is Michael Dunn-Barton. I'm the executor of the Lipinsky estate and none of that material was released to Miss Kates by me."

"We were told she had permission," he said.

"Did anyone bother to check? Don't you use fact checkers at the *Rag*?"

"We do, yes. We check all quotes, but these were written down. We had the assurance of the writer that all —"

"And since when do you take the word of a freelancer about something like that?"

"Mr. Dunn-Barton, I saw the diary myself, and some of those pics are from the Gay Archives."

"I don't think you understand. That diary and most of the pictures used were stolen from my home. You'll be hearing from my lawyer." I hung up.

A few seconds later, the phone rang. I let the machine pick up and went for a long walk.

Finally I arrived at Ronnie's old place. I found Ryan sitting on the back steps, smoking. Evidence of recent painting was on his T-shirt and hands.

A smile spread across his face as he saw me coming, then faded just as quickly.

"What's wrong?" he said uncertainly, his hazel eyes anxious.

"Didn't it occur to you I would find out eventually? That the damn article was going to be in a magazine for all to see? That I would see it?"

"Sure. That's cool, isn't it?"

"Cool? *Cool?* How could that be cool?"

"But it's like, a tribute, right? About what a great guy he was and that?"

"Is that what she told you?"

"Well, yeah. Why else would I help?"

"Money."

"She only gave me fifty bucks. That's not much."

"A few blowjobs would get you more than that."

"So? What's your point?"

I sat down beside him. For the first time in years, I longed for a cigarette.

Ryan laid his hand in the inside of my thigh and leaned in close.

"Not now," I said irritably.

"I don't get it," he said, removing his hand but still leaning against me. "How come you're pissed at me?"

"It didn't occur to you I wouldn't like you letting a stranger into the house when I wasn't there?"

"But she's not a stranger; she's a friend."

"No. She's my tenant. There's a difference. And you gave her access to private papers."

"They were just sitting there in an old carton," he said.

"It doesn't matter what the hell they were in, Ryan. They were private! Don't you get it?"

"I thought you'd be cool with it," Ryan said sulkily.

I stood up. "If you thought that, why all the whispering and secretiveness?"

"She didn't want me to tell you till the article was out."

"I wonder why."

"It was a surprise."

"You got that right." I paced around the small patch of greenery at the back, trying to think. Ryan watched me, smoking and pulling up bits of grass at his feet. "Let's see what you've been doing down there," I said, heading for the basement door.

Ryan perked up at once. "I'm almost finished," he said, trotting along behind me. "It looks real good, doesn't it?"

I agreed it looked real good. "When will you be ready to start on the hall in the front?"

"As soon as I finish the doors. Should only take another hour."

"Good. You can move into the apartment when the paint dries."

"You want me to live here?"

"Yes. While you finish the painting you can live rent free. After two months, you can stay and pay rent or move out."

"Can I come back to you then?" he asked in a small voice.

"No, Ryan. I don't think that would work."

"Fuck. She said it was a cool article," he said.

"It's not," I said. "She lied to you."

"The bitch!" Ryan exclaimed. "That fucking bitch!"

The next day Ryan and two of his scruffy pals moved all his things out to the basement apartment. I helped, mostly to make sure nothing walked out of my place that wasn't supposed to. I let him take the bed and bedding and pillows. There was a small dresser and old dilapidated armchair already there. There was a table and several chairs in the basement storage area, and I said he could have those too.

"What about cable?" Ryan said as he gave me back the key.

I just looked at him. He shrugged and grinned, his eyes sliding away from me. "See ya," he said with a wave.

My place seemed empty without him and his nervous energy, his rampant young sexuality that had oozed into every crevice of the old house. I aired out his room and decided it would make a good study. I spent the afternoon painting it and the next day bought a bright Bhutti rug, a desk, and a bookcase at IKEA. As I put it all together, which took another whole day, I tried not to think about Julie. I could hear her moving around sometimes, but I never saw her. In the old days, she would have been down like a shot to see what was going on. I imagined she had a pretty good idea and was lying low.

I ran into her at last in the supermarket. Literally. She rammed around the corner into my cart, talking into her tiny tape recorder and reaching up to the shelf for detergent. We stared at each other.

She snapped it off and slipped it into her bag. "Hey, sorry about that. I gotta watch where I'm going."

"I hope they paid you well," I said.

"The *Rag*? Yeah, they pay pretty well," she said, shifting her big bag up on her shoulder. "So what did you think? Good? Bad? What?"

I looked at the box of cleanser in my hand, dropped it into my cart. I felt very calm and very tired. "I'm suing the paper, and I'm thinking of suing you," I said. "I'm also giving you notice. It'll come in the mail. You should get it soon."

"What?" Her face flushed and she leaned forward, hands on her hips. "You're doing *what*?"

"You heard me."

"You have no right to do that!" she said. "Everything in that article can be backed up. It's all true!"

"And you didn't have the right to quote any of that material," I said.

"I didn't break in and steal it!" she cried. Heads turned. She didn't care. "You can't say I did! Ryan invited me in. He'll tell you."

"If you're counting on Ryan to stand up for you in court, you've made a big mistake."

"You're just doing this to ruin me, aren't you?" she snarled. "Because I'm a woman and you hate women!"

"We don't have anything to talk about," I said and pushed past her to the checkout.

"You go, girl," murmured a tall black queen sidling up behind me. "That youngster is way too pushy. Besides, she doesn't know how to accessorize."

CHAPTER TWENTY-FIVE

It rained the morning of the Dharman Foundation Garden Party. Poor Trish. Her luck improved, however, and by noon the sun was out, sparkling on the white gravel and flowers and dripping from the miniature trees in my garden. I was going to pick Laura up at her place at two fifteen. The event started at two, and Laura always arrived a careful thirty minutes late.

Trish had chosen the Old York Club as the venue. It had been built by a wealthy whiskey baron more than a hundred years ago and was now home to the golf, cricket, and lawn bowling set. I was surprised she hadn't chosen the Royal Canadian Yacht Club, but maybe there had been a date conflict. Or maybe this place gave more the feeling of being in someone's home.

Laura was impeccably dressed as always in a deceptively simple challis dress with pale mauve flowers painted on it around the hem. Her stockings were white as well, and her shoes a pale mauve to match the flowers. I was wearing the Indian cotton shirt I had bought in All American Boy in New York and the white linen pants. When Laura and I walked into the old entrance hall, I felt like a character in *The Great Gatsby*. Except I wasn't wearing a jacket. "Do you mind?" I asked Laura. "About the jacket, I mean?"

"Dear heart, of course I don't mind. I'm not wearing a hat, am I?" She laughed.

"Laura! Michael, how good to see you!" Dodie MacPherson bounced up from behind her table in the hall and leaned forward to greet us. I kissed her cheek.

"I'm surprised you still recognize me," I said.

"You haven't changed a bit, either of you," she said, taking the invitations we passed over and marking off our names on her list. "The art show is through there," she went on, pointing to a room to the right of the door into the garden. "All the paintings and photos are donated, and the sales go directly to the foundation. You've got a new house, Michael. Surely you need some paintings for your walls! Buy lots and lots!"

We made our way to the art show and wandered about, meeting and greeting, making appropriate comments. I found a lovely mixed-media piece I bought for my new study; then we went out into the garden.

I heard my sister's voice at once. "Isn't it a perfect day for a fete?" she was saying, her voice as usual just a little too loud. The spacious lawns, blue and white marquee, the waiters with their silver platters carrying golden champagne flutes, the beautifully dressed people standing about in groups were all from another part of my life, a part I rarely visited these days. But it was familiar and soothing in a way. No one here read the *Rainbow Rag*. No one would be so gauche as to bring up anything unpleasant. I took some champagne and stopped to make a toast.

"To you, Laura, for suggesting this," I said. Of course she had no idea why it was so right, just now, but she smiled with pleasure anyway, enjoying the thought. "You don't regret it, do you?"

"Not yet," she said, "but the day is young." And she laughed.

Everywhere we went I was greeted like the prodigal son, embraced, welcomed, made to feel wanted. I felt their curiosity as they looked from Laura to me and back again. Trish, however was not pleased to see me.

"What are *you* doing here?" she exclaimed, her face a study in astonishment when she finally noticed me. She had looked so happy a moment before.

"Helping the cause," I said.

"You've done an amazing job organizing all this, Trish," Laura said, laying a hand on hers.

"Thank you." My sister's face slid back to party mode, but having me there made her anxious. I helped myself to some hot hors d'oeuvres and wondered off in search of a chair. Far off on the terrace, I saw Monica Heising talking to a crowd of people, her gray-streaked hair blowing in the breeze.

"My, my. Look at the riff raff they're letting in these days," said a familiar voice behind me.

"Lew." I turned around and shook hands.

"I thought you and your esteemed sister weren't on speaking terms," he said.

"We still hiss a few well-chosen words at one another every now and then," I said.

"Oh good. I do so love a happy family."

"You remember Laura?"

"Who could forget the lovely Laura," he exclaimed, kissing her hand.

Laura blushed. "Really, Lew," she said. "You look fit and tanned. Have you been up to the lake?"

"Alas, no. The poor cottage is languishing. I'm going to try for a weekend soon, though. Michael, why don't you go up some time? Someone might as well use it, and it would give it a bit of a lived-in look."

"Thanks. I'll think about it," I said.

"I know you prefer Georgian Bay, but — My, my. Look who's here. I didn't know your sister knew *that*."

"Really, Lew," said Laura, but she turned around and looked, just as I did. "You mean that tall man with the long silver hair and the cowboy boots? Who is he?"

"Amadeo, the designer."

"I hear he just made a video with some rock star whose name escapes me."

"Well, unless he plays the harpsichord, it would, wouldn't it?" said Lew.

Laura was laughing. "You two," she said. "I'm going to talk to Cathy. I hear her husband is having an affair, and it's driving her back to drink, poor dear."

"Wait!" called Lew, but she slipped away into the crowd. "Damn, I hadn't heard that," he said. "Never mind. Did you know Amadeo and Ronnie were an item back in the '80s? He designed the gowns for some of Ronnie's shows. And he did that early Fashion Cares show, remember? With Ronnie as one of the models."

"I wasn't here then," I said. The sense of peace was evaporating, thanks to Lew bringing my two worlds back together again with an unpleasant jolt. I looked around for Laura, but she had disappeared.

Lew was still talking, looking over my shoulder, taking frequent sips from his champagne. "Well, your sister certainly has covered all the bases," he said, almost crowing with satisfaction. "Here comes Nigel Ross, large as life and twice as phoney."

"The guy making a run for the Conservative Party leadership?"

"Oh, if I ever opened my mouth about him, there's be no way he'd get that."

"Lew, you are the worst gossip I ever —"

"Listen, I happen to know for a fact —"

"Llewellyn ab Hugh," cried Trish, coming up to us with outstretched hands. I backed away, leaving the way clear between them. "I'm so glad you could make it," she went on. "Your office wasn't sure."

"I always make time for a Dunn-Barton," Lew said. Trish smiled graciously as he kissed her hand.

"Did you see Nigel Ross has just arrived?"

"Oh good. Enjoy the fete." She made a beeline for Ross's party.

"Smooth," I said.

Lew snagged another glass of champagne for both of us off a passing tray and edged me farther away from the crowd. "Listen, Nigel Ross used to date Bianca."

"Mick Jagger's Bianca?"

"No, ours. Bianca Bombe."

"You mean —"

"Yes, I do. I'd forgotten all about that until seeing him just now, pressing the flesh etcetera, and that jogged my memory. I remember him at the Queen's Birthday Bash back in the '60s, with Bianca and Luna and the rest. I was dating the guy who runs the thing."

"Bobby Mason. I was there. I went to pick Ronnie up, and he wouldn't let me stay. He said to go ahead, so I did."

"That's right. You came without him. And then Bianca got smashed and went out on the balcony and began to shout dirty lyrics to whatever song was playing on the stereo. Remember?"

"Oh right. I wasn't paying much attention because Ronnie showed up about then, reeking of marijuana, which was unusual. I blamed Glori."

"Right, and then someone called the police, and Nigel almost pissed himself getting out of there. He ran off, leaving Bianca to get arrested for disturbing the peace and some bawdy house crap."

"That I remember. And what were you doing all this time?"

"Climbing out the bathroom window, what else? But I bailed her out, which was more than Nigel was willing to do. Where were you?"

"Up on Bobby's roof garden, trying to find out what was wrong with Ronnie, but he was…in a really weird mood. Anyway, we missed all the excitement, I guess."

"So that's the dirt on Nigel Ross, prince of a fellow, queen for a day and all that. Think I'll go and say hi to the dear boy, just for old time's sake."

I watched him go, the crowds parting for him, closing around him again. He was a popular figure. Perhaps he should run for office. I looked over to where Nigel was standing. I watched the expression on his face, how it closed as Lew approached him, a mask sliding into place like armor. I doubted it would do him any good if Lew felt like going into joust mode.

"You just can't bear to let me have anything, can you?" Trish said quietly in my ear.

I spun around, surprised.

"Oh, don't look so innocent. I work my buns off, getting the right list of people, doing all the organizing, setting the tone, and you come waltzing in with Laura, monopolize the most notable guests, and who gets all the credit? You do. Everyone's talking about you. Just like when we were kids."

"What the hell are you talking about?"

"You bastard," she said, close to tears. She turned and almost ran into the house.

I was stunned. I looked around to find Laura standing behind me.

"She's always envied you," Laura said. "Don't take it to heart."

"But why?" I asked, feeling as if the ground had just slid out from under me.

Laura shrugged elegant shoulders. "Who knows? My brother killed himself. Do I know why?"

I opened my arms to her, and we held each other for a moment as the crowds chattered around us and the sun shone down on the string quartet that was just warming up under the marquee.

CHAPTER TWENTY-SIX

That evening, I had dinner with a former colleague who was in town for a few days visiting friends. She was only five years older than I but was contemplating retirement in spite of the penalties. She was organized, had it all planned out. I had always enjoyed her company. Even when disillusioned and depressed she managed to be upbeat and take matters into her own hands. I felt that no matter what she tackled, she would always be all right. She was an inspiration.

I arrived back home around ten thirty to a ringing phone. As I came in the door the machine picked up, and I heard Ryan's voice. He sounded panicky. I grabbed the receiver.

"What's the matter?"

"Michael, there's some asshole in a dress trying to climb up the fire escape to the third floor. I told him there was no one there. We all told him, but he's, like, stoned or crazy or something. He don't believe us. And he's got a knife."

"Calm down. I'll be right there."

I rushed back to the car and broke all the speed limits getting over to Ronnie's. Luckily I didn't meet any cop cars crossing Bloor Street. All the lights were on at number 145. Ryan and two of his pals were standing around looking up at the fire escape. Vince, the downstairs tenant, was standing to one side with his dog by his side. The dog was wagging his tail furiously, his tongue lolling out of one side of his mouth in a joyous grin. At least someone was happy.

Everyone started talking at once when I came up but it was pretty clear what was going on. I could see Bianca struggling up the narrow metal steps of the fire escape in high heels and a long flimsy dress. The wind had picked up and the dress kept billowing out and getting snagged on the rough metal. She had made it past the second floor and was shouting something I couldn't make out. Bianca was back in Neverland, looking for Luna La Dame.

I pulled Ryan to one side. "Someone's bound to have phoned the cops," I said. "Get inside and get rid of whatever you wouldn't want them to find in your place."

"But Michael —"

"Do it!" He turned and went around the back to the basement entrance. I went in the front door and up the stairs, unlocked Ronnie's door, and struggled with the window. It took forever to get it open. I could hear sirens in the distance now, coming closer. I climbed out onto the small landing. It seemed a lot flimsier than I remembered. I should have checked it out earlier. Bianca was toiling up just below me.

"Luna!" she called, looking up. For a moment I thought she would fall as she raised a hand to wave frantically. "You didn't answer," she said. "I was pounding on the door."

I started down the steps toward her, but she cried out in alarm and leaned out over the flimsy railing. I stepped back to the landing, afraid she would fall, or even jump.

"Bianca, it's Michael," I said, leaning over so she could see me in the light from inside. "Michael, remember?"

"Where you been, honey?"

"It took a while to get here," I said.

Bianca lurched to one side and cried out. One high heel was stuck in the slats of the metal stair.

"Just step out of it, Bianca," I said. "Come on."

"But it matches my outfit," she said.

I reached to catch her hand, but it slipped through my grasp.

"I'll get you another one, a new pair, okay?"

"Really?"

"Yes. Really. Come on." The sirens were much closer now. I was afraid if she saw the police she would panic completely. I started down toward her again, but she flung herself against the metal banister hard and screamed. The railing shivered and cracked. I held my breath, but it didn't break. It hadn't occurred to me to check the safety of the fire escape. I backed up to the landing again.

Two cop cars swung into place in front of the house, lights flashing red and blue streaks in the darkness. Bianca pulled her foot out of her wedged shoe and grabbed for my hand. She slipped and gashed her skinny leg on the metal. "Fuck!" she yelled. I lunged down two steps and grabbed both her arms and yanked her back to the landing. Her ravaged face was slick with sweat and streaked mascara. Lipstick made a red gash of her thin lips.

"The cops!"

"It's okay," I said. "We'll go inside and tell them everything's okay."

"Copasetic. Everything is copasetic. Luna always said that. Look, my dress is ruined."

I made soothing noises while trying to get her back inside. I could hear the heavy tread of police boots coming up the stairs. I yanked Bianca none too gently through the window into Ronnie's place. She looked around, and her face went even paler.

"Oh my God!" she said, putting both hands over her mouth. "Oh fuck!"

"Everything's okay now," I said. "You just wait here, and I'll talk to the cops."

Bianca sank onto the bed. She was shaking.

There were two cops, just like last time, and one herded me expertly into the living room while the other one talked to Bianca.

"She…he is having a difficult time adjusting to a friend's death," I explained. "His friend lived here until he died. He lived here for twenty-five years." I felt an unexpected lump of emotion well up in my throat. "Bianca… He's just out of the Clark," I went on. "He has bad moments now and then, but he's harmless."

"Did he threaten you or anyone else?" the cop asked. He looked like someone's father, broad and solid and kind, under the veneer of imperturbability.

"No, there were no threats. He just wanted to see his friend."

"And did he threaten to jump or anything like that?"

"No," I said. I wondered what madness Bianca was spouting in the next room.

The cop sighed. "You know there's no way we can take him to a psychiatric facility unless he's a danger to himself or to others."

"I know."

"What's your name, sir?"

"Michael Dunn-Barton."

"And his name?"

"I only know him as Bianca."

"That's okay. Maybe my partner got it."

I explained what I was doing there, why I had been called, and that was it. They went thumping down the stairs, and silence fell once again. I scooped up an old pair of shoes of Ronnie's and one of the leftover dresses that hadn't made it into the Wilde Nights wardrobe and went back to Bianca. She was crying, wiping her face with the hem of her dress, making even more of a mess of her makeup.

"I didn't do nothing," she said. "I never even saw the guy before. Ask Luna. She knew him. Not me."

"It's okay, Bianca, he was just a cop doing his job. They're gone now. Come on. Do these shoes fit?"

The dress and shoes distracted her at once. She thrust her long feet into the shoes, which were obviously too small, and insisted on wearing them. The dress she wrapped in her arms and said she would save for later.

"I'll drive you home," I said, offering my arm.

She smiled, a ghoulish effect, and took my arm as if we were about to enter a ballroom, batting her eyelashes. I felt my stomach turn.

As we made our slow progress down the stairs, she said,

"I gotta talk to Luna about that article in the paper, you know? They got it wrong. They never even mentioned me, and I was there, like, all the time, you know? How come they never mentioned me?"

"The article in the *Rag*?"

"It was all bogus."

"Yes, it was."

We were at the front door. Vince and his dog had gone back inside, and no one was there but Ryan, looking sulky.

"The cops never even came near us," he said. "You owe me, like, seventy-five bucks."

"Fuck off," I said.

Ryan flounced away, and I helped Bianca into the passenger seat, first throwing a bunch of papers into the back.

"What's all that?" she wanted to know.

"Oh, just notes for my book," I said, starting the car and swinging into the street

"Oh good! You're writing a book! You'll get it right, eh? You know, me and Luna, we go way back, right?"

"Bianca, it's not that kind of a book. It's —"

"Do you know Nigel?"

"Nigel Ross?"

"Yes! You do know him. You see, you're the right person to do this book, not that cunt reporter. And you can tell them I didn't do nothing. I didn't mean nothing by it. I didn't even know the guy!" She was getting agitated again. "And tell them about that bitch Glori…"

"Bianca, that's enough. You can't tell a writer how to write a book."

"Oh. Okay then. You were there. You know."

"Right," I said. I had no idea what she was talking about, and by this time I didn't care. "Where do you live?"

She told me and I took her to the place she called home. As I drove away, I prayed she would stay there.

When I got home I went through to the garden and put on the lights. I sat for a long time in the peaceful quiet, emptying my mind, listening to the hypnotic splash of the water, breathing in the sweet scent of the lavender and miniature roses. I felt calmer when I finally got up to go to bed. And looked at the pond. All my red goldfish were floating on the surface of the water. Dead.

CHAPTER TWENTY-SEVEN

I went back to the place I'd bought the fish and had them analyze a sample of the water. A little on the acidic side, but nothing lethal. I hadn't thought to bring in one of the corpses.

"Sometimes this happens," the owner said. "Even if you had brought one of them in, we probably couldn't tell for sure if someone had tampered with them."

"You said they were hardy," I objected.

"Once they're established, yes, up to a point. They'll even survive under the ice in the winter. Look, we'll replace the fish, since you hadn't had them for long. We'll change the water and start over again."

"And if it happens again?"

"If it happens again, bring in exhibit A."

I was sure Julie had done this, angered by the letter I had Lew write to her, threatening to sue, but I knew I couldn't prove it. Lew had told me I probably couldn't even get her out of my house if she refused to move. Not unless I needed the space for a family member. I thought of Trish and smiled. I thought of my niece, the one with the tasteful belly button piercing. Maybe, but Trish would never allow it. Just when I thought I was getting everything balanced in my life, the scales tipped again.

One thing that was moving along well, much to my surprise, was the Wilde Nights rehearsal. What I saw was a sort of patchwork quilt of the show, since I was there only every third time or so, and they rehearsed it out of sequence. Predictably, Ellis shone on stage. Less predictably, so did Jaym, tap dancing his way across the stage in a frenzy of movement and unexpected grace. He was never in drag, dancing as a man in the chorus line of chorines and one other guy. In another scene, he and the other guy danced together, just like in the old challenge type dances on the silver screen. It was very energetic. I believed him when he said it was great exercise.

After the next rehearsal, Glori sidled up to me as I was packing up my music and suggested we go for a bite to eat. I glanced at Jaym, who was putting his dance shoes in his bag near by. He smiled and motioned to Ellis with his head.

"If you've got something set up already," Glori began.

"No, no. That's a fine idea."

"You like Indian? There's a great place on Wellesley just past Parliament."

"Sounds good. My car's parked out front."

As we drove, I wondered if Glori had planned this beforehand. He wore no makeup or drag. No wig. He had rehearsed with a feather boa, which was now shoved into his shopping bag along with the heels. He looked like any other middle-aged man now, his color a little high and spreading middle attesting to a love of food.

We talked about the show and some of the people in it. We talked about our favorite restaurants. When we arrived at the modest house and were sitting down, we ordered. He was obviously known here.

"I come here often," he admitted. "I hear you and Bianca had a little bit of a to-do the other day."

So that was what this was all about. I shrugged. "It didn't amount to much," I said.

"What happened?"

I summarized the event as briefly as I could. "Maybe she was off her meds or something," I said.

"Sounds like it. You know, Michael, you can't trust a word that cow says. She's mad as a hatter."

"I sort of figured that out all on my own, Duane," I said.

He laughed.

"What's the scoop here, anyway?" I asked. "Why have you two got it in for each other?"

Duane sighed and fiddled with his silverware. "We used to share a house back in the '60s," he said. "It was me and Bianca and Lulu and two more ditzy young queens. The place was practically falling down and we got it cheap. They're all dead now but me and Bianca." He paused, rearranged the cutlery, and took a drink of tea. "We were all performing off and on here and there, mostly at private parties and the Manatee. No money in it really, but we loved it. We all had specialties, acts we did. But Bianca, we found out the hard way you couldn't trust her. She stole things."

"What kind of things? You mean money?"

"There wasn't much of that lying around, but if there had been, she would have taken it. She was like a magpie. Looking back, I think maybe she was envious, you know? Thinking that if she had something of ours she would be more like us. I don't know. Guess I need more therapy to figure it out."

"I think you're one of the sanest people I know," I said.

"Great thundering Jaysus, as my old man used to say, shows the kind of people you hang with, baby!"

The waiter brought the food, and there was silence for a few moments as we ate.

"But you know it wasn't that that soured me against her," he went on. "She stole my routines. That's what did it. The first time, I thought okay, she didn't do it on purpose. We all rehearse together, maybe she just absorbed it, you know, like osmosis or something. Then she used my material for an audition and she got the part. I was furious. She was making money on my material!" His face got red just thinking about it, even after twenty-five years.

"So it's professional jealousy," I said.

"Professional! That cow?" He snorted.

"Did she steal from Ronnie?" I asked.

"Probably. Ronnie never said. I don't know why he put up with her hanging around all the time. She didn't have an ounce of originality."

"They did an act together, didn't they?"

"Yeah, and I still wonder why."

"What do you mean?"

"Look, Ronnie was head and shoulders better than that cow, and I mean it. Never mind the fact I hate her guts. Ask anyone! Ronnie carried her for several years; then the drugs took over or she went round the bend or whatever, and Ronnie's career took off."

I took a drink of the Indian beer and thought for a few minutes. "Maybe she had something on Ronnie," I said softly. "Maybe she saw something, like Rey Montana's murder."

Duane got very still. He almost stopped breathing. "Great thundering Jaysus," he said.

Me and Luna, we go way back....

I drove Duane home and on the way asked about Nigel Ross.

"That prick," muttered Duane. "He was so in the closet he wouldn't even give Bianca his phone number, never mind address."

"He was in college then, I think. He was probably in residence."

"He didn't have a phone?"

"You were at the twenty-fourth of May party when the police came and he deserted Bianca, leaving her to get arrested?"

"Fuck, she wasn't the only one got arrested. Here's my building. Thanks for the lift, baby. Keep your powder dry." He rolled out of the car and up the walkway to his apartment building. I drove home. He had been so talkative until I mentioned the party. Had he been arrested too? Did he blame Nigel? Or Bianca, the one who had created the disturbance?

Nigel wasn't in the phone book. I knew his office wouldn't give out anything personal. Lew would know, but I didn't want to get into any explanations with him. I phoned Laura. We chatted for a few minutes about the Dharman event and how her old maid was getting along. When I asked about Nigel, she gave me the information without question. Dear, trusting Laura.

Nigel lived in a loft in the downtown core. At least he was practicing what he preached. Development of the downtown core as a living space was part of his platform. The place had a security guard and a concierge, who sat protected by a huge mahogany desk and banks of TV monitors, their cameras trained on every entrance and the parking lot too. I arrived at eight thirty that evening, knowing he worked late. Would he be out? How much did he socialize? I wished I'd called Lew after all. He probably knew all this and more.

I parked on the street, knowing I wouldn't be long, and marched up to the desk confidently.

"Michael Dunn-Barton to see Nigel Ross."

After a brief conference on the house phone, I was buzzed in by the concierge. I knew I was breezing along on the coattails of the foundation, doing just what I despised when others did it, but in this case, I had to know. I had come so far down this twisting road, in search of the real Ronnie Lipinsky and the true reason for the death of love. A mere twinge of conscience wasn't going to stop me now.

Nigel's door was at the end of the hall on the fourteenth floor. The door was opened by a tall man with the kind of boyish good looks that gave him a deceptively young appearance. He had a lot of white blond hair that tumbled artlessly over one eye, like an English schoolboy.

"I'm Rhys Evans, Nigel's campaign manager," he said, holding out his hand. Firm handshake. Lots of eye contact. Politics in action.

"Michael Dunn-Barton," I said, firmly shaking back.

"I hear the Dharman bash was very successful," he said, leading the way into the spacious loft. One whole wall of floor-to-ceiling windows showed the city lights spread out like winking jewels against the dark night. Ribbons of traffic streaked past in a steady curve of light. It was hypnotic. I found it hard to look away.

Nigel was coming toward me, a drink in one hand. He was shorter than Rhys, and more substantial, his once-luxuriant black hair thin on top and brushed with silver. His face was broad, bland, and difficult to read. His shirtsleeves were rolled up, and his shirt open at the neck. His feet, in their monogrammed leather slippers, made no sound on the enormous Persian carpet.

"Michael! I thought I saw you at the Dharman do, but I didn't get a chance to talk. Then you disappeared."

We shook hands. More firmness and eye contact. Nigel was definitely on the campaign trail, and he hadn't even officially entered the ring.

"It's so hard to really talk at those things," I said, letting him guide me to one of the leather armchairs grouped around the large glass coffee table.

"We were just going over a few loose ends from the office," he said, including Rhys with his smile.

Sure, I thought. I looked at the glass table in front of me, clear of everything but a few silver coasters. Life in the closet must be hell.

"Could I get you a drink? Scotch? Rye? Martini? Beck's?"

"Beer would be good," I said, settling back in the comfortable chair. Rhys went to get the beer, and Nigel settled into the chair opposite me. I wondered how long I would be here before they threw me out.

"You know, Nigel, it's been so long since we've moved in the same circles I'm surprised you recognized me today," I said.

He laughed easily. "At that event? Of course everyone knew who you were. After all, it's Dunn-Barton money that keeps the thing going. Always has been."

"The foundation has a lot of supporters."

"Now it does, yes."

I accepted an ice-cold glass of Beck's and took an appreciative sip. "Good stuff."

I noticed that Rhys hesitated a moment, unsure what his role should be. Then he sat down in the other armchair, leaned back, and crossed his ankles. His face looked older in repose.

"It must be tough for you," I said to him, without thinking.

His face was suddenly alert. He looked at Nigel.

"Rhys has experience managing campaigns. He knows what he's doing," Nigel said easily.

"I hope so," I murmured and took another drink.

"Do I take it we can count on you for support?"

Campaign funds. He wants money. Of course. I shrugged. "So far I'm uncommitted," I said, smiling. "You know, I had dinner tonight with another old friend of yours, Duane Kelley."

He shook his head. "Sorry. The name doesn't ring a bell. I meet so many people, you know."

"This is from the old days," I said easily. "When you were going with Bianca. She lived with Glori Daze, otherwise known as Duane Kelley. Ring any bells now?"

I had to hand it to Nigel. Nothing changed but the small lines around his eyes and the corners of his mouth. He shook his head firmly. "Nope. Sorry. Could you tell your sister —"

"You must remember Bianca," I persisted. "Remember that night in 1965 when the party was raided and you climbed out the window, leaving her to be arrested? It was just luck that Ronnie and I weren't arrested along with her, and in those days it could have been serious."

"You're mistaken. Michael, why did you come here tonight? To reminisce about people I don't know? I'm a busy man…"

"Nigel, look. I don't believe in outing people. I'm not a threat to you and Rhys."

"I think you should leave." He glanced at Rhys, who stood up.

"Nigel, I want to know if you went to Ronnie's place that night to pick up Bianca."

"In 1965. You expect me to remember some silly party with some girl I don't even remember?"

I didn't move. I lay back in my chair and watched his closed face. He remembered all too well. Rhys had moved to stand beside my chair. He was looking at Nigel too.

"You got to the party after I did. You came in when I was still in the hall, waiting for Ronnie. I didn't remember until I was talking to Duane this evening. I've been thinking about it ever since. I think you got to Ronnie's to pick up Bianca and walked in on something."

"That's enough! Rhys, call security." He was on his feet now, his face blotched and sweaty.

"Tell me what you saw!" I was on my feet too. I was slightly taller than he was. But Nigel stood his ground. Rhys was at the wall phone. He paused and looked back at his lover. Nigel waved him away.

"What do you want?" he said, his voice cold.

"I want to know." On impulse, I pulled out the picture I still carried of Ronnie and Haven outside Christopher's Curios in New York. "Take a look. That's Ronnie Lipinsky in 1965."

"You want to write a sordid, sensational article for the *Rainbow Rag*?"

"It's just for me," I said. "*I* need to know. No one else enters into it."

He looked at the picture, and I saw his expression subtly change. His head snapped up and he looked at me, his eyes hard and sharp. "Where did you get this?"

"In Ronnie's things. I had it blown up. You knew Rey Montana?"

He shook his head. "Never heard of him." He handed the photo back. "I can't help you about that other matter, either. Sorry you came down for nothing, but I'm afraid you've got me mixed up with someone else."

"Me and Llewellyn ab Hugh and Duane Kelley and Bianca…"

"Let go of the past, Michael. Good night and safe home."

He was steering me to the door, one hand on my arm. Rhys was on the other side. I was being herded by a couple of experts. "Give my regards to Trish. She did a bang-up job with that event."

I was in the hall. The door closed softly behind me. Nigel was good, but he couldn't hide the facts. He knew a lot more about that night than he was admitting. Had he walked in on something at Ronnie's the night of May 24, 1965? The night Rey Montana was murdered?

CHAPTER TWENTY-EIGHT

I sat in my garden as the night wore on, drinking Crown Royal and listening to the water splash. The Goldberg variations — the old Landowska recording — played on the speakers hanging just inside the door. Ronnie's cardboard box sat at my feet.

Ronnie's diary stopped May 21, with an entry that made me blush as he described our last meeting at my bachelor apartment in flaming purple prose. He then went on to rhapsodize about the coming party at Bobby Mason's, and how excited he was to be wearing the dress Bianca had loaned him. Glori Daze was teaching him to sew, and he would have to shorten the gown. They both said they were coming to help him get ready. He also mentioned I wasn't too thrilled by the whole thing, but he thought I'd come around. I did remember being a little skittish about going out with him in full drag. Everything was so new, perhaps I felt I could only handle so much. After that, there were a few pages of scribbled swear words, jagged, angry words scrawled across the page with such force the paper was torn. But not a word was written about May 24. From then on, there were no real diary entries at all, just a few lists, a disconnected note here and there. Then, a year or two later, the scrapbook took over, photos and crushed flowers and faded gift tags from boyfriends and admirers long dead or forgotten.

I thought back to the night of May 24. I had gone to pick up Ronnie. He was only half dressed and fussing with the wig he had bought for far too much money in my opinion. I still thought of this as dressing up for a costume party. For Ronnie it was much more than that, and this was hard for me to understand. I got tired sitting around, watching this rather unsettling change taking place. The room was too small to pace in. People kept dropping in: the girl from downstairs with some jewelry, Tucker Freemont for the rest of the wine he'd left there a while ago. I was drinking a terrible Chianti and smoking.

Finally Ronnie asked me to leave. I was making him nervous. I remember leaving money for a taxi, which made him angry. I remember some harsh words, which I regretted almost instantly. I guess this whole drag thing was getting to me. I had enjoyed it at first, but now I felt it was taking Ronnie away from me. I remember he wouldn't kiss me, because of the lipstick. It had been something I kept thinking about in the weeks that followed.

The night sighed around me. A cat yowled in the distance. Closer to hand, there was an eerie scraping noise. A shadow formed on the other side of the fish pool. Blond hair, graceful, raised arm. Tentative steps.

"Michael?"

I dropped my glass. It splintered on the flagstones, sending scotch and shards of crystal flying in the torch light.

"Jesus Christ!"

"Michael, it's me. Rhys Evans. I'm sorry to sneak up on you like this. I was trying not to startle you."

"You didn't succeed," I said.

"I'm so sorry. I heard the music. Here, let me help you."

"No, no. It's fine. I'll just clean it up." I went into the kitchen, leaving him standing in the shadows. As I swept up the mess, he hovered over me.

"I hope it wasn't crystal," he said.

"It was. Waterford."

"Tell me the pattern and I'll replace it."

I told him. "It's probably not made anymore," I added.

"I can track it down," he said. He wrote down the name in a small notebook.

"Well, now that you've made your grand entrance, you might as well sit down. Scotch?"

He nodded. "But not crystal."

"It's crystal or nothing." I was still feeling shaky and needed another drink. When we both had a glass in our hands, I looked at him expectantly. He put his drink down carefully on the small table.

"Nigel talked a lot after you left," he began.

"Does he know you're here?"

"No. He took a pill and went to sleep. He won't wake up till tomorrow."

"And you came here."

"You've got the wrong idea about him, Michael," he said leaning forward urgently. "He doesn't know that Rey Montana you were talking about, the one who was killed. But he did recognize the boy in the picture. He didn't want to tell you because you might make something of it that wasn't there. His name was Haven, and Nigel met him in New York years ago. Then the guy showed up on his doorstep about six months later. Nige was really upset."

"I believe it."

"Anyway, he explained to this guy he couldn't take him in or anything. He gave him enough money to get back to New York and that was that. He never saw him again."

"He never saw him again, Rhys, because he was dead," I said. "Haven was a stage name. A working name. His real name was Rey Montana."

Rhys was shaking his head. "No," he said. "You must be mistaken."

"Not about this," I said.

Rhys picked up his drink and took a long swallow. "Nigel didn't know that wasn't his real name," he said staunchly.

"Probably not, but that doesn't help."

There was silence for a moment. Ice tinkled in our glasses. "That was all a long time ago," Rhys said.

"Right."

"Everyone has something in the past they'd rather keep hidden."

I just looked at him. If my life had gone on the way it was going when I got married, I would be vulnerable to this subtle threat. Rhys was a politician. He had come here to deal, and I had stolen his ace. By the look on his face, I could tell he knew that.

"What now?" Rhys asked. "How far are you going to take this ruthless quest for knowledge?" His voice took on a bitter tinge I hadn't heard before.

"What I said to Nigel is the truth. I just want to know."

"And be damned to anyone who may get hurt."

"No one is going to get hurt."

"And you can guarantee that?" Rhys put his glass down again, adjusted his blazer, and stood up. "I'd better go. I shouldn't have come here. I just wanted you to know about Haven, that Nigel didn't… Shit."

"How long have you two been together?" I asked, getting up too.

"Three years, if you can call it being together, when I have to keep a separate apartment. One day maybe…"

"Yeah. One day." I ushered him through the house to the front door.

He stopped and faced me at the door. "Three years is a lot longer than you were with your boyfriend back then, as I understand it," he said. His pale hair glowed in the porch light, his eyes looked directly into mine. Then he turned and went down the steps to his car and drove away.

Yes, I thought, and maybe the one to blame is Nigel Ross.

Nigel and Haven. I couldn't get my head around that. What a shock it must have been, seeing the boy at his doorstep. And Ronnie. How did he fit in? I had thought Haven/Rey came to see Ronnie, but maybe I was wrong. I thought the boy wanted a share of the money his pal Ronnie stole. But maybe Ronnie was only a backup plan, someone else he knew in Toronto, someone to bunk with. Maybe his real mark had been Nigel, the wealthy closet case who had given the impression he was mad about Haven, mad enough to let slip his address. But in that case, why would Ronnie kill him? Or did Nigel follow Haven and kill him at Ronnie's? But then why did Ronnie cover it up? Money? Nigel had lots of it. Always had.

They say that money and sex are the great motivators behind murder. Was this just another sad example of the truth of that saying?

CHAPTER TWENTY-NINE

I woke up with a headache and a ringing in my ears. The ringing turned out to be the phone, which I had forgotten to turn off as I staggered to bed last night. Or was it this morning? I reached for the phone by instinct and mumbled a hello.

"Michael? Is that you? You sound funny. This is Monica Heising."

"Hi, Monica. Yes, it's me. I think."

"Late night?"

"Very. What can I do for you?"

"Good to see you at the Dharman thing. You were gone before I got a chance to say hello."

"I was surprised to see you there."

"I get money from the foundation. Least I can do is turn up and look grateful."

"Oh, that was the look you were giving everyone. It looked rather more predatory to me."

She laughed. "Which brings me to why I called at the obviously ungodly hour of nine thirty a.m. I wanted to ask you about a few of the people there as possible donors for Allegra House. Do you know the Rothenbergs?"

"No way. All their money goes to the opera."

"Okay, how about Judge Mooney?"

"Hmmm. As I recall, the old bird hangs out at the yacht club. Used to have a gorgeous sloop. Now, I don't really know. He supports the foundation rather handsomely, so maybe he thinks he's done his bit."

"Good point. What about Nigel Ross. You know him?"

I hitched myself up on the pillows. "Not anymore," I said.

"Didn't you go to school together?"

"He went to Trinity College School, I think. I went to Upper Canada."

"Funny, I thought I remembered you two knowing each other."

"Sure. But we weren't friends. I thought that's what you meant. Didn't you know him back then too?"

"I may have run into him a few times at parties. Anyway, the main thing is, he's got money."

"Pots of it. But he's also running for office. That takes a lot."

"Yeah, but it's good to be seen as generous to the right charities. I'll put him down. Can you think of anyone else I might hit?"

"You can put the Irving-Melvins on your hit list. I hear they're looking around for a tax write-off. And why don't you call Llewellyn ab Hugh? He's much more plugged in than I am." I gave her the phone numbers and hung up.

I lay there for a few moments, thinking over her words. I was sure she had been at Bobby Mason's party in '65, had talked to Nigel for some time on the stairs, just before the raid, but maybe I was misremembering. Or maybe she had forgotten. She had no reason for that party to be etched on her mind as it now was on mine.

I got up, had a shower, dressed. I was putting on the coffee when the doorbell rang. Jaym and the empty beer bottles. Already. He had phoned to tell me he was borrowing a friend's van for the morning to bring them over. I was so wound up in Nigel and Ronnie I had forgotten.

"Am I too early?" he asked, as I opened the door. He wore an old AIDS Walk T-shirt, washed-out red gym shorts and sandals. He looked wonderful. Two cartons of empty beer bottles were on the step beside him.

"I just put on the coffee. Here, I'll take those boxes."

We carried several loads of the empty bottles down to the rapidly filling basement and stacked them in a corner by the tubs of beer.

"It's nice and cool down here," Jaym said, heaving the last carton onto the pile.

I nodded, leaning on the other boxes. We were very close together, hemmed in by the tubs on one side, shelves holding old china and other miscellaneous things I hadn't unpacked yet and probably never would, and the bottles.

"Thanks for doing this for us," Jaym said.

"For you," I said. "I'm doing it for you."

We looked at each other, our bodies close in the confined space. His eyes were a melting chocolate brown, his compact body radiating energy. I could feel the electricity build between us. I reached out and ran my hand under his T-shirt and rested it on his bare waist just above the shorts. His skin was warm and moist under my fingers. He caught his breath. Neither of us moved.

The doorbell rang.

"Fuck," I said, pulling my hand away as if burned by his flesh. He dropped his eyes and moved aside, so I could get to the stairs. I felt disoriented for a moment, but I moved steadily to the front door and opened it.

"Trish." I stared at my sister as if I'd never seen her before.

She was holding the silver presentation tray she'd borrowed for the Dharman event. Her face had that closed, tight look she often wore around me.

"What's the matter with you?" she said. "You look flushed."

"Can't take the stairs like I used to," I said.

"Here's the tray." She thrust it out to me abruptly.

I took it. "Trish, it was a lovely afternoon," I said. "You did a great job."

She nodded and made a sort of small grunt of acknowledgment as she turned away.

"I ran into Nigel Ross yesterday," I went on, "and he was raving about it."

She paused and turned back to me.

"He said, and I quote, 'Your sister certainly knows how to organize a wonderful event.'"

"Nigel Ross said those exact words."

"Yes. Well, those exact sentiments anyway."

She smiled, her face opening up a little. She looked younger. "Thanks for telling me," she said.

"Do you want to come in?" I asked recklessly. "I've just brewed coffee."

She paused and I tensed, remembering Jaym. "I really can't this morning," she said. "Rain check?"

"Okay."

She waved and got into her car. I closed the door to find Jaym right behind me.

"I've got to go," he said, edging around me.

"Why? Is it something I said? Did?"

He shook his head. "I'm really attracted to you," he said, "but I don't want to go too fast. Okay?"

I shrugged. "If it's Ryan, you can forget about him," I said. "He's out of my life now."

Jaym leaned over and kissed me on the mouth, then fled down the path to his van.

I stood at the door, licking my lips and grinning as he drove away.

I felt strangely light-hearted for the rest of the day, as I went about my business. Even the inspection of my new office at the university didn't bring me down. A narrow slice of a room with half a window I would share with someone else, it was nevertheless a step up from last year's carrel at the end of a glassed-in hall. My desk was up against the old radiator and the bookcase we both would share stretched right to the molding of the high ceiling. I wondered what acrobatics would be involved in using the top shelves, since there was no room for a ladder. I loaded the books I had chosen to bring into my part of the lower shelves, moved the better chair over to my desk, and put the old brass nameplate I had had made years ago on top. I spent some more time waxing the drawers so they actually went in and out. I had had the forethought to bring floor wax for this purpose. Sometimes experience with old furniture comes in handy.

The rest of the day passed in a boring round of errands and chores: picking up dry cleaning, dropping off shirts, buying fish food and groceries and some gourmet goodies in case I could entice Jaym in for dinner sometime soon. I picked up the new light fixture for the tenant's front hall in Ronnie's building and got the replacement ceiling fan for the basement apartment. I thought about Julie and even got so far as ringing her doorbell, but there was no answer. Come to think of it, things had been awfully quiet up there recently. Maybe she was keeping a low profile, staying with her boyfriend. Or maybe she had gone? No. That I would have noticed, surely.

Over time, I have forced myself to learn something about cooking. It seemed that I never managed to pick a lover who could cook. All three of the men I had lived with over the years had no real interest in it. We ate out a lot. I ate out a lot now. But tonight, I stayed in and cooked pasta Alfredo with lots of garlic and diced chicken and a Caesar salad. I even baked an apple for dessert. Maybe seeing Trish had reminded me of one of our childhood favorites — cored apples stuffed with brown sugar and cinnamon, baked in the oven until soft. Not exactly gourmet fare, but it worked for me.

I was stacking the dishwasher when the phone rang.

"Michael, you'd better get over here. I mean it. That nutcase is back and he's got someone with him, and they're all up there screaming and yelling and —"

"Ryan, calm down. How did they get in? Just start from the beginning."

"Yeah, okay, so I come home and I see lights up there, right? So I go, okay, Michael's doing something or maybe he's with that real estate lady or something. So then I go into my place and order a pizza, and when I come out to pay for it, I hear them going at it up there. The pizza guy even says something. So I go up the fire escape, and the window's open and this nutcase is in there and someone else too, but I can't see him. So anyway, I shout at them and the nutcase throws something at me so I thought I better call you, like, before the cops, right?"

"So as far as you know, they got in the window? Are they still shouting?"

"I don't hear nothing, but maybe they're just, like, taking a rest or something?"

"All right, I'm coming over. Don't call the cops yet."

"Okay. And Michael? I think one of them's got a gun."

CHAPTER THIRTY

I broke all speed limits driving over to Ronnie's. Again. A playback of all those other times, racing to help. Trying to save Ronnie who didn't want to be rescued. But this time it was Bianca. The truth about that night twenty-five years ago was buried deep in her ruined mind and now I might get a chance to bring it to light. Or maybe not….

Crowds of people strolled along Bloor Street as I honked my way through, paying no attention to shouts and hand gestures from irate pedestrians. I was afraid I'd be too late. Too late to save poor, demented Bianca from whatever fate she was spinning to. I didn't believe there was a gun. I didn't think there was anyone with her, either. Ryan assumed the shouts were two people, because it wasn't sane to be shouting to yourself in an empty apartment. But Bianca wasn't sane.

When I pulled my car up in front of the house, there was another car already there, slewed at an abrupt angle into the street. Ryan was sitting on the steps, smoking, beside Vincent and his dog. A tall woman in a skirt and blouse stood talking to them, her arms crossed, hugging her elbows.

"This used to be a quiet house to live in," she said, bearing down on me as I emerged from my car.

"I'll handle it," I said.

"Putting this boy in charge is ludicrous," she went on, following along beside me up the path.

I couldn't remember her name. "He's not in charge," I said. "He's doing some painting."

"I'll move if this keeps up."

"Fine. Go home, everyone. Ryan, stay down here." I headed up the stairs to the third floor. Vincent's dog licked my hand as I went by.

It was quiet up there now. At least, I couldn't hear anything. Maybe Bianca had tired herself out. I remembered the last time, how she drooped when she got inside, sank onto the bed, and sat there, as if stunned. I quietly unlocked the purple door, pulled it open, and went inside. I smelled incense. Amber, I thought. Through the bedroom door I saw candlelight and heard a low murmur of voices. I felt pinpricks along the back of my neck. Ronnie used to burn incense. Light candles stuck in Chianti bottles. I walked into the bedroom.

Bianca sat on a cushion in front of the low window, surrounded by candles. Duane Kelley, aka Glori Daze, sat on the bed looking tense and red in the face. Bianca was wearing Ronnie's red dress, the one I had given her, and several long chiffon scarves attached to her wrists. Many cheap rings flashed in the candlelight. Her big, shiny, vinyl handbag was beside her. Duane wore expensive designer jeans and a dark green silk shirt. I wondered what he had been doing when lured away by Bianca.

"You finally got here," Bianca said, looking at me. Her eyes were very bright, her face over rouged, her mouth a gash of red that only approximated her lips.

"Hello, Bianca," I said. "How did you get in?"

"Through the window," Duane said tersely.

Damn. I must have left the thing unlocked after the last debacle. I looked at Duane, who merely shrugged his wide shoulders.

"I hear you're writing a book," he said.

"A book, yes!" cried Bianca. "Michael's going to get it all down, get it all right, about me and Luna and that. Right? That's why we all have to talk, to get everything…well, everything straight, like."

I opened my mouth to explain to Duane that I was doing no such thing, but his look stopped me. "Right," I said. "Why don't you tell me a little about it, and then we can all go home."

"Yes," said Bianca. She took something out of the bag, an old photograph, looked at it a moment, then touched it to the candle flame. "That one's not very flattering," she said. "Here's a better one." She handed over a picture of herself outside this house, young and vibrant and pretty in a tight turquoise satin mini-dress, waving at the camera.

Ashes fluttered around her and the smell of burning chemicals soured the air. I looked at Duane.

"Don't burn the place down, you idiot," Duane said suddenly, as she pulled another photo from her bag.

"You shut the fuck up, you ugly cunt!" Bianca shouted, the change so abrupt I was startled. "You have nothing to say! Nothing! This is my show!"

"You're right." I spread out my hands placatingly. "Bianca, why don't you start at the beginning, May 24, 1965. You came here to help Ronnie get ready for his first party in drag, remember?"

"Oh, for God's sake," Duane exploded.

"Shut up! I was there! And I saw you, Glori! I saw that man on the floor! But I don't know him," she added, her voice dropping to a whisper. "And Luna said it was okay, everything was copasetic, and anyway, we were all going to a great party! Except the man on the floor," she added.

"Was the man's name Haven?" I asked.

"No. No, I don't know. Maybe. Anyway, I didn't know him. Luna was scared of him, I think. So we decided not to talk about him. Ever. We swore a blood oath and did a ceremony and everything. So Glori, that cow, she starts to blab…"

"You fucking space cadet, I never said a damn word! I'm not the one with a few screws loose!"

"You ran away! I stayed to help Luna!"

"Help? Help! You poor, pathetic excuse for a queen couldn't even keep yourself out of the loony bin, let alone help Ronnie! He carried you for years, don't you realize that? Years!" Duane's face was getting dangerously red, his eyes watering with the smoke and emotion.

Bianca scrambled to her feet, clutching her purse. The long dress swayed perilously close to the dancing candle flames. "You coward!" she shrieked. "You broken-down old bitch! All you did was use other people's material! Over and over, never anything new! You only wanted the money!"

"What money?" I said.

Duane was on his feet now too. "You wouldn't know an original routine if you fell over it!" he shouted. "It was Ronnie who did all the routines!"

"Asshole! You weren't even here! How would you know?"

"Isn't this all a bit beside the point?" I asked, but they ignored me.

Duane took a few steps toward Bianca, who reached inside her purse. She pulled out a gun. I stepped back involuntarily. I had never actually seen a real handgun before, except safely in a policeman's holster. It looked as if Bianca had tied one of the chiffon scarves to the trigger guard of the thing, so she couldn't lose it. Or so no one could get it away from her easily.

Duane sank down on the bed again and gave me a look that I couldn't read.

But in spite of the gun, I wanted to get Bianca back on the track of the May 24 story. She seemed less upset by that than by Glori.

"Do you have any paper in that bag?" I asked. "I'll need to take notes."

Duane make an exasperated noise, but Bianca twittered on about always being prepared for anything and pulled out a small shiny silver book from the dollar store with a tiny pencil attached and threw it to me with a tittering laugh.

"Just the thing," muttered Duane.

"It'll do fine." I sat down on the one chair in the room and opened the book, pretending to write. "So, you were going to meet Nigel at the party, have I got that right?"

"Nigel?" She looked scared again, lost, as if she were five years old and couldn't remember where she lived. She was waving the gun around in an alarming manner. I wondered where the hell she had gotten it.

"Nigel Ross," I said.

"Oh, he wasn't here," she said, getting back on track again. "Weren't you here? I thought you were here?"

"I was here earlier," I said. "Then Ronnie said I was making him nervous, so I left, and waited for everyone at Bobby's house."

"As if she can process all that," muttered Duane.

"She was there." Bianca pointed the gun at Duane. "I remember that she was there, shouting orders at everyone, like usual."

"Someone had to do something!" Duane said.

"You're the one that got us all in that mess in the first place! You! You made Luna do all that…that…and then you ran away and left her in the shit!"

"Oh, for God's sake, you don't know anything."

Bianca suddenly aimed the gun at Duane and fired.

Noise filled the small room, booming inside my head. I clapped my hands over my ears. Duane's face went white. A whole gaped in the wall over his shoulder.

"Enough!" I jumped to my feet. "Give me the gun. Then I'll take the rest of my notes for the book."

"No! I told enough already. Enough talk. All talk, talk, talk. That one talked too much." She aimed the gun at Duane again, using both hands this time, trying to hold it steady.

I sprang at her, acting without thinking, going in on an angle that would knock her away from Duane. She screamed and twisted away from me, just as my shoulder slammed into her. A crash of breaking glass, and she went through the window, landing on the shaky fire escape beyond.

"No! No!" she shouted, leaning away from me as I lurched to my knees, reaching for her through the jagged window. A splintering creak and the rusty railing gave way. Bianca shrieked and fell backward through the warm night air, hitting the ground three stories below with a thud.

Duane and I peered though the broken railing at the shattered figure on the grass. The gun was flung out above her head, still tied to her wrist. Police sirens once again screamed toward us in the night.

"Jesus Christ," I said, my voice hoarse with shock. Blood splashed onto my shirt from a cut on my arm. Absently I pulled out a piece of jagged glass and dropped it into the wastebasket.

Duane whipped off a pillowcase, tore it into strips, and handed me one. "And that's the way it happens sometimes," he whispered in my ear. "Accidents, a chain of events. No real perp, as the cops say."

He was telling me something, something important, but I was too much in shock to take it in. The police were here. Again. Coming up the same stairs. Asking the same questions. It was good that they had come before; it was all on record. All Bianca's crazy behavior spelled out in the police computers.

"Where did he get the gun?" they asked.

"I suspect it's very old," I said. "I think it may be the gun that killed Rey Montana back in 1965."

They questioned us in different rooms. When they left I sat for a moment, looking ahead of me at the Wall of Death. Ronnie had lived with death for so long, and I had had no idea. While I agonized about his confusing behavior toward me, he was trying to cope with this hidden violence.

When I went back into the bedroom, Duane was sweeping up the shards of glass and putting them in a cardboard box he had found somewhere. "We'll have to cover that with something," he said, nodding at the window, which now had no glass in the bottom part.

I found some old plywood in the basement and together we nailed it up across the window. Didn't do too much for the look of the place. I'd have to get a glazier in and a plasterer to repair the bullet hole….

Bullet hole.

"Bianca always did leave a mess behind for others to clean up," Duane said.

"What's his real name?" I asked. "The police asked me, but I didn't know."

"Mark Vanderleez or something like that. Dutch. I don't remember exactly."

I led the way into the living room, away from the stench of candle wax and incense and death. I wondered how Ronnie had ever slept in that room again. No wonder he started using drugs so much.

We sat facing each other in the two white overstuffed chairs. Around us the mobiles whispered like ghosts in the breeze from the one open window.

"So I guess Bianca got you here with the gun," I said.

"Right. I was just about to go out to the movies. Then she went on about calling you. That you were writing a book about her, like I really believed that, and you needed to be here too. But I don't have a car phone, and this phone was disconnected. Was I glad when you showed up!"

"Ryan called me about the shouting and screaming. So what did go down here in '65?"

"Great thundering Jaysus, Michael. Give it a rest!"

"What happened?"

"Maybe you are writing a book about it," he muttered. "It was like tonight. Too many people in a small room, getting all overexcited. I was there helping Ronnie shorten the dress , and Bianca was twittering around being useless like usual, and then this guy shows up."

"Haven. Or did he call himself Rey?"

"No, he said his name was Haven. Ronnie went into shock seeing him, and then the guy began to demand money, something about his cut or something like that. Who knows? We thought it was crazy talk, thought the guy was high, you know? Half the world seemed to be high back then."

"That's not how I remember it," I remarked.

"Well, maybe not in the teachers' lounge," he said. "Anyway, then this guy pulls out a gun. Well, none of us had ever seen one. It was electric in there. And Bianca…"

"What did she do?"

"Bianca adored Ronnie. Nothing sexual, you understand, she just adored him. Thought he had everything. Fool. Anyway, she went ballistic when the guy got too close to Ronnie, waving that damn pistol. It was an unfortunate chain of events. Then Freemont came to the door and that distracted him. I grabbed him. Bianca got the gun."

"And Freemont?"

"He was on acid or something. He said something intelligent like, 'Solid, man,' and drifted out again with the rest of the mushrooms Bianca had."

"And then?"

"Then I forced the guy onto his knees so we could relax a bit, but someone else came to the door. The door bumped Bianca, who fired, and that was that. Right in the back of the head."

"Who was at the door?"

"For fuck's sake, who cares? It's over!"

"Nigel Ross."

"Let it be, Michael." He got to his feet and we went around checking the windows and locks, making sure all the candles were out. The scent drifted in the air, bringing back the pain of memories. Could I have helped? Was I so obsessed with my own coming out that I couldn't see Ronnie's pain?

Downstairs, I asked quietly, "Where did you get the leather?"

"I worked in a furniture factory back then. The one thing my father ever taught me was upholstery in the family business. I went back and got some of the stuff I'd been working on. It was ruined anyway for selling purposes, some imperfection. I thought we'd wrap the guy up for a while and then get rid of him somewhere. Then I got a chance to do a gig in New York. I had no idea the guy was still here."

"And no one thought to call the police?"

"In those days? In that neighborhood? A bunch of guys dressed up as women with a dead American on the floor. Sure. And anyway, Ronnie was afraid he'd be deported."

I walked him to his car. "And Nigel?"

"Nigel is good people, even if he is closeted. Leave it be, Michael. Just let it go."

I put my hand on the open window. "It wasn't Bianca, was it? It was you?"

We looked at each other for a very long time.

"One more thing."

Duane groaned.

"How did Bianca get to keep the gun?"

"That one I can't answer," he said. "I thought the wretched thing was in the trunk with the body." He shook his head. "You're a bull dog, Michael, but even a dog lets go eventually. Great thundering Jaysus." Duane sighed wearily and drove away.

Let it go. After all these years, just let it go.

CHAPTER THIRTY-ONE

So this is what a murderer looks like, I thought as I studied my face in the bathroom mirror next morning. I had killed Bianca, just as surely as Duane had killed Rey Montana. And I probably felt more guilty than he did. Duane was the organized one. The one who had the answers. The one who got results. And then he went away, and Bianca had never forgiven him for that. For being successful. Did he have help? Was it Nigel's money that had given him his start?

Bianca had finally made front-page news: Drag queen's suicide gives answer to thirty-year-old murder. They had matched the bullets from Bianca's gun to the one that killed Rey Montana. Ronnie was officially off the hook. With nothing to feed it, the whole thing would die in a day or two. They had no idea of anyone else's part in the murder, just that Bianca had known Ronnie. My name was mentioned as the landlord. *Thank you, Ronnie.*

But in spite of this, I felt strangely divorced from it all. It was over. It really was over. It was as if now I could put it all behind me and get on with my life. All these years I had been marking time, in a way, waiting to find out why I had failed with Ronnie. And now I knew. He had pushed me away because he loved me. Because he didn't want me to be involved in his sordid past. And I had let him. But now, I knew, and it was because Ronnie had taken me back at the end, made me his executor, knowing I would dig around until I found all the answers. He had given me the key to my future.

The phone rang as I was making coffee. I glanced at the clock. Nine a.m. on the dot. I considered letting it ring but decided against it.

"Hello, Michael. This is Rhys Evans from Nigel Ross's office."

"Good morning," I said.

"We saw the news story about the suicide in the paper," he said. "So I'm just calling to see how…"

"Rhys, put Nigel on the line."

"But…"

"Now, Rhys, or I hang up."

"Just a minute." He put me on hold. At least there wasn't any ghastly music dribbling in my ear subversively.

"Michael, Nigel Ross here. So sorry to hear you were involved in that unfortunate incident last night."

I didn't answer.

"I'm paying for the poor thing's burial. She was a constituent, after all."

"Indeed," I said.

"I understand you're writing a book?"

"Shame on you reading the yellow press, Nigel," I said. "You know they rarely get it right."

"So you're not writing a book on queens."

"On queens, maybe. Drag queens, never. I've had quite enough of them to last me a lifetime."

"I certainly understand how you feel," he said.

"I just bet you do," I said. "Look, Nigel, let's cut to the chase here. You've got a loyal supporter in Duane Kelley. And you don't have to worry about me, either, so relax."

"I certainly wasn't worried about you, Michael," he sputtered. "But it's best to let bygones be bygones."

"Couldn't have put it better myself," I said cheerfully and hung up.

As I drank my coffee in the solarium, I made a list of calls to make to workmen. I would be glad to get rid of the old place, if anyone would buy it, now that two violent deaths had happened on the third floor. But when I called my real estate agent, she seemed unfazed. "It'll be forgotten in a week," she said. "Location is all that counts in this market. Don't worry about it." Poor Bianca. She couldn't make a lasting impression even in death.

I spent the morning on the phone, going through the yellow pages until I found some workmen who agreed to actually come right now to do some work for an exorbitant sum. It would be worth it to get the place back in shape. I spent most of the afternoon making sure they actually did what I was paying them for, and by four o'clock I was home again, walking up my street past Logan's place. He was sitting on the front step.

"You're doing stairs these days?"

"My first try on my own," he admitted. He grinned his lopsided smile. "I phoned earlier, but you weren't in."

I sat down beside him. "I was hounding the workmen who were repairing last night's damage."

"I read about it. Suicide, eh?"

"Yeah."

"Sure."

I shrugged.

"So, you're satisfied?"

I nodded.

Logan hunched his shoulders and looked at his hands. "Fuck, Michael, I thought we were past this straight, gay, thing."

Startled, I looked at him. "I know a wall when I see it," he said.

"You don't know shit, Logan," I said. "Look, I really don't want to go into details on the street, okay?"

"Oh." He looked a little sheepish. At least that's how I decided to interpret the look.

"Can you make it to my place around eight? We can sit in the garden and talk there."

"Ah, the famous garden. Site of upheavals, sweaty young men, and dead fish," he said.

I laughed and got to my feet. "When are you coming back to rehearsal?"

"Oh, I don't think so."

"What better place to start? No one will even notice what key you're in."

"True."

"See you later." I waved and left him there, sitting on the step, a little closer to the life he had been watching from his window for so long.

Back home, I opened the door to find Julie in the hall, balancing a box on one hip as she dug her key out of her pocket.

"Moving back?" I asked.

"Earl kicked me out. His place is too small for two people anyway. So, are you going to kick me out too like you said?"

"No. Not unless you refuse to pay your rent," I added.

"So you're not pissed at me anymore, right?"

"Wrong," I said.

"Shit, Michael, get over it, okay?"

"I have," I said, "but that doesn't mean everything's back the way it was. I'm going forward, not back."

"Whatever that means," she muttered, sticking her key in the lock.

"It means no more dropping in, no more muffins and bagels and hanging out in the garden. What you do is your own business, but don't ever involve me again."

"Fine. I'm a journalist. Deal with it."

"Oh, I have," I said and went inside where a list of messages lay in wait. I phoned my sister first.

"I see you're on the front page again," she said.

"I expect to become completely un-newsworthy very soon," I said.

"I sincerely hope so. Can you come to dinner next Tuesday?"

"Good God, I didn't think I was that presentable."

"Well, if you're going to keep turning up at events like the Dharman gala, with your wife, even, I guess you are."

"Who else will be there?"

"Remember Adrian? Our cousin from England?"

"Of course. I haven't seen him in years."

"Well, he's in Toronto for a visit, and I'm inviting him."

"And you want the tray," I said.

"Well, yes, but I was going to invite you, anyway."

"Oh," I said, surprised. "Sure. Tuesday it is. We'll be there."

"We?" she said cautiously.

"Me and the tray," I said, and she laughed. "And Trish," I added, as she was about to hang up. "You can keep the tray."

Silence. "Really?" she said.

"You were right, you know. I don't look after it. And I don't entertain much anymore. You keep it. If I do decide to throw a big party, I can always borrow it back."

"Certainly," she said, real warmth in her voice for the first time. "Thanks, Michael. See you on Tuesday."

I hung up and looked at my father's sword hanging on the wall next to Ronnie's picture. I shook my head. Family. What an odd skein of conflicting feelings we wind around ourselves. Half the time we've forgotten the cause of the deep-seated resentment we drag around. Poor Trish. At least she now would have one thing she had always wanted.

And what about me? What did I want?

I glanced at my watch, then picked up the phone.

"Michael!" said Jaym, sounding pleased.

"I hate these newfangled devices," I grumbled. "Can't ever give anyone a real surprise anymore."

"Are you okay? After last night, I mean? I read in the paper —"

"I'm fine."

"Good, and you did give me a surprise. A nice surprise too," he said. "Unless you've called to tell me the beer has exploded or something."

"The beer's fine. I'm fine, thanks for asking, and I want to see you."

"Now?"

"Now."

"I'm on my way."

That was easy. I stared at Ronnie's picture that Jaym had done for me. I smiled. Food. We'd need food. Luckily, there was some in the freezer. And wine. There was lots of that. And Logan was coming at eight so I wouldn't have time to make a total fool of myself. I hadn't felt like this in years.

I set the table in the solarium. Chose the wine, put on music. While I waited, I got out Ronnie's box of memories and lit the fire. I would keep the diary, that dog-eared scribbler from the '60s that had caused me so much grief and pleasure. I would keep the early photos and some of the later ones. Everything else would go. It was only my memories that were important. My memories and Ronnie's final gesture of trust.

How much was I going to tell Logan? How much was mine to tell? He would know I was leaving things out. He had sensed that already. So be it. No one knows the whole truth about anything.

ABOUT THE AUTHOR

Caro's mystery, *Drag Queen In The Court Of Death*, was short-listed for a Lambda Literary Award in 2008. She is the founder of Bloody Words, Canada's annual mystery convention. Writing in several genres, her work includes the mystery *The Tangled Boy*, the SF series *The Danger Dance* and *The Abulon Dance* as well as two short story collections and five erotic gay novels under the nom de plume Kyle Stone. Caro's short stories have been published in many anthologies and gay magazines and she received the Derrick Murdoch award from the Crime Writers of Canada in 2002.

Website:
http://www.carosoles.com
http://www.bloodywords.com
http://www.kyle-stone.com

THE TREVOR PROJECT

The Trevor Project operates the only nationwide, around-the-clock crisis and suicide prevention helpline for lesbian, gay, bisexual, transgender and questioning youth. Every day, The Trevor Project saves lives though its free and confidential helpline, its website and its educational services. If you or a friend are feeling lost or alone call The Trevor Helpline. If you or a friend are feeling lost, alone, confused or in crisis, please call The Trevor Helpline. You'll be able to speak confidentially with a trained counselor 24/7.

The Trevor Helpline: 866-488-7386
On the Web: http://www.thetrevorproject.org/

THE GAY MEN'S DOMESTIC VIOLENCE PROJECT

Founded in 1994, The Gay Men's Domestic Violence Project is a grassroots, non-profit organization founded by a gay male survivor of domestic violence and developed through the strength, contributions and participation of the community. The Gay Men's Domestic Violence Project supports victims and survivors through education, advocacy and direct services. Understanding that the serious public health issue of domestic violence is not gender specific, we serve men in relationships with men, regardless of how they identify, and stand ready to assist them in navigating through abusive relationships.

GMDVP Helpline: 800.832.1901
On the Web: http://gmdvp.org/

THE GAY & LESBIAN ALLIANCE AGAINST DEFAMATION/GLAAD EN ESPAÑOL

The Gay & Lesbian Alliance Against Defamation (GLAAD) is dedicated to promoting and ensuring fair, accurate and inclusive representation of people and events in the media as a means of eliminating homophobia and discrimination based on gender identity and sexual orientation.

On the Web: http://www.glaad.org/
GLAAD en español:
          http://www.glaad.org/espanol/bienvenido.php

SERVICEMEMBERS LEGAL DEFENSE NETWORK

Servicemembers Legal Defense Network is a nonpartisan, nonprofit, legal services, watchdog and policy organization dedicated to ending discrimination against and harassment of military personnel affected by "Don't Ask, Don't Tell" (DADT).The SLDN provides free, confidential legal services to all those impacted by DADT and related discrimination. Since 1993, its inhouse legal team has responded to more than 9,000 requests for assistance. In Congress, it leads the fight to repeal DADT and replace it with a law that ensures equal treatment for every servicemember, regardless of sexual orientation. In the courts, it works to challenge the constitutionality of DADT.

SLDN
PO Box 65301
Washington DC 20035-5301
On the Web: http://sldn.org/

Call: (202) 328-3244
or (202) 328-FAIR
e-mail: sldn@sldn.org

THE GLBT NATIONAL HELP CENTER

The GLBT National Help Center is a nonprofit, tax-exempt organization that is dedicated to meeting the needs of the gay, lesbian, bisexual and transgender community and those questioning their sexual orientation and gender identity. It is an outgrowth of the Gay & Lesbian National Hotline, which began in 1996 and now is a primary program of The GLBT National Help Center. It offers several different programs including two national hotlines that help members of the GLBT community talk about the important issues that they are facing in their lives. It helps end the isolation that many people feel, by providing a safe environment on the phone or via the internet to discuss issues that people can't talk about anywhere else. The GLBT National Help Center also helps other organizations build the infrastructure they need to provide strong support to our community at the local level.

National Hotline: 1-888-THE-GLNH (1-888-843-4564)
National Youth Talkline 1-800-246-PRIDE (1-800-246-7743)
On the Web: http://www.glnh.org/
e-mail: info@glbtnationalhelpcenter.org

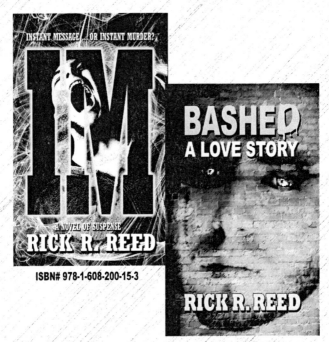

Lightning Source UK Ltd.
Milton Keynes UK
27 September 2010

160414UK00001B/23/P